Book 1 of the Billy Bowman Adventures

The Sun Never Sets

Stephen Archer

The Sun Never Sets
Book 1 in the Billy Bowman Adventures
© Stephen Archer
First published 2020

978-0-6487946-0-8

Cover design by Stephen Archer, images by Pixabay.

This is a work of fiction. Names, characters, businesses, places, events, locales, and incidents are either the products of the author's imagination or used in a fictitious manner. Any resemblance to actual persons, living or dead, is purely coincidental.

This work references some historical events but uses them in a fictitious manner. Some historical events have been entirely highjacked and re-written to create the world of this story. While the role played by historical figures in this narrative are entirely fictional, wherever possible (to suit the narrative and world of this story), they do abide by the generally known facts of the real person's life.

For Olivia and Isabel,
the Angels who inspired me to write these stories.

No book is a solitary effort. While the author sits down somewhere to write, there are numerous people behind the scenes who help and support the journey from idea to written word. My undying thanks go to my family and friends, who supported the creation of this book.

In particular, I'd like to thank Bec, who smiled indulgently at the recurring phrase "I'm just going to write for an hour before dinner", as well as Caitlin, Ryen and Harry, for their unconditional love.

I owe a huge debt to Sean Guy, who freely gave of his time, his advice and his own experience as a published author. I'm also indebted to Nicole Brown, for her enthusiastic reading (even from a hospital bed) and her feedback on some of the earliest drafts.

To all the early readers - Sav, Cat, Johanna, Alyssa, Cath, Debbie, Caitlin and Lotus - I thank you for your time and support for my stories.

I'd also like to give a shout-out to Melissa's Take Away in the Vic Hotel arcade in Darwin, for their delicious food and friendly service during my lunchtime writing sessions!

For more information on the historic events and persons interwoven into the story, please see the author's website.

Also by Stephen Archer

The Billy Bowman Adventures

The Sun Never Sets (Book 1)
Land of Hope and Glory (Book 2)
A Wing and a Prayer (Book 3)
The White Cliffs of Dover (Book 4)
God Save the Queen (Book 5)

Mark Bowman, RN series

Dawn Patrol (Novella)
The Dardanelles (Book 1)
ANZAC Cove (Book 2)

Author's Note: At the time of this publication, not all of these books are in print. Please check the author's website or social media accounts or contact the author via email for updated information.

Prologue

Caloundra, Colony of Queensland, Australia
June 1940

This was Billy's favourite time of the day.

The winter sun had set three hours ago, and the night had quickly closed in around their small home. The flickering light from the lamps was enough to cast a comfortable glow around the room, but it was the fire in the hearth that warded off the winter chill.

The cicadas were quiet now, and Billy could hear the ocean waves crashing on the beach - the faint, rhythmic sound of the surge and retreat of the waves carried on the gentle breeze that wafted up from the sea.

Dinner in the Bowman house had, as always, been a simple affair, with his parents insisting that the entire family spend each mealtime seated at the table. His mother, Mary, was an able cook, and although Billy's father didn't bring in a lot of money from his sales job for the Buderim Ginger Factory, the family always had enough to eat.

Now, Billy had helped with the clean-up after the meal, cleaned his teeth and was settled into bed, waiting impatiently for his father to come and read to him before putting out the lantern.

Yes, Billy loved the time his father spent reading to him in the evenings when he was home. Patrick Bowman needed to do quite a bit of travel for his job, across Queensland and even to the other Colonies sometimes, but on his return, he always made time to read to Billy.

Even though Billy was 10 and more than able to read himself, his father always created such a sense of realism and emotion from the words that Billy felt he was actually there in the story,

Of course, 'story' wasn't really the right word for it. The only book that Billy had was the only book that was approved by the Government - *The History of the British Empire.*

The History was factual and accurate in every way (it must be, for that was printed clearly, in large bold text on the back cover of every copy). It told how the Empire was held together by the benevolent and mighty will of the Royal Family, and how the peace that the Bowman family enjoyed, even in their far-flung colony, had been forged by the power of the Sovereigns of old and maintained by the King of today.

Billy knew much of the book by heart, as did all of his friends at school, his parents, their friends and their neighbours.

"So, what would you like to hear tonight, William?"

His father always asked what Billy wanted to hear, even though he was supposed to work through a set schedule of readings each year.

His father also always called him William, even though everyone else called him Billy. "It's a royal name" his father said simply, as if that was reason enough.

"Can we read about the rebellion, please?"

"Again? I read that to you last week."

"I know, but I like that story most of all!"

"Well, I suppose it is a turning point for our history. Without that, I'm sure we'd live in a very different world." His father shuddered slightly, as if the very thought of such a thing was unnatural and abhorrent.

Billy's father took *The History* from the shelf above the bed, and opened the volume carefully, almost reverently.

With barely a pause, he turned to the chapter titled 'The American Rebellion'. A black and white picture of one of the leaders of the rebellion was printed in an upper corner of the page, with the caption 'George Washington, convicted traitor'.

"By mid-1760," Patrick Bowman read, "the colonies His Majesty, King George III, had established in the Americas were doing well, producing ample products to maintain themselves, with a large surplus of important goods for export back to England.

"The colonies were trading between themselves, and prosperity was the norm for any colonist willing to work hard for King and Country.

"However, as the 1760s drew to a close, a number of dissidents and agitators began to emerge. Their cry was that, since they worked hard to produce the goods, then they were entitled to sell those goods to whomever they wanted and to keep the profits for themselves.

"Several of the Governors of the Colonies - men who had forgotten their allegiance to the Crown (perhaps because they were born in America, instead of being true Englishmen) - began to give credence to these dissidents. Some of the Governors even wrote to the King to implore His Majesty to let them keep the money for themselves.

"Of course, such notions of individual profiteering have no place in our vibrant and benevolent Empire. And so, the King, in spite of his overwhelming sense of decency and respect for all citizens, had no choice but to remind the Governors and the colonists that they were part of the Empire and must always do what was best for the Empire.

"And, His Majesty continued, it had come to his Royal attention that given their apparent affluence, the American colonies were not actually contributing a just and reasonable amount to the Empire. Hence, a Proclamation of an increase in both goods provided and taxes levied accompanied the reply from His Majesty to the letters sent by the Governors.

"Unfortunately, the Governors and the dissidents tried to resist the Royal Proclamation. At first, there were only a small number of objections, but over the following years, the colonists began to refuse to pay their lawful taxes and instead channelled that money into increasingly violent acts against the forces of His Majesty.

"Raids, bombings and destruction of property all increased during the 1770s, with the colonists becoming more and more unruly and disobedient to the Crown.

"Finally, in 1776, the colonists issued a declaration, stating they would be independent of England and no longer part of the Empire. This was, in reality, a declaration of war against the Empire that had founded the colonies, supported them in their lean early years, and required nothing more from them now than loyalty and a return on that initial investment.

"After a series of battles, the poorly organised and virtually untrained colonists were defeated by the magnificent army of His Majesty, King George.

"The rebel leaders, the men who had signed the declaration, were rounded up to a man, given a fair trial to defend themselves and their actions, before being found guilty of High Treason and sentenced to death.

"During the course of the rebellion, it became clear that the American colonies were being supported in their aggression against the Empire by the government of France. After the rebels were defeated, His Majesty determined that the French must never again be allowed to threaten the peace of the British Empire.

"The Government of France was therefore given a simple choice: the unconditional surrender of France and all her colonies to become a dominion of the British Empire, or face utter and total destruction. France chose to join the Empire.

"With the strength of the King, not only were the American colonies brought back to stability and prosperity, but the wayward French were also given the protection of His Majesty."

And with that, Billy's father finished the reading, as he always did, with a heartfelt 'God Save the King.'

Chapter 1

Caloundra, Colony of Queensland, Australia
Monday 7 September 1942

Billy woke early, with the first rays of the sun peeking through the curtains of his bedroom. Within moments, he'd thrown off the covers and was racing out of his room, down the hall, through the living room and into the kitchen.

His mother was busy at the stove, alternating between stoking the fire and shuffling the food in the skillet. Billy could smell the eggs and bacon from the hallway, but the scent didn't register until he got to the kitchen and saw his mother labouring over the pan.

"Morning dear," his mother called over her shoulder, not taking her eyes off the skillet, "Breakfast will be ready in a few minutes."

"Bacon and eggs?" Billy queried, "on a Monday?"

"Well, it is a special day, dear. I wanted to make sure you had a nice breakfast on your first day at secondary school."

Billy blushed a little, and was glad his mother had her back to him and didn't notice. It wasn't that Billy had forgotten he was starting in First Form today. Far from it, he'd been looking forward to this day for months.

No, Billy felt the wonderful tug of love and appreciation for his mother that came from her getting up so early to get him breakfast. He was humbled by her sacrifice, and once again reminded himself of his vow to follow her example and be selfless in everything he did.

"Always take care of others," she would say, "it makes the Empire strong. Good things will always come to us when the Empire is strong."

Down the hall, Billy could hear his father moving about. In a few moments, he would arrive in the kitchen, and the day could properly begin.

Billy took his seat at the small table in the kitchen alcove. He loved this spot, nestled into the bay window that looked out over the side garden. His mother had put a lot of time and effort into the garden, and even though the space was just a few feet across, Billy couldn't see the fence for all of the plants and ornaments that seemed to fill every available nook and cranny in the yard.

The weather had begun to warm as winter fell behind them, and the spring sun had brought many of the plants to their first bloom of the season. From the slightly open window next to Billy's seat, the fragrance of hibiscus and mint, damp soil and jasmine wafted into the kitchen, mixing in an almost raucous way with the smells coming from the pan on the stove.

As Billy's father entered the room, the kettle on the stove began to whistle. In a deft and well-practiced move, Billy's mother whisked the kettle off the stove top and poured the boiling water into the teapot on the bench next to her.

"Morning family," Billy's father called out cheerily, bustling into the room and taking his place at the head of the small table, "How goes it this fine morning?"

Billy's mother came over to the table, placing the teapot on the trivet at the same time she pecked her husband on the cheek.

"It's a wonderful day, dear."

"Is that bacon I can smell?"

"Aye. Special breakfast for our boy today."

"Fair enough, although I don't mind saying that I'd be very happy if there was enough left over for his Old Man to have a serving."

Billy's mother smiled indulgently at his gentle questioning. After all these years of marriage, Patrick Bowman knew full well that his wife would have cooked more than enough bacon for him and Billy to share. And Mary Bowman knew that this was his way of thanking her for looking after him and Billy.

Billy smiled at them both. He was old enough now to be well aware of the interactions between the adults in his life. He'd once overheard his mother say that Billy was far more attuned to the mood of those around him than most children of his age. At the time, Billy wasn't completely sure what his mother meant, but as he grew older it became more and more clear to him that he could sense how people were feeling.

This empathy for others had made Billy very popular in his primary school. His classmates soon discovered that Billy was a good listener and would be a friend that could be relied upon. Billy didn't have enemies, although some of the less mature students were jealous of his popularity. Rather, Billy had friends who didn't always like him. It was rare for Billy to have a cross word to say about anyone, and he stayed away from those would try to boost their own confidence and social position by gossiping or belittling others.

By now, the bacon and eggs were ready, and, for the first time, Billy was served first, ahead of his father. Billy looked at his father for a reaction to this breach of protocol, but Patrick was smiling indulgently at his son.

"Go ahead," Patrick said warmly, "today is the start of your journey into manhood."

He winked at Billy.

"My father did the same thing for me when I started First Form, so let's call it a tradition, eh."

Billy nodded solemnly, out of respect for his father, but at the same time he was ecstatic about being called a man and being given precedence at the meal table. Billy carefully cut a piece of bacon and some egg, savouring the smell as he slowly raised the fork of food to his mouth.

His father continued to smile at Billy for a moment longer, before turning his attention to his own plate of food. After a few minutes, his mother joined them at the table.

For the next few minutes, the family enjoyed their breakfast in companionable silence, before Patrick Bowman again spoke to Billy.

"So," his father continued, as if the silence had never happened, "are you looking forward to extending your education, William?"

"Absolutely!" Billy replied enthusiastically, "I can't wait to get started."

Billy's father chuckled, then grew serious for a moment.

"You know, it's not too late to join the Royal Navy. Your grandfather joined when he was twelve and spent a good portion of his life at sea, fighting for the Crown and defending the Realm."

"I thought about it very hard," Billy said equally seriously, "and I'm very proud of what Grandfather did for all of us, especially in the Great War."

Billy's father nodded, appreciating the sentiment, but also encouraging Billy to continue his explanation.

"A good number of my chums joined straight after school finished."

Billy grew a little sad at the thought of all the friends he wouldn't see again for years, if at all. Then his face took on a more determined look.

"But I did well enough in school to be offered a place at the secondary college, and not everyone gets that chance."

What Billy didn't say, although everyone in the room knew it, was that not everyone from their social class - the middle class - was given the opportunity to advance their education beyond the primary school years.

Everyone in the Empire, male and female, regardless of their social standing, was guaranteed education until the end of the primary years. The Empire ensured every citizen could read, write, do basic arithmetic and understand the key parts of *The History*.

But once that schooling was completed, many in the lower and middle classes would need to work to help support their families. Others simply did not have the grades to advance to secondary education. Those without the means to support themselves, or the skills to study, would be gainfully employed in the factories, or would serve in the lower ranks of the Navy.

This was the way of things in the Empire, and everyone recognised that it was for the good of every citizen that each person accept their place and their role in society.

Billy's face took on a determined look, before he continued his explanation to his parents.

"I have been given a wonderful opportunity, and I intend to make the most of it. I want to do well at school and seek my Commission when I graduate."

"Well done, my boy, well done!" Billy's father enthused, a twinkle of pride in his eyes.

"You'll make a fine officer, I'll wager. You might even become a Captain of your own ship one day, like your Grandfather."

For the second time that morning, Billy blushed.

oOo

After breakfast, Billy helped his mother clear the table and stack the dishes in the steam-driven automated washer, while his father retired to the living room to smoke his pipe and read the paper.

With the chores completed, Billy and Mary joined Patrick in the living room, to await the Anthem. All three Bowman family members settled in their chairs, looking up at the large portrait of King George VI that hung in a gilt frame above the fireplace.

Every home in the Empire had the same portrait. It was provided to every house and building by the government, installed as part of the construction process and only replaced if damaged by some accident or in the event of a change of Monarch. This particular portrait had been in homes for the last six years, since King George VI had taken over from his older brother, after King Edward VIII had died suddenly after less than a year on the throne.

On the stroke of 8 o'clock, the speaker above the portrait clicked on, and a recording of the chime from Big Ben, the Westminster Quarter, was played through every home in the colony.

Habitually, Patrick Bowman removed his pocket watch from his waistcoat, and flicked it open to check its accuracy against the sounding of the Quarter. Satisfied, he returned the watch to his fob pocket, taking care to ensure the thin silver chain didn't get caught on any of the buttons of his waistcoat.

With this ritual complete, he rose from his easy chair, standing ramrod straight and ready for the anthem to begin.

"All men and women of the Empire owe a duty of loyalty and respect to the Crown," he had taught Billy from the age of four.

"We must always remember that we owe our peaceful way of life to the hard work our Sovereigns have done, now and in the past.

"This is why the entire colony stops, at 8 o'clock each morning and at 8 o'clock each night, to honour our King as his anthem is played."

Once Patrick had stood up, Billy and Mary joined him, standing tall and silent, respectful and obedient to the Throne.

As the last note of the Westminster Quarter died away, the speaker began to play the soaring tune of the Anthem, performed by a magnificent orchestra.

All across the Colony of Queensland, the voices of every man, woman and child began to sing the Anthem to their King.

"God save our gracious King, Long live our noble King,

God save the King!

Send him victorious, Happy and glorious,

Long to reign over us,

God save the King!

"Thy choicest gifts in store, On him be pleased to pour,

Long may he reign!

May he defend our laws, And ever give us cause,

To sing with heart and voice,

God save the King!"

As the last notes of the Anthem died away, Billy heard the faint click as the speaker above the portrait switched off.

"Right, everyone," Billy's father announced, "time for work!"

And with that, he kissed his wife on the cheek and patted Billy affectionately on the head, before picking up his umbrella and briefcase, popping on his hat and heading out the front door.

"Time for you to get ready for school," Billy's mother told him, her hand resting on his shoulder.

"You only have about 20 minutes until you need to leave."

Billy didn't need to be told twice. He raced down the hall to his bedroom, to begin getting dressed.

Chapter 2

Near Grodekovo, Siberia, Russia
Monday 7 September 1942

"It is warmer today, Comrade Volkov," the Trooper opined.

Volkov didn't bother to reply. He had very little time for small talk. He was here to complete a mission, and that was the only thing that concerned him. The apparently desperate need of the Troopers to fill the silence with their inane chatter was at best a distraction. At worst, it had the potential to compromise his mission.

Not for the first time this week, Volkov considered whether ridding himself of the Troopers might increase his chances of successfully completing the mission. Also not for the first time, he reminded himself that despite their inability to remain silent, they would become a necessary part of the operation if he needed to cross the border into China.

This was not a typical mission for Volkov, but he knew his duty and would perform his role with professionalism and skill.

He had been recruited into the Soviet Security Division when he was 12 years old and had quickly established himself as highly capable and diligent. There were few forms of training in which he didn't excel.

The one area of his training that was not of such a high standard was his teamwork. His preference was to work alone, and when he was given latitude to complete his mission without interference, he was without peer. However, when required to work with a squad, even when he was their leader, he would struggle to complete the mission.

His dedication and skill made him a formidable operative. But his disdain for teamwork was seen as a liability.

"You must learn to include others," his Instructors had informed him, over and over again, "It is not sufficient to be a lone wolf. You must learn to work with the pack."

One of the Senior Instructors, though, saw this weakness as a new skill he could embrace.

"Other people are weak," she had told him, "compared to you. You have resilience, strength, tenacity. Other people are looking for someone who will guide them, as they cannot make their own decisions.

"Do not despise these people, do not avoid them. Embrace them, guide them, give them the leadership they so desperately crave. And in doing so, manipulate them into doing the things that are necessary for our survival and our country."

Upon graduation from training, he had been given the codename Volkov - 'The Wolf'. In the fifteen years since then, Volkov had become one of the most decorated officers of the Division.

Whenever a small group of sympathisers needed to be stirred into action, Moscow would send in Volkov. If an opportunity arose for planting the seeds of dissent and causing disruption to the insidious, overbearing, totalitarian British Empire, Volkov would plot and coordinate and manipulate to maximise the impact.

But this mission was different. This time, Moscow had sent him to the Sino-Russian border to observe a small village. Moscow had not told him what he was looking for, simply that he was to keep watch.

When receiving his orders, Volkov had briefly wondered if he was being punished for some unknown transgression against the State.

"Do not fret, Comrade Volkov," his Commanding Officer had informed him, as if sensing the doubt in his mind, "you have done nothing wrong. You are simply the only available agent at this time."

Now, a week later, Volkov turned his ice blue eyes to the Trooper, staring at him coldly.

His dispassionate stare was one of his most highly effective tools for changing the behaviours of the men and women around him, manipulating them into doing what he wanted done. His stare made people shiver involuntarily, and was one of the trademarks of The Wolf.

The Trooper was no different to the other weak willed and weak-minded people Volkov dealt with. His voice trailed off under the withering stare.

"Apologies, Comrade Volkov," the Trooper mumbled, before resuming his watch of the border town.

Volkov continued to stare for a moment longer, knowing that the Trooper would be feeling his gaze bore into the back of his head. Volkov also knew that the Trooper would share this moment with his fellow soldiers after his shift.

"I tell you, it was a narrow escape." he'd inform his comrades, "I was certain I was a dead man when I saw those eyes turn upon me."

Volkov rarely needed to resort to such extreme measures. The Senior Instructor had been correct. Once he honed his skill for manipulation, Volkov did not need to employ the violent methods of some of his fellow operatives.

He maintained his lethal skills, of course, as all operatives were required to do. His preference, though, was to engineer situations that met his goals, creating events by manipulating people to do the work for him.

Volkov was the first to admit, though, that his reputation as The Wolf - single-minded, dedicated, unstoppable, full of tightly controlled aggression - made this job much easier. He always liked it when Moscow gave a few days' notice to the area he was going to next. It meant they would be on edge when he arrived, and that made them much less likely to try to resist his orders.

"Maintain your watch," he ordered the Trooper, "and inform me immediately if anything changes in the village."

Volkov turned and stalked away to the Command Post.

oOo

Volkov sat in his small office, at the back of the Command Post. As always, the door to the office was open, so he could hear everything going on outside. His staff couldn't see him, of course, but they knew he was always listening.

"Fear," he mused, "is an excellent motivator."

Volkov ran a gloved finger over the scar on his face. It was wide, almost as wide as his index finger, and ran across the left-hand side of his face from his chin to his ear.

The scar was a relic from the Sino-Soviet conflict in 1929. Not far from where he was standing right now, he had gone into battle against a Chinese machine gun nest. He had graduated training just a year before, and when the order to attack was given, he had realised he probably would not live to see his seventeenth birthday.

Only a few paces into the attack, Volkov had been hit by two machine gun bullets in his thigh, causing him to fall. As he dropped to the ground, a third bullet had whipped across his face, tearing the flesh and leaving him with a bloody wound.

Volkov had been rescued some hours later by the medics, and he received excellent treatment for the wounds in his thigh. The doctors were not, however, interested in performing cosmetic surgery on the face of a sixteen-year-old boy, so the wound to his face was cleaned and dressed, but only roughly stitched.

The scar was a constant reminder to Volkov of the things that were truly important. His looks were not important, and the fight for freedom has a price that needs to be paid, sometimes in pain, sometimes in blood. He was a revolutionary, in a country that had revolted against their imperial masters.

What he could not understand, though, was why the people who craved freedom were often so unwilling to fight for it. Were they afraid? Did they think that someone else should be responsible for their freedom?

And what about the people who still suffered under the tyranny of the British Crown. Surely they could see that they were trapped in a life of servitude and obedience to their Empire? How could they not stand up against their Monarch, as his people had done in 1917, and demand their freedom?

Volkov's thoughts were interrupted by a knock on his office door. He momentarily chided himself for not remaining focussed on the task at hand, but he responded to the knock as if he was thinking of nothing other than the mission.

"Da," he said sternly.

Volkov liked how the Russian word 'Da' carried so much more authority that its English equivalent, 'Yes'.

"Comrade Colonel," the Private standing at the door began, before being silenced by a sharp look from Volkov.

The young soldier realised his error and froze. Volkov did not permit use of his military rank, even though he was one of the youngest officers in Russia to have risen to that high level. Volkov found his code name - and the reputation that went with it - to be a far more effective tool than his military status.

"Comrade Volkov," the young man quickly corrected himself, "we have received an encoded message, recalling you to Moscow."

"Finally," Volkov thought, although his face betrayed no emotion, "Moscow has a more suitable mission for me."

"Da," was Volkov's only reply.

Chapter 3

Caloundra, Colony of Queensland, Australia
Monday 7 September 1942

It only took Billy about 20 minutes to make the trek from his home to the College gate, so he arrived with some 15 minutes to spare before the first class of the day was scheduled to begin.

As Billy entered the gate of the Caloundra Colonial College, he stopped on the edge of the path. He was trying to remember all the details from his tour of the College earlier in the year.

"Right-o," he said to himself, "where is everything on campus?"

To his right, he remembered, was the original school building, built near the end of last century. The long, low, sandstone building, now known as 'College House', was bright and solid, lending a sense of decorum and stability, dependability and strength, to the College.

Originally the only building on campus, College House was now the administrative hub, with the offices of the Masters clustered together on one side of the central entrance door, and the office and residence of the Headmaster on the other.

A newer building, the Assembly Hall, had been built onto the back of College House, so that the entrance way connected the two buildings. If the Assembly Hall was the vertical part of a capital letter 'T', College House would be the horizontal part. A visitor or new student could enter College House through the front door, walk past the reception desk and through the corridor that ran across the building, then down a small flight of stairs to enter the Assembly Hall.

"Good." Billy thought, congratulating himself on his memory, "Now, what's on the far side of the Assembly Hall?"

The main part of the campus consisted of four smaller, single-storey buildings, arranged like the sides of a square, creating a large, central courtyard inside. The courtyard was well shaded by trees, and small pathways linked cleared spots where students could sit on the grass or at picnic tables.

Each building was the home for one of the subjects in the curriculum. E block housed the English Department, M block was for Mathematics, and H block was for the History Department. S block, which contained a series of laboratories as well as classrooms, hosted the Science Department.

Between the academic buildings and the Assembly Hall was the oval. A gymnasium containing locker rooms, a boxing ring, and space for other indoor sports stood next to the oval.

At either end of the oval were combination goal posts, allowing students to play either rugby or football, without needing to change the goal posts. The vertical posts were the correct width apart and rose to regulation height for rugby.

By a clever arrangement of hooks built into the crossbar and the lower part of the uprights, a football net could be quickly strung up. Special connections were sunk into the ground behind the posts, allowing the net to be tightened into place.

Billy had seen both sports played on the oval during his visit, with rugby practice for Third Form taking place in the morning, and a scratch game of football being held at lunchtime between the Fourth and Fifth Form students.

While the rugby practice was quite serious, as the team was representing the College in the upcoming zone carnival, the football match was full of fun and good-natured rivalry. Trick shots were the norm, as the talented players tried out some fancy manoeuvres with the ball. Both teams had made dribbling the ball into an art form, and the strikers were pin-point accurate on every attempt at goal.

Billy was snapped out of his reverie by a sharp cry, coming from somewhere off to his left, away from the buildings. Turning towards the sound, Billy saw quick, furtive movements between the storage sheds, where the groundskeeper kept his machinery and chemicals.

Without a second thought, Billy dropped his satchel and took off at a run towards the sheds. His instincts told him someone was in trouble, and his immediate reaction was to step up to the problem and help.

As Billy rounded the corner of the equipment shed, he slid to a halt. With his back pushed up against the rowing shed, Billy saw a boy about his age, wearing wire-rimmed glasses, surrounded by three older, bigger, boys. The younger boy was probably another First Former, Billy thought, although he was quite a bit shorter than Billy.

The boy had a thin trickle of blood coming from the corner of his mouth, and his school uniform had leaves stuck to it. To Billy, it was clear he'd been punched and knocked to the ground, but the boy had gotten back up again and was facing off to the gang, his fists raised defiantly in self-defence.

No one had heard Billy arrive on the scene, and one of the gang members was taunting the young boy.

"This is Third Form territory," the biggest of the older boys sneered, "no one else gets to go through here without paying the toll."

"Yeah, you tell him, Sean," laughed one of the other boys.

"Seems to me," the young boy quipped, with only a slight quaver in his voice, "this area is for the groundskeeper."

The ringleader took a step forward, but the younger boy stood his ground. Although he'd taken a hit, he was clearly not cowed by the bullies and was standing up for himself.

Billy was touched by the bravery of the smaller boy and felt a protective surge rush over him.

"You know," Billy said, "he's got a point."

All three bullies whirled to face Billy, their initial shock at being caught relaxing into sneers as they realised Billy was a student, and not a Master.

"Mind your own business," snapped Sean, "or you'll get the same treatment as the little runt here."

"Now, that's very interesting," Billy said evenly, as he advanced slowly towards the group.

Billy kept his hands in his trouser pockets, as the bullies watched him warily.

"I was always taught," Billy went on, unhurriedly, "that if someone had a grievance, he should sort it out man to man.

"I don't ever recall it being proper for three people to beat up a younger, smaller man," Billy paused for effect, locking eyes with the ringleader, "unless one or all of them were cowards."

At this harshest of rebukes, all three of the Third Form boys sucked in a loud, collective breath.

The boy called Sean took a step towards Billy.

"Is that really what you want?"

Billy kept his gaze steady on the older boy. "It's not about what I want. It's about whether you're going to be a man or not."

The other two bullies took a step forward at this challenge to their leader, and Billy cocked his head to one side, questioningly.

Sean held his arms out to the side, stopping the other boys in their tracks. He then took another step forward and Billy nodded.

"Marquis of Queensbury rules?" Billy asked.

The older boy nodded.

"Very well, then."

Billy eased effortlessly into a boxing stance, his weight moving forward onto the balls of his feet, his hands moving up into defensive positions near his head.

The older boy took a similar stance, although he lacked the grace that Billy brought to the pose.

The Third Form boy was nearly a foot taller than Billy and had a much longer reach. Billy knew that physical strength alone would not be enough to see him topple this older boy.

After a few moments, Sean lunged forward, swinging a roundhouse haymaker at Billy's head. Billy saw the move coming and ducked easily under the punch. Darting in under the swinging arm, Billy landed two quick, powerful jabs to the solar plexus of his opponent, winding him.

The older boy was off balance and struggling to draw breath. Billy stood up and drove a sharp blow directly onto the bridge of the boy's nose. Blood spurted out of his nostrils to the sound of a loud crack, and he fell backwards onto the seat of his pants.

Billy returned quickly to his fighters' stance, waiting to see what Sean would do next.

After a moment, the bully held up his hands.

"Alright," he said between gulps of air, "I yield."

As Billy had suspected, Sean was like most bullies. He intimidated others with the threat of violence and his physical size, but he was not able to maintain his bluster when someone stood up to him.

Billy took two steps toward Sean, still seated on the ground and breathing hard. His gang stood dumbstruck, unable to believe that their leader had been so quickly and thoroughly beaten in a fight. As Billy moved in towards the fallen boy, all eyes followed him to see how he would treat his foe.

Instead of continuing the beating, or taunting the older boy, Billy reached out his hand. After a moment, Sean grabbed the hand, and Billy helped him to his feet.

"I'm Billy Bowman," he said, simply.

"Sean Byrne," the older boy replied.

Billy shook his hand, then nodded his head towards the younger boy.

"Are we right to go now?"

Sean nodded.

"Thanks, Sean," Billy said evenly, before turning to each of the other boys in the gang and giving each a nod of acknowledgement, "Gentlemen."

Billy turned on his heel, and without another glance at the older boys, started walking back towards College House.

Stephen Archer

Chapter 4

Caloundra, Colony of Queensland, Australia
Monday 7 September 1942

The younger boy quickly caught up with Billy, and just as they turned the corner of the shed, he stuck out his hand to Billy.

"I'm Ian," he said, "Ian Landsborough".

"Billy Bowman," Billy said, shaking Ian's hand warmly.

"Thanks for stepping in, Billy, I wasn't really looking forward to starting school with a beating."

"How did you happen to be over behind the shed?" Billy asked.

"It's a shortcut for me," Ian said, "I live on the other side of the river behind the College.

"A little way upstream, a large tree's fallen across the river and you can use it to scoot across, without having to go all the way round through the town to get to the front gate."

"And no one told you the Third Formers would demand a toll for passing through that way." Billy mused.

"Exactly," Ian agreed, "I've never heard of such a thing! Very unsporting, if you ask me."

Billy nodded in agreement.

He always tried to find a way to peacefully settle disputes and fighting like he'd done this morning was his last, not his first, resort. But in this case, honour had demanded that he call cowardice on the bullies and then back up his accusation.

As they got closer to the main path leading from the gate to College House, Billy started looking for his satchel. He'd dropped it somewhere near the pathway in his haste to assist Ian. His satchel didn't appear to be anywhere on the ground, and Billy had a sinking feeling that someone might have picked it up and taken it.

Suddenly, Billy looked up and saw that his satchel was being held tightly to the chest of a young girl. She was looking around anxiously, her long red hair in braids that were swinging in time with the movement of her head. She was taller than Ian, and only a little shorter than Billy.

The girl let out a delighted squeal as Billy and Ian got closer.

"Mouse!" she cried, "where have you been? I've been waiting here…"

Her voice trailed off as she saw the leaves still stuck to his hair and the dribble of dried blood coming from the corner of his mouth.

She ran over to him, grabbed his shoulders and held him at arm's length as she examined him for injuries. Her brow was furrowed in concern and her mouth was set in a thin line of barely concealed anger.

"What happened?" she demanded.

"Nothing much, Jane," Ian said reassuringly, "I just had a bit of a disagreement with some Third Formers about rights of access into the school."

"Third Form!" she harrumphed, "They should be reported for this!".

"Slow down, slow down," Ian chided, gently, "it's all sorted out now."

Jane turned her head slowly, looking at Billy as if she'd only just noticed he was standing there.

"Billy," Ian said formally, "may I present Miss Jane Everington-Smyth. Jane, this is Billy Bowman, who gallantly assisted me in my recent difficulties with Third Form."

Billy bowed slightly and offered his hand to Jane. Jane slowly reached out her own hand, allowing Billy to gently clasp her fingers. Then, both of them broke into delighted grins, as their hands fell away.

"Thank you for minding my satchel for me," Billy said.

"What? Your satchel?"

"Yes, I'm afraid I dropped it here when I went to...", Billy paused, glancing at Ian, "...to assist Ian."

"Ah, yes, I see," stammered Jane, "well, in that case, you're welcome."

Billy continued to grin, slowly turning his head between Jane and Ian.

"So, how do you two know each other?"

"We were at Primary School together, and we became friends over the years," Jane said.

"Well, it helped that we're both reasonably good at our subjects," Ian added, a sly grin creeping across his face.

"That's a bit of an understatement, don't you think?" Jane laughed.

"I don't want Billy to think we're just a couple of eggheads who do nothing but study and ace our exams."

"Well, we're certainly not just that, Mouse!"

They both started laughing, in the comradely way that only the best of friends can manage.

Billy looked at the two friends, one eyebrow raised in question.

Jane and Ian noticed the look from Billy and began to explain.

"We're both explorers," Ian claimed proudly.

"When we were 9, we realised that there were parts of *The History* that happened around this area," Jane's arms swept wide, taking in the whole of the town and the hinterland surrounding them, "but the events happened years ago."

"So, we started combing through *The History*, and the newspapers in the library, to try to find clues that might tell us where to look for some of the relics from those events."

"We must have spent..." Ian paused, looking at Jane.

"About a year."

"...About a year gathering all the evidence," Ian continued, "and pouring over the maps of the settlement and some of the old Admiralty charts."

"And then, when we were ready," Jane chimed in, "we set off early one Saturday morning to look for evidence of the men from the *Queen of the Colonies*, who were marooned in 1863."

Billy thought for a moment, recalling that part of *The History*.

Some of the passengers from the ship *Queen of the Colonies* had become lost in a tiny boat, when a storm blew up while they were returning to the ship from a landing party. Eventually, the group were cast ashore, and they survived for a fortnight on shellfish and berries, before they were eventually located by a search party sent out, at great peril, from Brisbane.

Billy let out a gasp of astonishment.

"You're the ones who found the Pandanus Tree!"

Ian blushed a little, while Jane nodded ever so slightly.

Their discovery had made the front page of the newspaper a couple of years earlier, and Billy's father had read the story enthusiastically to the whole family. The newspaper told how two intrepid young local explorers had located a pandanus tree that had the name *Queen of the Colonies* carved into the trunk, near the spot where it was now believed the little boat had been driven onto the shore.

"That's right," said Ian, "we thought we might have worked out the route their boat took in the storm and started exploring along the coast where they might have landed."

"So you two actually added to *The History*!" Billy exclaimed.

"It's only an extra paragraph," Jane said quietly, but Billy could see how proud she was of their achievement.

All the while they had been talking, the other children attending the College had been moving past them towards the entrance to College House, and the Assembly Hall beyond.

Now, with a clank and a hiss of steam, a small squat machine mounted on the wide verandah at the front of College House sprang into action. The exposed gears on the machine whirred quickly in one direction, before slowing down, stopping, and then spinning the opposite way, increasing their speed as they turned. A solid metal arm protruded from the top of the machine, connected to a brass bell. As the gears turned, the metal arm moved the bell, first in one direction, then in the other, causing a rhythmic ringing.

One of the Masters had come out onto the wide verandah at the front of College House, and looked at his pocket watch as the bell started ringing.

He caught sight of Billy, Ian and Jane standing on the path, and called out to them, smiling.

"Come along, children, we're about to start the school year."

Chapter 5

Caloundra, Colony of Queensland, Australia
Monday 7 September 1942

By the time Billy, Ian and Jane had scampered through College House and down the steps into the Assembly Hall, the large room was almost full.

Ahead of them was the stage, with a podium in the centre. On the left side of the stage were seats for the Head, the Masters and dignitaries, while to the right was a small section for the College band.

From the stairs at the back of the hall, a central walkway ran all the way down to the front of the stage, with neat rows of chairs branching off from both sides.

A tall, slim boy, with the last traces of acne still visible on his face, was standing in the walkway, just behind the last row of chairs. His blazer was carefully tailored and immaculate, and he wore a glittering gold badge engraved with the word 'Prefect' in deep blue copperplate script.

"New chums?" he asked quietly.

Billy, Ian and Jane nodded in unison.

"First Form?" the Prefect continued.

Again, the three students nodded.

"Move quickly and quietly down to the front," he instructed, "First Form students sit in the first two rows. Hurry now, the Head's about to start."

With Ian and Jane leading, and Billy just a step behind, all three moved down the walkway to the second row of seats. All of the seats on the left-hand side were taken, but there were three empty seats on the right-hand side, some 5 or 6 places in from the aisle.

Rather than trying to squeeze past the legs of the already seated students, Jane looked pleadingly at the students in the row. Without a murmur, all of the seated students quietly stood, shuffled three places to their right, and then sat down again.

As Billy, Ian and Jane took the newly vacated seats, all three nodded their thanks to the students who had moved to let them in.

This simple action, taken without complaint or concern, reminded Billy once again of the core values of the Empire. It wasn't about individual rights or looking after oneself at the expense of others. The Empire was built on the solid foundation of caring for others. Those in higher stations, born into greater privilege, had the greatest responsibilities to others, but no one, no matter what their social status, was exempt from looking after those around them. This was one of the fundamental tenets of their Empire, and it served them all well.

After a moment, a grey-haired, rather stooped man rose from his seat on the stage and shuffled carefully to the lectern, putting much of his weight on the stout cane he held in his left hand.

When he reached the lectern, he took a few seconds to look across the hall at all of the students, before speaking.

"I am Headmaster George Carpenter," he intoned, in a voice that clearly carried his authority.

Then, a twinkle came to his eye, and he smiled gently at the assembly.

"Welcome everyone, to the 1942-43 school year.

"We will start with the playing of the Anthem by the College band. As most of you know, the band only performs the Anthem twice each year - at the opening and closing ceremonies.

"Will the band members please take your places on the stage."

Several students began moving from their places around the Assembly Hall toward the right side of the stage, where the instruments stood ready.

Billy noticed that Sean Byrne was part of a small group of Third Form students who were moving to the band area. Sean had cleaned himself up since Billy had last seen him, although his nose was still swollen and his eyes were red. Billy rather hoped Sean didn't play a wind instrument and that he wasn't one of the singers.

As the band members took their places, Sean moved to the upright piano and settled quickly into his seat. Billy breathed a soft sigh of relief that his altercation with Sean hadn't cost the older boy his place in the band.

One of the Sixth Form girls moved to the front of the band and picked up a short baton from a music stand. She turned to bow to the Headmaster, who nodded kindly at her, before turning back to the band.

"Please rise for the Anthem." called the Headmaster.

The students and the Masters quickly stood to attention in their places. Only the band members remained seated.

The conductor tapped her baton lightly on the music stand, then raised her arms in the air. At this movement, every member of the band took up their playing positions, ready to strike the first note.

After the briefest of pauses, the conductor began directing the band, and the singers began one of the most beautiful renditions of the Anthem that Billy had ever heard.

As the last notes died away, the Headmaster again spoke to the assembly.

"God save the King!" he cried.

"God save the King!" came the enthusiastic response.

"Please, be seated," the Headmaster instructed.

"For some of you, this is your first year here at Caloundra Colonial College, and you may be finding things a little overwhelming."

The Headmaster straightened slightly and looked directly at Billy and Ian.

"While others in First Form," he continued, not shifting his gaze away from the two boys, "may already be working out how things *should* be done."

Billy and Ian glanced at each other out of the corners of their eyes, not daring to move their heads.

The Headmaster held their gaze for just a second or two longer, before once again turning his attention to the rest of the students.

"Some of you are beginning your final year with us, and we want to congratulate everyone who is now in either Fifth Form or Upper Sixth Form. You've all done very well to get here, and we are looking forward to bringing you through the final stage of your secondary education.

"Normally, at this point in proceedings, I would try to impart some words of wisdom to you," the Headmaster continued, "something to inspire you to achieve great things during your time here at the College.

"But today, you will not hear words of wisdom from me. Instead, we are honoured to have a very special guest speaker address you."

The Headmaster paused, looking off stage to the left. From his seat, Billy could see a young Air Force Officer with gold braid on his uniform, standing just behind the curtains on that side of the stage.

As the Headmaster looked over, the young Officer gave a nod, indicating for the Head to proceed.

Headmaster Carpenter returned his gaze to the auditorium and drew a deep breath.

"Ladies, gentlemen, students," he said solemnly, "pray stand for His Excellency, Group Captain the Honourable Sir Leslie Wilson, GCMG, GCSI, GCIE, DSO, the Governor of the Colony of Queensland."

Chapter 6

Caloundra, Colony of Queensland, Australia
Monday 7 September 1942

Every person in the auditorium shot to their feet, as the speaker above the large portrait of King George, hanging at the back of the stage, played the first six bars of The Anthem as a Vice-Regal salute.

As the music was playing, a tall graceful man strode out onto the stage. As he passed the young Officer, who must have been his Aide-de-Camp, the Governor was discreetly handed a slim folder.

Resplendent in his Royal Air Force dress uniform, with gold aiguillette, rank insignia and gleaming pilot 'wings', Sir Leslie was the picture postcard of a Senior Officer in the service of His Majesty.

When he reached the podium, the Governor carefully placed the folder on the lectern, but did not open it. His eyes were piercing, looking out at the students from atop his bristling moustache.

Billy could see a striking intelligence in those eyes, as well as compassion and maybe even a hint of mischief. Sir Leslie had Billy enthralled before he even started his address to the school.

"Thank you, Headmaster," Sir Leslie said, with a nod to the older gentleman who had now taken his seat beside the other staff.

"We live in a golden age of peace and prosperity across the Empire." the Governor began, not taking his eyes off the students seated before him.

"We have not needed to bear arms in any significant conflict since the Great War of 1914-16 drew to a close, with the defeat of Germany and the inclusion of the Axis nations into the British Empire.

"As you all know, only three areas of the globe - Russia, Japan and China - still remain outside the Empire, and His Majesty has stated He is prepared to wait until they are ready to become part of His realm.

"However, we must remember that the revolutionary forces which destabilised Russia in 1917 could still spill beyond the borders of that great, frozen land." Sir Leslie said firmly.

"The Japanese maintain their isolation from the world, ignoring our overtures of friendship, so we cannot know their future plans outside their island home.

"China too remains largely closed to us, and what little we know of them suggests they are warlike and feudal, vying among themselves for power. It is not impossible that a warlord may one day conquer all of China, and perhaps even seek to expand his influence to our colonies which lie nearby.

"I do not say any of these things to scare you," Sir Leslie continued, scanning the assembled students and making eye contact with each young person in the room.

"I say these things to remind you that we must not let this great age of advancement and peace lull us into a false sense of security. We must not become complacent about our duty to protect the Empire.

"I have had the honour to serve five Monarchs, both in times of war and in times of peace.

"I have seen action as a Royal Marine in Africa at the end of last century, and I fought beside some of your grandparents at the Gallipoli landing in 1915. I have seen the battlefields of France from the sky, after I transferred to the Royal Air Force in 1916.

"You should all pay heed to the Masters, sitting here to my right," Sir Leslie gave a sweeping gesture, encompassing all of the academic staff of the College.

"See how each one of them wears the medals of honour, courage and service, bestowed by our King, for their dedication to duty in wars gone by.

"But do not feel that military service is the only way to fulfil your duty," Governor Wilson continued, "I have also served as an Aide-de-Camp to the Governor of your fellow Australian colony, New South Wales.

"I have been Governor of India, and am now your Governor, here in the colony of Queensland.

"But this will be my last posting in the service of His Majesty," Sir Leslie said, a little sadly.

"My time of service is coming to an end, but your time is just beginning.

"Young Gentlemen and Young Ladies, you hold the future of our Empire in your hands. How you act in the years to come is critical for the continuation of our way of life.

"Do not feel your part is too small to matter," the Governor continued, "every part of the Empire is needed to make us strong and stable.

"And so, young people, I will give you my three best pieces of advice to help you fulfil your role and your responsibilities into the future.

"I call it The Triple-A Rule," Sir Leslie chuckled, a devilish grin appearing on his face.

"Firstly, always remain Aware. Notice what is going on around you. Is it good or bad? Does it meet the values of our Empire, or does it undermine the things we hold to be true? Remember, if something does not support the Empire, it cannot continue. Apathy and lethargy are some of our greatest enemies.

"Which leads me to the second 'A', Application. Seeing a problem and doing nothing about it will lead to our destruction. To say, 'it's not my problem', or 'I'm not important enough or strong enough or influential enough' will not suffice. Apply yourselves to everything you do. No matter what task you are given, no matter what challenges are thrown your way, no matter what injustices or wrongdoing you see, give your all to achieving your best effort.

"And finally, binding the Triple-A Rule together, at the heart of everything I am sharing with you today, is Attitude. If your attitude is positive, generous, courageous and dedicated, all things are possible."

Sir Leslie paused for a moment, as if allowing time for the students to consider his words.

"You have all proven yourselves worthy of being here in this next level of education." he intoned sombrely, "Do not waste this opportunity."

Once again, the Governor scanned the room, before smiling again at the assembly.

"I wish you every success in your school life."

And with that, Group Captain Sir Leslie Wilson, Governor of Queensland, turned on his heel and left the stage, to the triumphant strains of the Anthem playing from the speaker.

As the Governor left, the staff and students quickly scrambled to their feet, too overwhelmed by the power of Sir Leslie's speech to even clap or cheer.

It was only much later in the day that Billy realised His Excellency hadn't once looked at his speech, the thin folder had remained closed the entire time. Billy became even more certain that Sir Leslie was now his role model.

Chapter 7

Caloundra, Colony of Queensland, Australia
Monday 7 September 1942

After the assembly, the older students quickly separated into their Form groups and headed to the classrooms. The First Form students remained in the Assembly Hall for orientation.

While the older students were getting organised to leave the Hall, Billy quickly reached into his satchel and took out a pencil and a small leather-bound notebook. For a moment, he reverently held the notebook in his hand, enjoying the touch of the cool leather against his fingers.

The notebook had been a gift from his grandfather for his 10th birthday.

"This is a special book," Grandfather Bowman had said, "for keeping the important things in your life close at hand.

"The world around you is an amazing place, William. You will see strange, beautiful and wondrous things in your life. And when you do, pay close attention to them, take note of them, write about them or sketch them. In here."

His grandfather tapped the black leather cover of the notebook, looking resplendent with its bright red leather stripe on the spine and matching leather triangles on the outside corners of the covers.

"From time to time, you'll meet people who will say something that strikes a chord in your heart. Don't worry too much about they are of high station or not, William. Concentrate on what they say, not who they are."

Billy nodded, in awe of this amazing gift.

"If you are very, very lucky" Grandfather Bowman said with a wink, "you might need more than one notebook across the years of your life."

Billy's grandfather reached into his little bag, the one he always carried with him, and pulled out his own small notebook.

Mark Bowman's notebook was worn down by years of use. The leather covers were scuffed and scratched, and did not quite meet properly any more. The edges of the paper were a little warped, looking like a gilt-edged wave between the covers. Billy could see stains on the notebook, some of which were probably dirt, while others could have been dried blood, perhaps from seeing service with his grandfather in one of the wars.

"When I die, this book will pass to your father," the old man said softly, "and then eventually, it will go to you.

"But before then, William, I want you to make your own book, for your own treasures and precious memories."

In the two years since getting the notebook, he had already filled almost a dozen pages. Now, with the words of Sir Leslie echoing in his head, he used his neatest handwriting to inscribe the three words of the Triple-A Rule in a vertical list on the inside cover of his journal - 'Awareness', 'Application', 'Attitude'.

With a contented sigh, Billy put the notebook and pencil back in his satchel, and turned his attention to the Headmaster, who was now approaching the First Form students at the front of the Hall.

oOo

The Headmaster only addressed the group briefly.

"I'm very pleased to see all your eager faces here at the College," he said, "and I hope you'll all enjoy your time here."

"Now, I must dash, but Mr Gibson will take things from here."

The Headmaster turned to Mr Gibson and touched his hand to the brim of his mortarboard cap in salute. Mr Gibson returned the gesture, before taking a step towards the students as the Head shuffled away towards College House.

Mr Gibson was a rather squat man, with a round face and horn-rimmed glasses perched precariously on the end of his nose. Underneath his nose was the largest, bushiest moustache Billy had ever seen.

"Good morning, I'm Mr Gibson, the Head of Mathematics," he informed them, in a voice that was thick with the accent of the Highlands of Scotland. He began rocking gently on his heels as he spoke.

"While you'll all be doing the same units of study this year." he continued, "I will be conducting a special examination two weeks from today, for any student who wishes to be considered for the Advanced Program."

Billy heard a little squeak from the seats next to him. He looked over to see Jane and Ian almost bursting with excitement at the news of an extra exam and an Advanced Program.

"However," continued Mr Gibson, "I must warn ye that if you're accepted into that program, it will be extra study, and will nae replace the normal units. You'll still be expected to complete the same studies as e'ry one else."

As Mr Gibson turned away from the students and re-joined the group of staff, a very prim and proper lady stepped forward, her grey hair tied back in a neat bun. Her dress sense was impeccable, and she carried a small lace fan in one hand.

For a moment she looked at Mr Gibson, as if expecting him to introduce her. When he made no move to present her to the group, she smoothed her dress and turned to the students.

"Good morning, children," she began, in a voice that might have come straight from the Manor.

"My name is Mrs Franklin, and it's lovely to meet you today," she said, smiling politely.

"I will conduct your lessons in the King's English. I look forward to reading your first compositions."

Mrs Franklin turned slightly, to look at the group of staff. She caught the attention of a rake-thin man, wearing large round glasses and carrying a slightly stained and worn laboratory coat draped over one arm.

Mrs Franklin turned back to the group.

"Children, I'd like you to meet Mr Isaacs, our Sciences Master."

Mr Isaacs bowed ever so slightly, then shuffled forward.

"H-h-hello," he stammered, "I don't h-have a special exam for you."

Then he smiled warmly at the students.

"But I think you'll like the experiments we'll do together in the lab."

Billy noticed that Ian and Jane seemed even more happy to hear about the Science experiments than they were about the Mathematics exam. He smiled to himself as he remembered that this was exactly the sort of thing one should expect from the *Queen of the Colonies* explorers.

The next Master was the opposite of Mr Isaacs. He was tall and tan, with broad shoulders and incredibly short-cropped black hair.

The Master took one athletic step forward before introducing himself.

"My name is Roberts," he half-bellowed, in a voice that was only slightly toned down from the sound of a coach on the sidelines of a rugby match.

"I'm the Sports Master," he continued, without changing the volume level of his voice, "see me in one of the breaks if you want to play".

He began to turn away, then quickly snapped back around, causing some of the students seated closest to him to flinch a little.

"And make sure you bring your PE kit tomorrow. Boxing practice for boys and gymnastics for the girls is after lunch."

Mr Roberts did another snap turn and took an energetic step to re-join the group of Masters.

The last staff member to address them was a lady who looked like she hadn't yet reached the age of 25. Her hair was plaited into a long braid, that she wore down the centre of her back. Her dress was subdued, but fashionable, as if she was the daughter of a middle-class banker or merchant.

As she stepped forward, her eyes sparkled with intelligence and humour.

"I'm Miss Wellington," she introduced herself, confident and sure despite appearing quite young compared to the other Masters, "and I'm the History Master."

"I make sure I spend time with every student, in every Form, each week," she continued, "I'm sure you all know how important it is to the Empire that every student understands *The History*. It is my honour to serve the Empire by helping each and every one of you learn about our past glories."

"If you ever have any questions about *The History*, or our Empire, please book a time to talk with me. My door, as they say, is open."

As Miss Wellington stepped back, Mr Gibson stepped forward again.

"Now that the introductions are over," he said, with just a hint of a smile peeking out from under his moustache, "it's time to git to work."

"First Form, please follow me to M-Block. It's time for some Mathematics."

Chapter 8

Near Grodekovo, Siberia, Russia
Monday 7 September 1942

Volkov was just finishing up his hand-over for the operative who would relieve him, when an urgent cry came from the control room.

"Unidentified airship approaching," announced the radar operator, "20 kilometres and closing fast."

Dealing with an incursion by the forces of the Chinese Army was not, strictly speaking, within his mission role. However, Volkov knew that if an attack was under way, his skills and experience would be invaluable.

As Volkov moved to the doorway of the office, to better observe the control room, the Major in charge of the outpost stepped into the middle of the room.

The Major looked over at Volkov, silently offering command to the operative. Volkov waved a gloved hand dismissively, making clear his intention was to observe.

"Unless, of course," Volkov thought, "you make a mess of things Comrade Major. I won't put my life at risk if you lack the competence to deal with an attack."

The Major moved smoothly into action.

"Report," she demanded of the radar operator.

"Single airship approaching, Comrade Major. She's small and fast. Could be a bomber or a transport airship."

"Time till arrival?"

"Seven minutes, Comrade Major."

The Major turned to her operations officer, a newly graduated Lieutenant, who was looking very pale and uncertain in the face of this hostile move. The Major leaned over to the young officer and made eye contact with him.

"Courage in front of the men, Comrade Lieutenant," she whispered, "always show courage in front of the men."

The Lieutenant swallowed hard, then squared his shoulders.

"Alert all field guns and have the men stand-to in their weapons emplacements," the Major ordered.

The Lieutenant leapt to his station and began barking urgent orders to the runners.

Satisfied that the Lieutenant was now able to perform his duty, the Major turned to Volkov.

"Would you care to join me for a stroll, Comrade Volkov?"

For a moment, Volkov wondered if the Major was challenging him. Then, he saw the determined grin on her face, and realised that the Major intended to face the enemy in the open, not hiding in an underground bunker.

Impressed with the Major's courage, Volkov gave a humourless grin in return.

"Da," was all the response he needed to give.

The Major and Volkov strode out of the command post together.

oOo

Out on the tundra, a few metres away from the Command Post, was a small hillock. The snow-covered lump in the ground was more a pimple on the landscape than an actual hill. But it did provide a view over the border into China, and the two Russian officers effortlessly climbed to the top of the mound.

They planted their feet firmly, and stood side by side, ready to stare down the airship should it cross the border into Soviet airspace. Each peered into the distance, silently wanting to be the first to spot the enemy craft.

Behind them, a voice was shouting, trying to get their attention.

"Major! Major!"

The Major turned to see the radar operator running towards them, shouting and pointing wildly. After a stunned and surprised moment, the Major realised the soldier was pointing back behind the Command Post, away from the Chinese border.

"What is it, Sergeant?"

"Ma'am," the man panted breathlessly, "the airship is coming from Siberia, not from China."

"It's one of ours?"

"Da," the radar operator almost whispered, deeply embarrassed by his error and terrified of the reaction of his commander.

The radar operator stole a glance at Volkov, a sudden terror gripping his soul at the thought that his Major might hand him over to the Wolf for punishment.

The Major clenched her fists, locking her arms by her side. There was a vein pulsing in her neck. If the Sergeant didn't know what red-hot anger was, he need only look at the face of the Major to discover the meaning of the term.

"Return to your post," the Major ordered through gritted teeth. "I will convene a court martial in the morning, to determine your fate."

The radar operator scampered away so quickly, he left a spray of fine powdered snow hanging in the air behind him, puffed up from his frantically moving feet.

The Major turned to Volkov, mortified.

"Comrade Volkov," she began, "I apologise for the incompetence of my men. I will deal with this man in the harshest way imaginable. It will be a long time before he sees anything except the snows of Siberia."

To her surprise, the Major saw something that she never imagined was possible. Volkov had a hint of a smile on his face, and a mischievous twinkle in his pale eyes.

"Comrade Major," Volkov asked, maintaining a straight face, "am I to understand that your radar operator got confused, in the heat of the moment, and read his radar screen upside-down."

The Major nodded, uncertain if Volkov was angry or amused.

"I see," continued Volkov, "and would you say that, if we ignored this error in judgement, he is a quite competent radar operator?"

"Da," the Major agreed, although perhaps a little reluctantly.

"Comrade Major, you may do with the man as you see fit," Volkov said, before pausing for effect.

"But if, as you say, he is a competent operator most of the time, perhaps it would be a shame to lose his expertise to the salt mines."

The Major paused, considering the situation.

"Perhaps you are right, Comrade Volkov. Mother Russia has spent a great many roubles training him in the radar system."

"Perhaps, he has simply become complacent, with his current rank and role."

The Major grinned at the suggestion from Volkov.

"Yes, I believe you are correct, Comrade Volkov. Perhaps a stint as a Private, will allow him to refresh his skills and his dedication."

Volkov nodded.

"Shall we go meet the airship now, Comrade Major?"

oOo

The airship was moving in for final approach to the landing pad behind the Command Post. Her propellers were whirling up snow as she descended.

The radar operator may have had trouble telling direction, but he was absolutely correct in his assessment of the sleekness of the airship.

The large tube shape of the balloon was long and thin, tapering to a near point at the front and back. Most people described the balloon as cigar-shaped, but Volkov found this a very crude description for this marvel of air travel.

Beneath the balloon hung the gondola, where the passengers or cargo would be carried. The gondola also housed the bridge of the airship, while the engines and crew quarters were tucked up inside the lower section of the balloon.

As the airship got closer to the ground, Volkov realised that she had a very small gondola, perhaps only big enough for six or eight passengers. Combined with her large, thin balloon and four massive propellers, it was hardly surprising that she was very fast and, Volkov suspected, very manoeuvrable.

Four crewmen raced out from the support hanger on the side of the landing pad, spreading themselves out around the gondola. Volkov realised that the airship had stopped descending and was now hovering some 10 metres above the ground.

With a hiss, four ropes launched themselves out from the four corners of the gondola. Each crewman grabbed a rope and ran the end out to a circular hitch imbedded in the ground. When the crewmen had secured the ropes to the hitches, they raised both arms above their heads.

The captain of the airship must have been waiting for this signal. As soon as the fourth crewman raised his arms, the ropes began to be reeled back into the gondola by a hidden mechanism at each corner. As the airship got lower to the ground, Volkov could see the crew manipulating brass levers, to keep the giant ship descending evenly.

When the airship was just 30 centimetres above the ground, the mechanisms came to a screeching halt, locking the ropes in position and holding the airship rigidly in place. It would take a gale to dislodge the giant ship from her current position.

The door on the side of the gondola opened, and the airship captain stepped out and walked the few paces to the Major and Volkov.

"Comrade Volkov" he said, saluting, "I have been sent to collect you. You are required in Moscow at all possible speed."

Volkov nodded and strode past the captain on his way to the airship. He didn't look back at the Major. His entire attention was now focussed on his new mission, whatever that might be.

Chapter 9

Caloundra, Colony of Queensland, Australia
Monday 7 September 1942

Along with the rest of the First Form students, Billy spent the first hour after assembly in one of the Mathematics classrooms, as Mr Gibson recapped everything they had learned during their primary school years.

At first, Billy couldn't understand why they weren't doing any new work. Then he realised that not everyone in the Form had the same grasp of basic mathematics. Mr Gibson was conducting an informal assessment of the students, working out who would need additional tutoring to help them get ready for the new material.

When the clock in the classroom struck 11am, Mr Gibson pulled his pocket watch out from his waistcoat, hidden under his academic robes. With a nod of satisfaction, he returned the watch to his pocket.

"Time for your morning break," Mr Gibson informed them, "Make sure you're all at S-Block for Science class by 11:20."

As the students stood up, Mr Gibson walked towards the classroom door. When he'd left, the students began to exit the room, splitting up into groups as they moved away from the room and onto the various pathways that ran through the large courtyard outside.

Billy looked for Ian and Jane, but the two students were nowhere to be seen.

With a shrug, Billy wandered along one of the paths, until he came to a small stone picnic table, with built-in bench seats along the two longest sides. The table was nestled under a towering gum tree, and since no one else was sitting there, Billy sat down on the shady side of the table.

Reaching into his satchel, Billy pulled out his notebook and a shiny red apple.

Billy liked to use small breaks like this one to read through his notebook. He found it very comforting and motivating to leaf through the book and remind himself of all the things he had 'discovered'.

As he skimmed through the book, Billy began eating his apple and quickly became lost in thought.

"Do you mind if I sit here with you?"

Billy looked up to see a young lady with blonde hair, bleached almost white by the sun, standing next to the table and looking at him expectantly.

It took Billy a moment to understand that the girl had been speaking to him. When realisation struck, he recovered his wits quickly and stood up.

"Of course," he said, "I'd be delighted. I'm Billy Bowman."

"Hello," she replied, with a slight smile on her face, "but tell me, is it really Billy, or is that short for something?"

"William," Billy gulped, "it's William. But only my family calls me William."

"Well, it's delightful to meet you William. My name is Ann. Ann Roberts."

She offered her hand to Billy, which he quickly shook, then motioned for her to take the shaded seat, while he moved around to the other side of the table.

"Are you in First Form too, Ann?" Billy asked, once they were seated.

"No, William," Ann replied, with a hint of an Irish accent in her voice, "I'm in Third Form. I'm afraid I'm just a bit small for my age."

Billy was a little taken aback by this revelation. Ann wasn't as tall as Jane, so he'd simply assumed she was his age.

"I'm sorry, Ann, I didn't mean to presume."

"It's quite all right, William. You're not the first and I doubt you'll be the last. It is simply the way things are."

"Well, I must say, that's a very positive way to look at a situation."

Ann nodded her thanks.

"I really should apologise, William," Ann changed the subject, "I interrupted you when you were reading."

Billy smiled. He had put his notebook on the table as he stood up to greet Ann.

"I have read this little notebook many times," Billy said, smiling, "and I shall read it many more times in the years ahead. It was no hardship to be interrupted."

Again, Ann nodded, smiling this time at his chivalry.

Billy couldn't help but notice how her entire face lit up and her eyes sparkled when she smiled. It was then that Billy noticed how the blue of her eyes was the richest, deepest blue he'd ever seen. They were almost cobalt blue, Billy realised, with an intensity that was mesmerising.

A comfortable silence settled between the two students, as they continued to look at each other.

Then, Billy blushed, as he realised he was staring at Ann. He quickly looked away, embarrassed.

After a moment, he glanced up to see if she was angry about his impertinent stare. Ann let him see her smile and Billy looked relieved.

He was about to ask her about her classes, when the sound of the brass bell rang out across the campus. Billy cocked his ear quizzically at the sound.

"That's the five-minute warning bell," Ann informed him, laughing gently at his expression, "it lets everyone know that the next classes are about to begin, and all students and Masters should make their way to the correct room."

Billy nodded and began to rise from the stone bench.

"May I escort you to your next class, Miss Roberts?"

"That's very kind of you, Mr Bowman," Ann replied with equal formality, although Billy could see she was working quite hard to stifle a grin at his unexpected courteousness.

"However, I fear that you and I are not travelling in the same direction this morning, and I would not like to be responsible for you being late to one of your classes."

Billy bowed slightly in acknowledgement.

"Until next time we meet, then."

"Until then, William," Ann said as she rose and moved gracefully towards the English building.

Billy stared after her for a moment, mesmerised as he remembered the blue of her eyes.

Then, with a shake of his head, he broke the spell and began trotting towards the Science building for his next class.

Chapter 10

Caloundra, Colony of Queensland, Australia
Monday 7 September 1942

The Science building contained three laboratories at one end and two classrooms at the other, with a storage room in between. The entrance to the building led into a long corridor, with the classrooms to the left, the laboratories to the right, and the storage room directly in front.

As Billy rushed into the corridor, he could see through the window that the storage room was full of shelves overflowing with scientific equipment, glass beakers, test tubes, and a wide range of sizes of specimen containers.

The laboratories themselves were quite spacious, to accommodate the tall lab benches that ran in four rows from the front of the classroom, on either side of a central walkway. There were three wooden stools at each bench, and additional benches ran along the side walls of the laboratory.

When Billy arrived at the laboratory where the First Form students were gathered, he could see Ian and Jane, deep in conversation, at one of the front benches. Most of the rest of the class were spread out at the other benches.

Billy quickly moved to the bench where Ian and Jane were and sat down at the third stool.

Jane and Ian looked up from their conversation.

"Hello Billy," they said in unison, smiling.

Billy grinned back at them.

"Hello Jane," he said, "hello Ian."

"I say, old chap," Ian said earnestly, "after our little scrape this morning, I think it perfectly reasonable for you to call me Mouse."

"Thank you, Mouse, that's very decent of you."

"Not at all, old bean," Ian replied, smiling broadly.

"That makes you part of a very select group," Jane chimed in, "there are only perhaps a half-dozen people who have been invited to call him Mouse."

"In that case, Mouse, I am honoured."

At that moment, Mr Isaacs strode into the laboratory. He was now wearing his lab coat, and unlike the shy, uncertain man who had addressed them in the Assembly Hall, Mr Isaacs was now full of confidence and control. Clearly, this was his most comfortable environment.

The last couple of students from First Form scurried into the room behind him.

"The other Masters and I will make allowances today," he said firmly, "as it is your first day at the College. But only for today. The bells give ample notice for students to make their way to class, and tardiness is not an acceptable quality for the young gentlemen and ladies of the Empire."

The students who had arrived late muttered an apology to the Science Master, who nodded in response.

"Very good. Let's begin by looking at the Sciences we study in this modern age. Who can tell me one of the three branches of science?"

A scattering of hands were raised around the room, although Billy noticed that Ian and Jane raised their hands like a shot.

"Landsborough?" Mr Isaacs looked at Ian.

"Mechanisms, Sir," replied Ian.

"Very good, Landsborough. Mechanisms is the science of machines. It has everything to do with cogs and wheels, steam and propulsion."

"What's another branch of science?" Mr Isaacs continued, again looking around the room. After a few moments, he paused.

"How about you, Marks?" Mr Isaacs gestured towards a rather pimply young lady sitting in one of the back rows of benches.

"Umm, I'm not sure Sir."

"Would you care to take a guess?"

"Umm," Marks paused, before realising Mr Isaacs wasn't really giving her a choice about responding.

"Organisms, Sir?" She said quietly and hesitantly.

"Well done, Marks," Mr Isaacs smiled at the nervous student, who blushed a little at the attention.

"And who can tell me what the Science of Organisms studies?"

Jane hadn't lowered her hand since the questioning had begun.

"Smyth?" Mr Isaacs said, looking directly at Jane.

"It's Everington-Smyth, Sir,"

Mr Isaacs nodded, and Jane continued smoothly with her answer.

"The Science of Organisms is the study of all forms of life, both animal and plant. It includes the study of the individual species, as well as the relationships and interactions between species."

"Outstanding, Everington-Smyth," Mr Issacs boomed, "Well done!"

Billy thought the room got a little brighter because of how broadly Jane smiled at this recognition.

"And so, class, that leaves just one more branch of science."

Mr Isaacs was looking around the room, waiting to see who might respond with the final answer. He ignored the raised hands of Ian and Jane, wanting another student in the group to be given the opportunity to respond.

"Really," he said after a moment, "no one?"

Ian and Jane were almost standing up in their attempt to have Mr Isaacs acknowledge them. The Master continued to ignore their efforts.

"Very well," Mr Isaacs sighed, "the last branch is the Science of Compositions, which examines the component parts of all materials, both natural and manmade."

oOo

For the remainder of the period, Mr Isaacs introduced the students to the various pieces of scientific equipment, and the enormous list of safety rules that had to be followed when working in the laboratory.

As they were seated in the Compositions Laboratory for the start of the period, Mr Isaacs started by showing the students the Bunsen burners, and the correct technique for lighting them using a safety match. Each of the students was allowed to use, under supervision, a pipette to transfer a small quantity of a blue coloured liquid from a beaker to a test tube.

They then labelled their test tube with their name and the date, and carefully placed the tube in a rack on one of the side benches. Mr Isaacs explained that they would re-examine their samples later in the week and would be expected to note any changes.

In the Organisms Laboratory, which was the room next to the storage room, Mr Isaacs showed them the herbarium, where various species of plants and fungi were grown. He explained that the First Form was responsible for the care of the herbarium, and that each student would be placed on a roster to water and feed the plants.

The middle laboratory was the Mechanisms Laboratory. After visiting that laboratory, Ian, Jane and Billy almost needed to be dragged away from the flashing lights and large brass dials of the display that Mr Isaacs had set up. Even after returning to the Compositions Laboratory, the three students kept looking wistfully at the interconnecting door that joined the two science spaces.

After what seemed like only minutes, but in reality was over an hour, the College bell could again be heard ringing across the campus.

Unlike every other male Billy had ever seen, Mr Isaacs did not pull out his pocket watch when he heard the bell ring. Rather, he raised his left arm and turned his wrist towards his face. With his right hand, he gently pulled up the sleeve of his lab coat and his suit jacket.

Mr Isaacs had two thin brown leather straps running around his wrist, with a gold buckle holding the ends of the straps together. On the top of his wrist, Billy could just make out that the other ends of the leather straps were cradling a gold disk.

The disk looked like a small pocket watch, and Billy could see what appeared to be an hour and a minute hand, but there was no chain or fob to be seen.

It was then that Billy realised that Mr Isaacs was wearing a wristwatch, one of the latest inventions to come from the brilliant minds of His Majesty's Science Academy.

A masterful piece of miniaturisation, the wristwatch was part of the latest developments in the field of Mechanisms. Billy had seen a drawing of one in the newspaper, but he'd barely paid it any attention, thinking it was some sort of poor cousin to the pocket watch.

For Billy, and all the adult males he knew, there was something special about the debonair and sophisticated movement that came from checking one's pocket watch whenever a clock bell chimed. It was an outward sign that one was not only a man, but a gentleman, with social status and a proper upbringing.

But now, seeing this marvel in real life, on the wrist of one of the respected Masters of the College, Billy began to reassess his perspective on the pocket watch as a symbol of status in the Empire.

New wasn't always better, he knew, but that didn't mean new should be ignored either.

For the first time ever, Billy had come across two new things - the words of Sir Leslie and the wristwatch - worthy of inclusion in his notebook in a single day. And it was only just time for luncheon.

Chapter 11

**Caloundra, Colony of Queensland, Australia
Monday 7 September 1942**

Ian, Billy and Jane left the Science block together, making their way into the large enclosed courtyard. They were the last students out of the building after the class, as they'd all stayed in the hallway, peering through the now locked door of the Mechanisms Laboratory at the gleaming, gently hissing and humming contraption Mr Isaacs had put together.

Finally, Mr Isaacs left the laboratory where they'd had their class, and seeing the students steaming up the glass panes in the door, he tutted and hustled them outside.

"And no sneaking back in there after I'm gone." he chided, as he walked along the central path that led back to his office in College House.

The three students looked about, trying to decide where they should go for their lunch. Without speaking, they all knew that they wanted to find a nice shady spot in the courtyard, where they could sit and chat while they ate their lunch.

Without a word, Ian turned to the left-most path and started off. Without even a pause, Jane was at his heel, following Ian along the path. Billy shrugged to himself, then set off after the other two students.

As they neared the corner where the Science block came to an end and the History block began, Ian slowed, then stopped. To his left was the Science block, in front of him was the History block, but to his right was a large eucalyptus tree that towered above both of the buildings. Ian's gaze was drawn to the flat, clear ground under the tree. The canopy of the tree was so dense and wide that nothing grew underneath, and only a soft carpet of fallen leaves lay at the base of the thick trunk.

"Perfect," Jane said, and Ian nodded.

Reaching into his satchel, Ian pulled out a tightly woven bundle. With practiced ease, he undid a clasp at each end and placed the bundle on the ground.

"Stand back a little, old chap," Ian said to Billy, who was moving in close to see what the bundle was.

With a flick of a hidden switch, the bundle began to wriggle and writhe, letting out tiny puffs of steam and a gentle hissing sound. With a metallic

---

clank, the bundle expanded, opening up and spreading out across the ground.

In a few moments, the tightly woven bundle had become a large, cushioned mat, matching the contours of the ground and providing a perfectly level, padded surface on which they could all sit.

As the final hissing sound died away, Billy whistled softly.

"I say," he said, clearly impressed, "I had no idea anyone had that sort of thing. That's dashed impressive, Mouse!"

"They're not yet in full production," Ian replied, "but Jane and I sometimes get asked to test out new items when we go exploring. The scientists at the Academy like to find out if their inventions are of any practical use in the field."

Once again, Billy had to remind himself that even though Ian and Jane were also 12 years old, they had achieved far more than many people who were much older. Billy considered himself quite lucky to be their friend, and their sense of adventure was quite infectious.

All three students sat down on the large mat. Billy was surprised by the feel of the material. He'd expected it to be rubbery or hard, but it was more like a jelly that changed shape to accommodate his body and give him support wherever he needed it. It almost felt like floating on a calm pond.

"I think we should claim this spot," Ian announced.

"So long as you don't feel the need to impose tolls on people walking past," Jane chuckled at him, good-naturedly.

"Hardly," Ian harrumphed, "but since we'll be here at the College for the next few years, I think it's a good idea that we have a spot that we can always go to."

"I think that's a fine idea, Mouse," Billy agreed.

Ian reached into his pocket and pulled out a small pen knife. He got up from the mat and began searching through the nearby undergrowth. After a moment, he returned to the mat with a short, slab of quite thick wood that had fallen away from one of the smaller trees nearby.

Ian quickly and expertly wielded his pen knife to strip the bark from the slab, then began carving letters into the wood. After a few minutes, he'd created a sign saying 'Explorers Club', which he wedged carefully into a fork in the eucalyptus tree.

Ian stepped back and admired his handiwork. Billy smiled happily, and Jane clapped her hands with glee.

"That's brilliant, Mouse," she enthused, "well done!"

Ian, Jane and Billy spent the remainder of their luncheon break eating and chatting about the day, the times and the future, under the shade of the tree.

In his notebook, Billy wrote about attending the inaugural meeting of the Caloundra Colonial College Explorers Club.

—

oOo

After the luncheon break, the First Form students met at the gymnasium.

Each student was assigned a locker in one of the change rooms. They were all reminded of the need to bring their PE kit to school tomorrow and were told to place their kit into their locker before the first class of the day.

They were also told that they would be expected to get changed into their PE kit straight after the luncheon break, so they were ready for either boxing or gymnastics, in the afternoon.

The students were then sent back to the Assembly Hall for the final hour of the school day.

When they arrived at the hall, the Head was waiting for them at the front of the room, and again he was accompanied by a military man. However, Billy quickly noticed there was something very different about the uniform of this rather young-looking officer.

The Headmaster cleared his throat as the students took their seats.

"Good afternoon, everyone," he began, "I hope you've all enjoyed your first day at the College."

Without pausing for a response from the students, he introduced his guest.

"This is Cadet Lieutenant Callum Hodges, from the Empire Service Scheme. He's here to brief you on your obligations under the scheme."

"Mr Hodges," the Headmaster said, by way of handing over the group of students to the Cadet Lieutenant, before turning and shuffling away.

"Thank you, Headmaster," Hodges said crisply.

"As some of you may know, the Government established the Empire Service Scheme in 1909, in preparation for the possibility of a war against our Empire. Under the scheme, all citizens must serve in the Cadets from the age of 12 until they are 18 years of age.

"For efficiency, 12-year-olds are enrolled in the Junior Cadets on their first day of school, instead of on their birthday. You will attend a schedule of training sessions and camps - known as bivouacs - each year as part of your training.

"Once you turn 15, you'll be transferred the Senior Cadets. Again, for efficiency, this will happen on the day you begin Fourth Form. You'll remain in the Senior Cadets until you reach the age of 18, unless you join one of the services as a full-time soldier, sailor or airman before that age."

Ian put up his hand to ask a question. The Cadet Lieutenant paused for a moment, then nodded at Ian.

"Yes?"

"Are you in the Senior Cadets?"

"I am," replied Hodges, "I've just started Lower Sixth Form, and will turn 18 early next year, but I was selected last year to join the Cadet Officer program."

"Thank you, Sir."

Again, the Cadet Lieutenant nodded at Ian, before continuing.

"If you choose not to join one of the Services as a full-time member, you'll be required to serve part-time in the Militia force from the age of 18 to 26. This is one of the ways we contribute to making our Empire strong.

"For the remainder of this afternoon, you'll be undergoing your medical examinations to determine if you have any medical conditions which might prevent you from becoming a Junior Cadet.

"Kitting for all new Junior Cadets will be held at 3:45pm on Friday, here in the Assembly Hall. Your first parade will be held at 0900 hours on Saturday.

"Are there any questions?" Cadet Lieutenant Hodges asked, scanning the room.

No hands were raised.

"Very well, please form a single line at the back of the hall and the Doctor will see you in turn."

Billy, Ian and Jane looked at each other, then raced to the back of the hall.

It looked like their next adventure was about to begin.

Chapter 12

Moscow, Russia
Wednesday 9 September 1942

"The Director will see you now, Comrade Colonel."

Volkov looked at the Aide for a moment, then stood up from the straight-backed wooden chair in the ornate anteroom. He chose to ignore the use of his rank. Either the Aide didn't know any better, or the young man felt protected enough by his position to not care.

He barely glanced at the priceless artwork on the walls or the ornate timberwork. He knew these trappings were designed to overwhelm the senses of the visitors to this place. But Volkov didn't think of himself as a visitor. He felt more at home in this place than anywhere else in the world.

The Aide opened the enormous solid wooden door that led to the outer office. Three secretaries were busy typing or taking messages. None of them looked up at the handsome young agent, and Volkov felt a particular pride and respect for their dedication to their work.

Volkov was ushered straight through the outer office and into the inner sanctum of the Director.

"Good flight, Volkov?" the Director asked from behind a large wooden desk.

She was tall and thin, incredibly muscular for a woman of her age. Many would have allowed their promotion to a desk job to rob them of their fitness, but the Director had maintained her physique, and could return to field work tomorrow, if necessary.

While her hair was a uniform grey now, there was no doubt about the intelligence that lurked behind her clear, green eyes. Like her fitness, that insightfulness had not faded over the years.

"Yes, thank you Comrade Director, Volkov replied.

"Good, good. And what did you think of our new toy?"

"The airship? She's a fine example of Soviet engineering."

"Hmm," the Director mused, "not really an answer to the question I asked. But then, you have a knack for answering the questions you want to answer, instead of the ones that are posed to you."

"You taught me well, all those years ago, Comrade Director," Volkov nodded his head in acknowledgement.

"We have need of your talents, again, Comrade Volkov.

"Please, sit, we have much to discuss."

oOo

Two hours later, Volkov left the office of the Director, his head swimming with the possibilities of his new mission. To be entrusted with such an important task was an honour beyond anything Volkov had previously experienced.

Volkov was also acutely aware, for the first time in many years, of the pressure he was under to perform this mission. To be selected was an honour. To actually achieve the outcome was demanding in a way that he had never experienced before.

The magnitude of this mission was staggering. If he were to achieve the mission objectives, it would start a chain reaction that could shatter the British Empire and depose the King.

He had much to prepare before he would be ready to depart Russia to begin his mission. The Director had given him a month to make the necessary arrangements.

"Time is precious, Comrade Volkov," she had explained in the meeting, "and so is secrecy. You must be ready to depart for your mission by the end of the first week in October, but no team can be trusted to help you prepare."

Volkov looked up in surprise at this revelation. For a mission this complex, he would usually have at least three staff to organise logistics and weapons, while he concentrated on planning.

"Secrecy is too important on this mission," the Director continued, "You will have space in this building to work, and access to any equipment you need. But you cannot have a team to help you."

"I understand, Comrade Director."

oOo

Volkov stood at the entrance to the cavernous basement of the headquarters building, stunned by the sheer size of the labyrinth stretching before him.

The noise coming from all around the space was low, but constant. Every now and then, the background sound would be punctuated by the ringing clangs of metal striking metal, or the hissing discharge of steam from some machine.

He had never visited the development laboratory before. On previous missions, one of his team members had collected the latest equipment and cutting-edge weapons for him.

Now that he was standing here himself, Volkov realised he was disoriented and more than a little overwhelmed. He could not recall a time when he hadn't stridden purposefully into a room. Even when he entered the Director's lavish office, he was full of confidence and determination. The development laboratory seemed to rob him of those feelings.

A balding old man shuffled towards Volkov. His back was bent from years of working over a lab bench, and his white coat was stained and, Volkov noticed, a little singed in places.

"Do you know what you need?" the old man rasped, with a voice that had been exposed to far too many chemicals over the years.

"No, I don't know what you've developed since my last mission."

"Hmm," the old man harrumphed, "area of operation?"

"Classified."

The old man looked at Volkov for a moment, then shrugged.

"Come with me," he instructed.

Leading the way to a long bench on one side of the basement, the old man pointed to a series of shining brass instruments and leather cases.

"This is the current set of standard issue equipment for field operatives," he wheezed, running a hand lovingly across the items.

"First, the Tokarev TT-33 semi-automatic pistol, standard issue for all Soviet officers."

Volkov shook his head. While he was more than capable of using a pistol, he found that carrying one was too distracting for those he was trying to manipulate.

"Very well," continued the old man, "perhaps something more modern."

The scientist picked up a fountain pen from the bench and began to demonstrate for Volkov.

"This fountain pen has a small needle inside, which can be extended by pushing the clip downwards. The ink canister inside contains a powerful neurotoxin. When you extend the needle and jab it into your victim, the toxin is automatically injected, causing paralysis for up to three hours."

"Can they still breathe?" Volkov asked, intrigued.

"Hm, what? Oh, yes," the scientist mumbled, as if he'd lost his train of thought when the agent interrupted him.

"The toxin only affects the voluntary muscles. Heart and lungs are not affected. During testing, we found that in a small number of cases the victim could even talk a little, but it took great effort for them to do so and they were unable to speak above a whisper.

"This canister," he said, holding up a small metal cylinder, "contains a 20-minute supply of oxygen. Should you need to swim underwater for an extended distance, or remain underwater for a period of time, this canister will supply the oxygen you need.

"We are particularly proud of these," the old man's eyes glinted with delight, as he held up a pair of brass goggles, with green glass eye pieces.

"These have only just been perfected." he continued, "They allow the wearer to see in the dark."

Volkov looked sceptical.

"No, I assure you, Comrade, when these goggles are turned on, the mechanism amplifies the existing light, no matter how feeble, making it seem like daylight.

"The goggles also have the same functions as binoculars."

"So, there would be no need to carry binoculars as well, if you had these goggles?"

"Da, Comrade."

"And what is the purpose of this antenna?" Volkov asked, pointing to a small dish-like attachment above the left eyepiece.

"That is the sound amplifier. When turned on, the antenna will capture any sound it is pointed at, amplify it and send it to the wearer through this earpiece built into the strap of the goggles."

"Ingenious!"

"You can hear a whispered conversation from 30 metres away," the old man beamed at Volkov.

"Very good," Volkov thought, "very good indeed."

"Send the equipment to Room 307," he instructed, before turning and walking out of the basement, his earlier disquiet about the laboratory now forgotten.

Chapter 13

Caloundra, Colony of Queensland, Australia
Saturday 12 September 1942

The sun had barely crossed the edge of the eastern horizon when Billy opened his eyes and sat up in bed, wide awake. He listened intently, but the house was silent. Even his mother wasn't awake yet.

Billy lay back down on his bed, and let the past week replay in his mind. It had all been such a blur, as he settled into his new First Form classes. He'd had several periods with each of the Masters and was beginning to get comfortable with the class schedule.

"Actually," he thought, "it's more like a rhythm than a schedule."

The flow of the students around the grounds, the mechanical precision of the bells keeping time. It was almost as if the school was a living, breathing creature, and all of the Masters and students were the cells in the organism.

Billy smiled at that thought. Jane, with her fascination with the science of Organisms, would be particularly amused by that idea he imagined. Billy found that he always smiled when he thought of his new friends.

Billy looked over at the wardrobe in his bedroom. Up until yesterday, he'd always thought that having such a large wardrobe seemed a bit excessive. He only had a few shirts and trousers, and a couple of pairs of shoes, and yet his wardrobe had three doors across the front, with hanging space behind two of them, and shelves behind the third. There were also three deep drawers across the bottom, and the whole wardrobe took up nearly an entire wall of his bedroom.

"Don't worry about it, dear," his mother had said when he asked why he had such a grand piece of furniture in his room, "you'll need the space one day."

After the kitting session for the Empire Training Scheme yesterday afternoon, Billy realised that day had finally come. His wardrobe was now full of an amazing array of uniforms and military kit.

Billy now had a dress uniform, complete with patent leather shoes and an olive-green tunic with gold buttons down the front and a wide black leather belt with a gold buckle that cinched tight around his waist. The Quartermaster, a gruff man with a wide moustache and mutton-chop sideburns, had shown the new cadets that the belt had to be worn on the outside of the tunic, and that a different, thinner belt was used to hold up the trousers.

He had also been issued with three sets of field uniforms, each one made up of a pair of drab olive-green trousers and a matching smock. He'd been given a pair of black boots to go with the field uniforms, as well as brand new undershirts, three pairs of green socks and a webbing belt to wear with the trousers.

He had needed to clear an entire shelf of his wardrobe to house the hats the Scheme had issued to him. The dress uniform, which the Quartermaster had called 'Brass Buttons', included a slouch hat with a wide puggaree of coloured cloth and a gleaming gold badge. He also had a floppy, cloth hat in olive green, which could be worn during field exercises when the slouch hat would be too cumbersome.

Billy still had his PE kit in a small bag in one of the bottom drawers of the wardrobe. The other two drawers were now crammed full with his field pack and webbing. The pack was a bulky but fairly comfortable affair, in olive green, used to carry his sleeping bag, ground sheet, mess set and, when in the field, his spare field uniform items.

The mess set was quite the modern marvel. The inside of each of the two nested metal pannikins was coated in a special substance. When you had finished eating, you sprinkled a fine powder, almost like ash, into the pannikin, which then reacted with the coating to cause the powder to turn into a hissing, bubbling foam. After a minute, a small amount of water could be used to wash out the foam, leaving the pannikin hygienically clean. By placing your cutlery into the bottom of the pannikin before adding the powder, you could clean your entire meal utensils in just 60 seconds.

Billy's webbing was also very cleverly designed, with a wide belt and a harness. The harness started from the back of the belt, moving up through the centre of the back and then branching into a Y-shape between the shoulder blades. One of the straps then passed over each shoulder, before coming down the front of the wearer and joining again at the front of the belt, near the hip. A large knob was mounted chest high on the right-hand strap. When the wearer turned the knob, a series of cables, woven inside special channels in the fabric, would compress, tightening the entire webbing arrangement against the body of the wearer. This gave the webbing a tailored fit, without the need for fiddly adjustment of buckles and connectors, and helped with freedom of movement by making the webbing behave as if it was attached to the person.

There were a number of pouches attached to the webbing, for holding ammunition, supplies, a field medical kit and other small items. At the back of the webbing, sitting in the small of the wearer's back, was a long, narrow pouch. This was the protective coverall.

By slapping, rather than turning the knob on the right-hand strap of the webbing, a spring-loaded mechanism would push open the pouch and a small steam canister would then deploy a raincoat up the back of the wearer, around their sides and over their shoulders. Once the pieces of the lightweight, breathable fabric were in position, special fasteners would connect the various panels, sealing the raincoat at the seams.

Billy had been told that the webbing issued to the militia and the men and women in full time service contained a more advanced raincoat that would deploy faster and could be extended to create an airtight seal around the wearer, to protect against chemical weapons and poisonous gas.

Billy marvelled at the ingenuity of those who worked in the Academy of Science. He knew that they were some of the most imaginative people in the Empire. And while it was true that almost all of their inventions were created for the military, many of their ideas were eventually filtered down to the average citizen.

Ian's fold-out rug, that was now permanently in place under the eucalyptus tree was a perfect example of a piece of military equipment that was being made available to the general public. Billy imagined a day, not too far in the future, where everyone would have a raincoat pre-loaded into their belt.

Although he didn't have a watch of his own, and the only clock in the house was on the mantle above the fire in the living room, Billy sensed that he had about an hour until he needed to get up for breakfast. Rather than trying to go back to sleep - he was far too excited for the day ahead - Billy decided to re-read the précis the new cadets had been issued.

Although *The History* of the Empire was the only book available to the public, the Empire allowed many other publications. Newspapers were available every day, and many pamphlets, handbooks and small guides were created to keep the citizens up to date with the latest news, or to inform them on such things as decorum, civic responsibilities and other matters that were important to their lives. The Customs and Traditions of the Military: Empire Service Scheme Edition, was just such a handbook.

The handbook was a slim volume, designed to fit in one of the button-down pockets on the shirt of the dress uniform or the field uniform smock. Billy had noticed how much smaller it was than his notebook, so he stored his précis inside the front cover of the notebook when he wasn't wearing his uniform.

Even though it was small, the handbook was filled with important information for Cadets. Billy read through some of the most important parts, trying to commit them to memory before he had to report for the parade. The last thing Billy wanted to do on his first outing as a Cadet was to make a blunder in military etiquette.

Billy spent some time studying the pictures of the rank insignia, learning the hierarchy of ranks from Cadet at the bottom to the most senior of the

Non-Commissioned Cadets, the Company Sergeant Major, or CSM as they were usually called.

In a second column on the table of rank insignia were the Commissioned Officer ranks, from the most junior, the Second Lieutenant, all the way through to Colonels and Brigadiers, and then a host of different types of General.

Billy closed his eyes and pictured each of the rank insignia in his mind. He knew that as a brand-new cadet, everyone out-ranked him. But he also knew from the handbook that only the Officers had to be saluted.

As he moved through the sections on the appropriate way to address various people, and the multitude of rules concerning dress, grooming and bearing, Billy began to realise that not only were the requirements simple common sense, they were exactly the things that his parents had been teaching him his whole life. Billy wondered whether this was something that had come about because of his grandfather's extensive military service. Perhaps that service had exerted enough influence to lead to Billy being educated in the correct way to behave and the right way to present himself in public and in private. Certainly, both his father and grandfather stood ramrod straight and carried themselves with confidence.

Just then, Billy heard the faint chime of the mantle clock striking 7 o'clock, and he realised that he should get up and help out with breakfast. His mother would be getting up shortly to start cooking, and Billy needed to collect firewood from the woodpile, stoke the coals in the stove, and add the firewood before his mother got to the kitchen. With a grin, Billy leapt out of bed and headed out his bedroom door.

oOo

After breakfast and the Anthem, Billy returned to his room to get dressed for the parade. Knowing he had 20 minutes before he had to leave, Billy took his time. He knew which uniform to wear today, since Cadet Lieutenant Hodges had 'briefed' all of the new cadets before the kitting started yesterday afternoon. Billy wasn't sure what being briefed had meant, but Mouse had spotted the confused look on his face and leaned over towards him.

"A briefing is where someone, usually an Officer or Senior Cadet, tells us important information," Mouse whispered to Billy, "and it's always done very formally."

Billy nodded, realising this was one of the special words the military used instead of normal ways of speaking.

"I may need a glossary," Billy whispered back.

Mouse grinned but didn't respond.

"Listen up Cadets," Hodges began, in a strong, confident voice that easily carried to the back of the group.

He paused for a moment, ensuring everyone was quiet and looking at him.

"Tomorrow morning at 0900 hours, all cadets in the Caloundra Colonial College Unit of the Empire Service Scheme are to parade on the oval of the College.

"Cadets are to form up, under the control of the NCOs, by Form, with First Form closest to the Assembly Hall. Dress for all cadets will be field uniform with slouch hat. Packs and webbing are not required.

"Are there any questions?" Cadet Lieutenant Hodges asked, before looking around at the faces of the students.

After a moment, a hand was raised by a slim girl in the front row.

"Yes," said Hodges, "Cadet Green, isn't it?"

"Yes Sir," responded Green, "how will we know what field uniform looks like, or how to wear it properly?"

"Good question, Green. Along with all your uniform items, the Quartermaster will issue you with an instruction card on how to wear your uniforms. On one side of the card are the instructions for field uniform, and on the other side are the instructions for dress uniform."

"Thank you, Sir."

"Are there any other questions, Cadets?"

A rather timid hand was raised near the back of the group, and Cadet Lieutenant Hodges almost didn't see it.

"Yes, Cadet?"

"Sir," the young boy stammered a little, "what's an NCO?"

Some of the cadets started to giggle, thinking this was a rather silly question. Lieutenant Hodges silenced them in an instant, with a glare.

"If anyone in the Scheme doesn't know something," Hodges said with an edge to his voice, "it is the responsibility of everyone else around him or her to make sure they understand.

"We do not make fun of those who know less about some topics than we do," he continued, "because it is almost certain that those people know far more about other things than we ever will. The Empire stays strong when we all do our part and we all help each other. We must work together and support each other. It is the way of the Scheme and it is the way of the Empire."

The students who had laughed hung their heads and murmured their apologies to the Cadet Lieutenant.

"Now, Cadet Armstrong, you had a question?"

"Yes, Sir, I don't know what an NCO is."

"An NCO," explained Hodges, "is a Non-Commissioned Officer. The first of the NCO ranks is a Corporal, followed by Sergeant and Staff Sergeant. There are also some higher ranks, the Warrant Officers, after which the Officer ranks begin."

"Thank you, Sir."

"Cadets, this discussion of the rank structure is important, and there are many other important things you will need to learn in your time in the Empire Service Scheme.

"For this reason, you will all be issued with a précis, a small handbook full of essential information for cadets to know. I recommend you all become very familiar with the contents of this document, very quickly."

Mouse leaned in to whisper to Billy, but he had already worked out that when an Officer said they "recommend" something, it's just a polite way of giving them an order.

For this reason, Billy had his instruction card on his desk as he carefully pulled out the items that made up his field uniform. After laying out all of the items on his bed, he began getting dressed, frequently referring to the card to ensure everything was being worn correctly.

After 15 minutes, Billy was satisfied that he was wearing his uniform correctly. With a final tug on the hem of the smock, to ensure it was sitting straight, Billy picked up his slouch hat and went to the living room to say goodbye to his mother.

Mary Bowman was waiting for him in the room, the family box brownie camera in her hands. The camera had been in the family for years, but was only brought out for special occasions, as the cost of developing the film was quite high.

Billy raised an eyebrow at his mother when he saw the camera.

"We have a photo of each of your grandfathers on their first day in uniform," she explained, "and your father, and your uncles, on both sides of the family. We're not breaking the tradition for you, young man."

While her voice sounded quite firm, Billy realised she was actually holding back tears of pride and joy. He was certain she would cry once he left the house.

"Well, in that case," he replied, gently, "how could I possibly refuse."

"Good. Stand over there, so the light from the window shines on you."

Billy moved to the side of the room, opposite the window, and carefully balanced his slouch hat in the crook of his left arm. Drawing himself to his full height, he stood with a straight back and a stoic expression on his face, while his mother carefully composed the picture.

"Alright, William," she said eventually, "One, Two, Three."

The camera made a soft click, as the shutter opened to expose the film. Mary Bowman carefully wound the film on to the next frame, then placed the camera on the nearby side table.

She moved towards Billy with her arms outstretched, and for a moment, he imagined she was going to hug him, but instead she held him by the shoulders and stared into his eyes.

"I'm very proud of you, William." she whispered at him, the tears starting to well in her eyes again, "I'm certain you're going to achieve great things in your life."

Billy didn't quite know what to say, but after a moment, she released her grip on his shoulders, and turned towards the kitchen.

He stared after her for a moment, then, with a glance at the mantle clock, he quickly headed out the front door of the house.

Chapter 14

Caloundra, Colony of Queensland, Australia
Saturday 12 September 1942

By the time Billy arrived at the front gate of the College, Ian and Jane were already there, waiting for him.

"Good morning," they chimed in unison, with enormous grins on their faces.

Billy couldn't help but smile in return.

"Hello, Jane. Hello Mouse."

"I say, old chap," Ian said, cocking an eyebrow at Billy, "who do you imagine our Corporal will be? Jane and I have been playing a bit of a guessing game about it since yesterday after the kitting, but we just can't work it out."

Billy laughed, amused by the things that entertained his friends.

"What!" Billy exclaimed in mock surprise, "you two can't solve a puzzle!"

Jane and Ian stared at Billy for a moment, pretending to be shocked, before breaking into laughter themselves.

"Well," Billy said, after they'd taken a moment to control their laughter, "I guess there's only one way to find out."

And with that, the three students, in their field uniforms and slouch hats, walked purposefully through the front gate and headed towards the oval.

oOo

The other First Form students were standing in a small group on the edge of the oval, just next to the Assembly Hall. A broad-shouldered cadet was standing in front of the group, facing them. As Billy, Ian and Jane approached, they could only see the back of the boy, but it was clear from his position that he was the NCO for the First Form cadets.

The NCO must have heard the three students approaching, for he turned sharply towards them, rotating his body by spinning on the heel of one foot and the ball of the other. As he turned, the first thing Billy saw were the Corporal stripes on the boy's sleeve. An instant later, Billy recognised him as Sean Byrne, the Third Form boy who had bullied Mouse earlier in the week.

———

Billy was immediately concerned. He knew enough about military protocol to know that Sean Byrne was in a position of power and authority over the First Form students, and that he could easily use that power to continue to bully the younger students. Given that he might have a grudge against Ian and Billy, it was quite possible Sean would make their experience in the Scheme very unpleasant.

"Corporal," said Ian and Jane, as they passed Sean.

"Cadets,' he responded.

As Billy went to move past, Sean stopped him.

"Cadet Bowman, a moment."

Billy stopped, standing in front of Sean and making sure he kept his face neutral.

"I've spent the whole week thinking about what you did to me on Monday morning," Sean said quietly, so that only Billy could hear him.

Billy felt his whole body go tense, not knowing what was coming next, but ready to react if he needed to.

"I'm quite ashamed by my behaviour," he continued, speaking even more quietly, "and I wanted you to know that I'm going to behave like a gentleman from now on."

"I'm very glad to hear that, Sean."

"I felt it was important to let you know," Sean continued, "I didn't want you to think that I would hold a grudge."

"I appreciate that, Sean."

"Very well, Cadet Bowman," Sean said loudly, straightening up a little, and winking at Billy, "join the rest of First Form now."

Billy quickly moved past Sean and joined the group of students. Ian and Jane watched him all the way to the group, with curiosity and a little concern clearly evident on their faces. Billy gave them a small 'ok' sign with his hand as he got to the edge of the oval, to let them know that his conversation with Sean had gone well.

oOo

"Line up," shouted Corporal Byrne, "Three ranks. Quickly now, quickly now."

The First Form students stumbled over each other a little, but Sean moved in close to the group and pointed out to individual students where they should be standing. When the whole of First Form was in rough position, Sean moved back to his spot, in the middle of the front rank, and a few feet forward of that row.

As the automated bell rang to signal 9 o'clock, Sean performed another of those spinning turns, so that his back was now to the First Form students.

—

A moment later, Cadet Lieutenant Hodges marched crisply from the side of the oval, to a position directly opposite the students. With a stomp, he halted, then paused for a beat before making a quarter turn to face the assembled students. Billy noticed that when the Lieutenant turned, he used that same heel-toe spin that Sean had used, even though he only made a ninety-degree turn.

"Markers" bellowed Lieutenant Hodges.

With this command, three students from the other groups started marching smartly forward, toward the Lieutenant. To Billy, it looked like they were moving to predetermined positions on the oval, as when each cadet reached their allocated spot, they halted, while the others continued forward.

While this was going on, Corporal Byrne did another smart turn, to face the First Form students again, before explaining what was going on.

"The oval is now considered to be a parade ground," Sean informed the wide-eyed students.

"The three Cadets who moved forward are called Markers. They mark the front corner of each group of cadets when they are lined up on parade. In a moment, the Cadet Lieutenant will call for the remaining cadets to fall in. When he does, the rest of the cadets will march onto the parade ground and line themselves up with their Marker."

"After that, there'll be a number of drill movements, to line up the cadets neatly and evenly, to raise the Union Jack, and to enable the senior Officers to inspect the Cadets."

"We'll stay here to observe, as you haven't been taught any of the drill moves yet. Over the next few weeks, though, we'll teach you everything you need to know to participate in a parade."

oOo

After the parade had finished, Corporal Byrne took the First Form cadets into one of the classrooms in the Mathematics block. Waiting at the front of the room was an older Cadet, who was wearing a rank insignia with a large crown on her shoulder. The students stood behind the desks in the classroom, waiting for instructions.

"Good morning, Cadets," she said brightly, "please be seated.

"My name is Cadet Warrant Officer Samantha Golding. I'm the Company Sergeant Major, or CSM, for the Caloundra College Cadet Unit.

"I wanted to welcome you all to the Empire Service Scheme, and to this unit in particular. We have a very strong tradition of service, with many of our graduates taking up commissions in the Army, Navy or Air Force.

"I myself have started Fifth Form this week, and yesterday received a letter of offer to join the Australian Fleet of the Royal Navy when I graduate next May.

"Many of you may be offered a place in one of the services in just a few short years. If you find yourself in that position, the skills and experience you will gain here as a Cadet will make your Service training a little easier and more enjoyable.

"I have one critical piece of advice for you," she continued.

"One of the things you may find most difficult, as you adjust to the Scheme, is that your friends from school may not always be your peers on parade. The Scheme values initiative, courage and leadership in Cadets. Promotion to the various ranks is based on a combination of skill and experience, not on time in the Scheme.

"Do not expect to be promoted to a higher rank each time your start a new Form. Some cadets will be promoted each year, others may take more time to move from one rank to the next.

"Sometimes, a particularly capable Cadet will be promoted even more quickly, moving ahead of the others in their Form. Remember, not every cadet will become a Warrant Officer, and only one of the cadets who do reach that rank will be selected to become the CSM.

"You may find that you become an NCO before your friends. In that case, you must learn to separate your time in the school from your time in the Scheme. When you put on your uniform, you also put on your rank, and all of the responsibilities that go along with that. Sometimes, that will include disciplining your peers, or even your friends. Take care to ensure this does not sour the friendships you have outside the Scheme.

"The same applies in reverse, for those of you who are not promoted so rapidly. If a friend or a peer one day outranks you, be supportive of that person, and remember you can be friends outside the Scheme, even if they are your superior on parade days."

CSM Golding paused for a moment, shaking her head slightly.

"I didn't learn that lesson very well when I started in the Scheme. I was promoted quite quickly, but I lost friends, close friends, in the process, because I had trouble separating the Scheme from the school. My behaviour while in uniform continued on when I was at school, and my friends would not tolerate my attitude of superiority.

"Learn from my mistakes," she said firmly, looking around the room at the new Cadets, "and remember your friends, regardless of rank.

"Now, I'd like to introduce you to your instructors."

"This is Cadet Sergeant Michael O'Meara," she said, indicating a tall, slim cadet with incredibly short-cropped blonde hair, who was standing to her right.

"And this," she continued, indicating the cadet to her left, "is Cadet Corporal Sean Byrne."

Both of the NCOs nodded their heads at the group but did not otherwise respond.

"We have three hours remaining for our parade this morning," Warrant Officer Golding stated, after glancing at the clock on the opposite wall of the room, "Sergeant O'Meara, the Cadets are yours."

"Thank you, Ma'am," he said, snapping to attention as the CSM turned and marched out of the room.

"Alright, Ladies and Gentlemen," the Sergeant said smoothly, "take out your précis. We have a lot to go over this morning."

Chapter 15

Melbourne, Colony of Victoria, Australia
Saturday 12 September 1942

"We cannot allow this to continue!" thundered Arthur Fadden, standing on the floor of the chamber to address the Members of the House of Commons.

The other members of the Opposition Party stomped their feet on the green carpet of the House.

"Hear, Hear," they cried, supporting their leader.

"We are in the greatest period of peace the Empire has known," he continued, "and yet we have unknown terrors to our north.

"Terrors," he continued after a dramatic pause, "about which this government does nothing.

"Does the Prime Minister expect that the people of the Colony of Queensland, my Colony, will bear the full responsibility of dealing with this threat, simply because, as the northernmost Colony, we will be the front line if hostilities arise?

"Japan is only a few hours away from our shores by airship, and we have not the faintest clue about their military capability. Beyond Japan lies the great unknown of China, and revolutionary Russia beyond that.

"With such pressure from the north, from nations whose populations far exceed our own, how are we to prepare? These nations are not part of our glorious Empire, and if they are not with us, then surely they are against us!"

The Opposition Members exploded with cries of support for their leader. When the cries had died down a little, Mr Fadden continued.

"Mr Speaker, I ask the Honourable Prime Minister to share with the Members of this House, how he intends to deal with this grave issue."

The Opposition Members were now hooting at the Government Members, sitting opposite them across the floor of the chamber.

"Order," shouted the Speaker, "Order!"

The Prime Minister rose from his seat, with the calm dignity of a man who knows far more than those around him. Although he was slim, with wire-rimmed glasses, John Curtin had an almost overpowering presence when he stood to speak.

"Mr Speaker," began the Prime Minister, in grave tones, "His Majesty has decreed that Japan, China and Russia are free to join our Empire whenever they choose to do so. These nations, according to our King, are no threat to us or anyone in the Empire.

"However, if the Honourable Leader of the Opposition feels that His Majesty has made a mistake, and that one of these nations is, in fact, actively plotting against the Empire, I would see it as my duty to immediately present Mr Fadden's evidence of the error to His Majesty, in person, in London."

This time it was the Government benches that erupted in jeers and hoots at the Opposition.

"Shame!" came the cry from the Government Members, "Shame!"

oOo

As the debate raged on in the chamber, the Chief watched impassively from the visitors' gallery.

It was quite rare for him to attend a Parliamentary Sitting. Usually, he simply sent one of his staff to observe, and report back on anything of interest or concern. But a Saturday Sitting was unusual, especially in peacetime, and so the Chief had decided he had best attend the session himself.

So far, however, it was disappointing. He had initially wondered if Mr Fadden might have finally obtained some information that might challenge the Prime Minister. Perhaps even force Mr Curtin to reveal some of the sensitive information the Chief had obtained for him through the efforts of his Directorate.

But, sadly, no. Mr Fadden was a good man - there was no doubt of that - but he was far from the political equal of the Prime Minister.

Instead of presenting evidence of incursions into the Colonies, Mr Fadden had simply thrown up the usual 'terror in the north' rhetoric and tried to manipulate it into a commitment to support Queensland should a war break out in the Pacific. It was all just a little too predictable, and it was hardly surprising the Mr Curtin had been able to deal with the accusations so smoothly.

The Chief turned to one of his staff, who was sitting in the row behind him in the gallery.

"I don't think there's much to see here today, Birdwood. But stay here and observe. If anything unusual happens, contact me immediately."

"Certainly, Chief."

Everyone called him 'Chief'. None of the staff had any idea what his real name was.

There was a rumour in the Directorate that a few years ago, some unkind souls had whispered that it had been so long since the Chief had used his real name that even his mother had forgotten what it was.

No matter how quietly they said it, no matter how carefully they checked to see if anyone was listening, those people soon discovered that, in the Directorate, someone was always listening. According to the rumours, those whisperers no longer worked for the Chief. Or for anyone else, for that matter.

"Let's go," the Chief said firmly to his Aide.

The young woman didn't respond. Instead, she stood and, looking carefully at everyone around, moved in front of the Chief and began clearing a path out of the gallery.

One part secretary, two parts bodyguard, the young woman projected restrained danger, from her hair tied into a tight bun to her well-defined muscles under her business suit and the lithe way she balanced on the balls of her feet, like a mountain cat ready to pounce on any prey that happened to get into her sights.

This entire projection of lethality was reinforced by the small lumps that could just be seen on either side of her torso, under her jacket. Those who were potential threats to the Chief would instantly recognise these as her pistols, hanging in shoulder holsters and ready for instant use, should the need ever arise.

The Chief had no idea what her name was, nor did he particularly care. All that mattered was that she was efficient and discrete. In the event of an attempt on his life, she would take every step to protect him, including sacrificing herself if necessary.

After exiting Parliament House, the Chief climbed into the carriage that was waiting for him on the concourse. He was pleased that his aide had called ahead when they left the chamber, to ensure his carriage was waiting for him. He knew that her action was to minimise his risk, by not having to stand waiting in the open, but it had the added advantage of being convenient.

"Well done," he said to the woman, who simply nodded in response.

She only stopped scanning the area for potential threats after she had climbed aboard the carriage herself.

The Chief had incredible instincts when it came to recognising threats to the Empire. It was the main reason he held his position as head of the Directorate, and why he was so very, very good at his job.

This unexpected sitting of Parliament and the clearly agitated state of the Opposition Leader made every nerve in his being twitch. The ineffective way in which Mr Fadden raised the issue did nothing to alleviate his sense of foreboding.

"Something must be going on in Queensland." the Chief mused, "something's spooked Fadden.

"When we get back to the Directorate," the Chief instructed his Aide, "send a message to Commander Bowman in Queensland. I want him in my office on Monday morning, ready to brief me on the current situation in his Colony."

oOo

Caloundra, Colony of Queensland, Australia
Saturday 12 September 1942

Billy almost didn't hear the knock at the front door of their house, over the sound of the mantle clock striking 9 pm. Patrick Bowman, though, heard it instantly.

"William, would you answer the door, please."

Billy got up from his chair in the living room. After finishing his homework, he had come to the living room to read his précis yet again.

"Telegram for Mr Patrick Bowman," announced the young boy standing on their front porch.

"I'm his son. I'll accept it for him."

"I'm sorry, but my instructions are to hand this telegram directly to Mr Patrick Bowman."

"And, he must sign for it," the boy added.

"I see," Billy mused, "very well, wait here."

Billy partly closed the door and turned back into the living room. His father must have overheard the conversation, though, as he was already out of his chair and making his way towards the front door.

"Thank you, William," his father said, "I'll take care of this."

"I'm Patrick Bowman."

"I've been asked to request identification, Sir."

"Very well," Patrick responded evenly, reaching for his wallet and extracting his Citizenship Card.

The telegram boy leaned forward to look closely at the photograph stapled to the buff coloured cardboard identification document, before looking up at the Patrick.

"Thank you, Sir. Please sign here," the boy said, as he passed over a small clipboard.

After Patrick Bowman had added his elegant signature to the document on the clipboard, the messenger handed over the telegram.

"Good night, Sir," the boy called, as he turned and left the doorstep.

"Yes, good night," Patrick responded, distractedly, closing the front door and reading the telegram.

To: Patrick Bowman

From: Chief of Operations

URGENT

Report to head office, Melbourne, 9am Mon 14 Sep

STOP

Update required on current situation in your area

STOP

Passage booked on train to Brisbane and airship to Melbourne

STOP

Train departs Caloundra 10am Sun 13 Sep

STOP

Patrick Bowman carefully folded the telegram and placed it in his shirt pocket.

"Is everything all right?" Billy asked.

Looking at his son, Patrick paused for a moment, then smiled warmly.

"Oh, yes," he replied, "everything is fine. I just need to go to Melbourne for some urgent business for the Ginger Factory."

"Melbourne," Billy exclaimed. "That's so exciting!

"But it'll take you days to get there by train, won't it?"

Patrick chuckled.

"Not this time, William. The work is so urgent, that I'm apparently going to travel by airship."

Chapter 16

Caloundra, Colony of Queensland, Australia
Sunday 13 September 1942

Billy was hurrying down the street, moving quickly towards the College. He wasn't rushing because he was late. He was in a hurry because he was looking forward to what the day would bring.

His father had left for the train station immediately after the Anthem that morning, and Billy had waved to him from the front porch until his carriage was out of sight.

Then, Billy started getting ready for the adventure that he was sure the day would bring.

After the parade yesterday, Mouse and Jane had invited him to spend the rest of the afternoon with them, but Billy had politely declined. He wanted to make some notes in his notebook about the parade and the Scheme, while the events of the morning were still fresh in his mind.

Billy felt a little bad about the situation. He really enjoyed spending time with Mouse and Jane, and he wanted to share in their adventures.

"How about this, then," Billy had countered, "I'll go home and finish my chores and my homework this afternoon and have dinner with my family tonight. Then, tomorrow, I'll be free, and we can go and do something together. What do you think?"

"I think," responded Jane playfully, "that you have just had an excellent idea, Billy."

"I agreed," added Ian, "and that gives Jane and I the afternoon to work out the best way to spend our Sunday."

"Alright, let's meet at 9:30 tomorrow morning at the College gate."

"Do you mean 0930 hours?" laughed Jane.

"Why, yes I do, Cadet," Billy responded, trying but failing, to keep a straight face.

Billy had spent the rest of the day working quickly to get everything done. By dinner time, he'd chopped and neatly stacked the wood his mother would need for the stove during the week and had moved the tree branches his father had cut down on Saturday morning into the drying stack in the back corner of their yard.

After the family meal and the 8:00 pm Anthem, Billy had retired to his room to complete his homework. As it was the first week of the school year, the Masters had only given revision work to the students to complete by Monday morning. Billy was finding the Mathematics and English quite easy, as they were still reviewing the primary school studies to find any gaps in their understanding.

Science was a little more challenging, as they had begun their first unit in the field of Organisms. Billy liked Mechanisms, and had a basic grasp of Compositions, but his primary school had done very little in the Science of Organisms, and he felt more than a little overwhelmed by all the new terminology.

Jane, he had discovered, had something of a passion for Organisms, and was apparently far ahead of the rest of the class in this field of study.

"It just makes sense to me," she had told him, when he asked her why she knew so much about the subject.

"It's like you with *The History*," she continued, "When Mouse and I read *The History*, we see the facts and figures, names and places.

"But you, Billy, you see the connections and the flow and ... and the life in the stories, creating a vivid picture of our history and our Empire.

"I see the life in the world, the plants and animals, in much the same way - connected and flowing together to create a rich tapestry of existence."

Now, as Billy rushed excitedly towards the College gate, he had his Organisms homework in his satchel. No matter what was planned for today, Billy needed to spend some time with Jane, sorting out this part of his homework.

Jane was already waiting at the gate when Billy arrived.

"You're early," he remarked after bidding her a good morning.

"So are you," Jane replied, laughing gently, "I guess we're both keen to find out what we're doing today."

"What do you mean?" Billy asked, puzzled, "I thought you and Ian were going to organise something yesterday afternoon."

"We were, but then Ian got called away. Some sort of urgent family matter or something."

"I wonder what's going on," Billy mused, "or if Mouse is even still coming this morning!"

"Oh," Jane shrugged, "I hadn't thought of that."

oOo

A few minutes later, a shiny black Hansom Carriage, drawn by a beautiful black horse, pulled up in front of the gate.

Billy stared at the carriage. The timber was painted a deep gloss black, with so many coats of wax it shone in the morning sunlight. The windows sparkled and were framed with thick red velvet curtains.

But most startling of all was the driver of the carriage. Sitting in the driver's seat was an automaton. The mechanical driver wore a black suit and peaked cap, but the polished silver and bronze face and hands were visible, complete with tiny cogs and gears. Billy had never seen an automaton up close before, although he'd heard about how they were becoming more and more sophisticated. He'd even heard some, less educated people calling them 'robots', which sounded to Billy like far too vulgar a term for such an impressive feat of engineering.

"This must be important," Jane said matter-of-factly, "Ian almost never uses his carriage."

Billy looked from the carriage, to Jane, and back again, shocked.

"I do beg your pardon," Billy said tentatively, "I must have mis-heard. I thought you said his carriage."

Jane smiled, and opened her mouth to reply, when the near-side door of the carriage was flung open. Ian immediately leaned out and beckoned his two friends to climb aboard.

"Come along," he said brightly, "I'll explain it all on the way to the beach."

Chapter 17

Caloundra, Colony of Queensland, Australia
Sunday 13 September 1942

Inside the carriage were two bench seats, facing each other. Ian was sitting on the bench seat that faced the front of the carriage. Billy and Jane took seats on the opposite bench, facing the rear of the carriage.

Once his friends were inside, Ian pressed a small red button on the side wall. A beep sounded from the speaker above the button, and when the tone had finished, Ian leaned over and spoke into the speaker.

"Leach Park."

Another beep sounded from the speaker, then a whirring sound could be heard. After a few moments, the whirring sound stopped and the speaker beeped again.

"Leach Park," a clearly mechanical voice intoned, "Estimated travel time, 10 minutes."

The speaker clicked off and the carriage began to trundle down the road under the command of the automaton. As the carriage gained speed, a faint hiss could be heard as the suspension system began to compensate for any rough spots in the road.

Ian turned to his passengers. Jane was sitting on the edge of the plush leather seat, waiting impatiently to hear about what had happened. Billy, on the other hand, sat dumbstruck, his mouth open in shock.

"Oh dear," Ian said plaintively, "I do apologise, Billy, I thought you knew."

"Knew what?" Billy asked, recovering his senses, but still looking around the carriage and at Ian in wide-eyed wonder.

"About my family," Ian said simply.

After a moment, Billy made the connection.

"Landsborough," he said, "Ian Landsborough."

Ian nodded.

"Guilty, I'm afraid." Ian chuckled, "My great-great-grandfather was William Landsborough."

"The great explorer?"

"Yes."

"The man who led not one, but two missions in search of Burke and Wills?"

"That's him."

"The William Landsborough who was presented with a gold watch by the Royal Geographical Society for finding a practical route from north to south through Australia?"

"One and the same."

Ian was grinning broadly by now, and Billy whistled softly.

"You certainly keep a low profile, Mouse," Billy grinned.

Ian inclined his head and winked.

"I'll take that as a compliment, Billy." he said, "My family has a long history, and Caloundra and it's surrounds have been good to us.

"But I am my own man. I will choose my own friends and I will not use my family name or connections for personal gain."

Billy nodded, realising the strength of character that Ian had displayed by not using his family name to his advantage.

"Now," Ian said, firmly, "to the business at hand.

"As Jane knows, but Billy you don't, my grandfather passed away last year."

"I'm sorry to hear that, Ian," Billy offered.

"It's quite alright, old bean," Ian said, "We were quite close, but it's been a long time since the funeral. Besides, stiff upper lip and all that."

Ian drew a breath, before continuing.

"On Friday, while we were at school, my parents took the train to Brisbane to meet with the family lawyer. Apparently, Grandfather had left instructions that his will was not to be opened until one year and one month after his death."

"I wonder why?" Jane asked.

"I have absolutely no idea," Ian replied, "and neither does Father. But we're both quite sure Grandfather would have had his reasons.

"My father decided that he wouldn't tell me about the trip or the will until yesterday afternoon. He knew I was excited about starting Cadets and that I had quite a bit of prep work to do to be ready for the parade yesterday morning. He didn't want me to be distracted."

Jane and Billy nodded their understanding.

"Father expected me home after the parade, so when I decided to spend the afternoon with you, Jane, Father worked out where I was and sent the note telling me to come home immediately.

"I didn't know what it was all about at that time, Jane," Ian continued, "I'm sorry I had to rush off like that."

Jane smiled and nodded, acknowledging the apology and at the same time, encouraging Ian to continue.

"Most of the will was about Mother and Father, and the wishes of Grandfather regarding how they should manage his estate and property. But there was one clause in the will about me.

"It seems that Grandfather was so impressed with the exploring I've done with you Jane, that he decided to leave me something in his will that I suspect is going to be quite valuable in our future explorations."

Jane and Billy both edged forwards in their seats, happy for Ian, but ever so slightly frustrated that he was prolonging the revelation of his inheritance.

Suddenly, the carriage stopped and the speaker in the side panel crackled.

"Destination reached," the mechanical voice intoned.

"Ah," said Ian, "we're here. Perhaps it's better if I show you."

oOo

After alighting from the carriage, Ian led the way along the boardwalk towards the southern end of the park. The boardwalk stopped at a small rotunda, with some bench seats where people could sit and watch the waves rolling onto the sandy beach. At this time of the morning the rotunda was empty, and Ian completely ignored it. Instead, he walked through the rotunda and stepped off the wooden structure on the far side.

Billy and Jane followed close behind and realised that they were now travelling on a small sandy path, barely visible through the undergrowth, shaded by the soaring Golden Wattle trees. The salty smell of the ocean blended with the sticky sweet scent of the wattle, creating an aroma that Billy always associated with his hometown.

The path meandered through the trees, and it took the group a few minutes to arrive at a small clearing. Nestled in the clearing was a long, narrow boathouse. The front of the boathouse touched the sandy edge of the beach.

In the side of the boathouse nearest the path was a small door, secured with an ancient looking padlock. Ian reached into the pocket of his trousers and pulled out a metal ring with several equally ancient looking keys attached. He walked up to the door, looked at the padlock, then carefully examined the set of keys.

Selecting one of the keys, Ian gingerly inserted it into the padlock. All three friends collectively held their breath, as Ian turned the key and the padlock sprung open with a surprisingly loud click.

"Well now, that's interesting," Ian said, turning to the group, "it would seem that Grandfather had the internals of this very old padlock replaced with a modern mechanism."

Ian chuckled to himself.

"That would have given any would-be thief a shock."

"How so?" asked Jane.

"Modern padlocks have additional security built in," Ian explained, "If you try to open it without the correct key, it sets off a piercing whistle that will shatter your eardrums."

"Well in that case, I'm very pleased you took your time selecting the right key, Mouse," Billy quipped.

"As am I," Ian replied, grinning.

Ian looked at the door, noticing a second lock set immediately below the doorknob. Again, he looked carefully at the ring of keys, before selecting one and putting it into the lock on the door. The key turned effortlessly, and Ian reached up to turn the doorknob, removing the key from the lock as he did so.

Ian pushed the door, and it swung almost silently open. Inside, the boathouse was dimly lit, with most of the light coming through the dirty glass skylight panels mounted in the roof.

"Shall we?" Ian asked his friends, before stooping down to walk through the low doorway without waiting for their reply.

Jane and Billy looked at each other for a moment, then stepped through the doorway to join Ian inside.

—

Chapter 18

Caloundra, Colony of Queensland, Australia
Sunday 13 September 1942

The light inside the boathouse was dim, and it took a moment for Billy and Jane's eyes to adjust.

As their sight began to clear, they realised that a large shape, long and tall, loomed over them. It seemed very dark and forbidding in the gloom.

"Ah-ha," they heard Ian say, somewhere off to their right, "there it is."

Suddenly, there was a loud click, followed by the tinny, whooshing sound of gas rushing through narrow metal pipes. Somewhere in the dark recesses of the roof of the shed, a series of muffled whump sounds could be heard, as the gas in the pipes reached the series of large lanterns that were suspended above.

As each lantern received its supply of gas, the wick was ignited by an automatic striker, and the lantern began to glow with a soft orange light that grew in intensity until it was a bright orb of white that seemed to float above their heads. With all of the lanterns lit, the inside of the boathouse was as bright as the morning outside.

Billy and Jane stared in awe at the giant shape in front of them. What had seemed menacing in the gloom now appeared delightful in the lantern light.

In front of them, just barely fitting inside the boathouse, was a steam yacht. The dark timber of the hull and superstructure were polished to a sheen, and every brass fitting glinted in the lantern light. Rising through the centre of the yacht, up through the superstructure, was a smokestack painted gloss black and reaching up towards the roof of the shed.

Most of the deck was taken up with the superstructure. In front of the smokestack was a spacious wheelhouse, with large glass window panes wrapping around, giving the captain a clear view to the front and both sides of the vessel.

Behind the stack was the main cabin, with panoramic windows to give passengers a view of the ocean around them. Billy could see a saloon arrangement of lounges, with built-in side tables, through the windows of the cabin.

Behind the saloon was an open area of deck, although the roof of the cabin extended through to the stern, creating a covered verandah at the rear of the yacht. The verandah area was almost as large as the saloon.

Ian came to stand next to his friends.

"So, what do you think?" he said, spreading his arms wide.

"She's magnificent, Mouse!" Billy opined.

"This is the *Sea Gypsie*." Ian said, lovingly patting the side of the yacht.

"Grandfather had her custom built, to his personal design. She's 28 feet long and can cruise at up to 10 knots.

"After our Pandanus Tree adventure," Ian continued, "Grandfather brought me here to show her to me. I was smitten, and he spent the next few years teaching me how to sail her."

Jane's mouth was set in a firm line, and she had raised an eyebrow, clearly miffed at not having been told about the boat until now. Ian looked at Jane, apologetically.

"I'm terribly sorry I didn't tell you about the yacht, Jane," he said sheepishly, "Grandfather swore me to secrecy."

Jane considered this for a moment, then her face softened.

"It's all right, Mouse," she said gently, "I understand. I would have been far more disappointed if you had broken your promise to your grandfather."

Ian smiled gratefully at Jane, reaching out to pat her hand.

Suddenly, Billy realised that they were standing at the level of the deck of the *Sea Gypsie*, and he leaned forward to peer down the narrow gap between the floor of the boathouse and the side of the yacht. Below them was a trench, carved deep into the floor of the boathouse. As Billy looked down, he could see that the hull of the *Sea Gypsie* was nestled into some sort of cradle resting at the bottom of the trench.

"Mouse?" Billy asked, hesitantly, "How do you get the boat from here to the sea? Do you have to wait for high tide?"

"Nothing so primitive as that, old bean," Ian laughed, "Grandfather was very, very clever with Mechanisms."

"I say, would you like to take a cruise in the *Gypsie*?" Ian asked, "I can show you how to launch her and we can take a Sunday tour of the coast."

Jane and Billy almost fell over themselves with excitement at the prospect.

"Yes please!" the pair exclaimed, almost in unison.

Mouse laughed, caught up in the excitement himself now.

"Come aboard, then," he waved graciously at the *Gypsie*, "and join me please in the wheelhouse."

oOo

The inside of the wheelhouse was beautifully panelled in rich, oiled timber. Just below the level of the windows, running the full width of the wheelhouse, was a console full of switches, gauges and levers, the polished brass fittings gleaming in the light. Rising out of the centre of the console was a ships wheel, again crafted from magnificently oiled timber.

Ian moved confidently to the wheel, gently running his hand along the timber. He motioned for Jane and Billy to stand behind him, one either side of his central position.

"Everything required for launch and recovery can be controlled from here in the wheelhouse," he explained, "The *Gypsie* connects via radio waves to the mechanisms built into the boathouse."

With a flourish, Ian flicked a large switch on one side of the console.

A loud bang rang out in front of the vessel, and then the seaward doors of the boathouse unsealed in the middle and the two halves began to slide apart, folding onto themselves like a concertina. A shaft of bright morning sunlight began to pour into the boathouse though the vertical opening between the doors, competing with the glow from the lanterns above.

Once the doors were halfway open, Ian began to turn a large red knob on the side of the console. As he turned the knob, the beach in front of the boathouse began to shake, revealing a long, thin, black line in the sand, running straight from the boathouse to the ocean.

As Billy and Jane stared on in amazement, the line became wider and deeper, opening into a long trench, wide enough to house the *Gypsie*. Ocean water began to flood into the trench, but it didn't reach all the way to the boathouse - the tide was too low to have enough water to completely fill the trench.

"Now," announced Ian, "for the clever bit."

Billy and Jane looked at each other. They had both thought everything they'd seen so far was the cleverest thing in the world.

Ian selected a large lever on the console and gently pulled it downwards, until the mechanism it controlled engaged with a satisfying click. The sound of a powerful engine could now be heard from somewhere behind the *Gypsie*, and this was soon joined by the sound of water rushing through large pipes somewhere under the ground.

"A steam engine drives a pump that sucks sea water through an underground pipe. The pipe dumps the sea water into the trench below us, where it flows out through the channel.

"The rate of flow of the water is fast enough that the trench and channel will fill with sea water, lifting the *Gypsie* off her cradle and allowing her to float down the channel to the ocean.

"All I need do now," Ian continued, "is to start her steam engines, and drive her down to the ocean once the trench is full."

Ian flicked two more switches on the console, then depressed a red rubber button for a few seconds. After a moment, the *Gypsie* shuddered slightly, as the twin steam engines in the bowels of the vessel began to chug, before settling into a steady rhythm that gently vibrated the floor beneath their feet.

Less than a minute later, the trio felt the *Gypsie* rock slightly, as she came free from the cradle.

When Ian judged that the channel held enough water for the *Gypsie* to clear the bottom, he placed his left hand on the ships wheel and his right hand on a double lever arrangement. Easing the lever forward, the engines of the *Gypsie* sprang to life, and the boat began to ease forward. Ian watched the doors of the boathouse carefully, using tiny turns on the wheel to keep the *Gypsie* moving straight through the opening.

Once clear of the boathouse, Ian continued to carefully guide the boat down the channel, until the *Gypsie* was clear of the beach and bobbing gently in the swell of the bay. Ian grinned broadly and turned to his friends.

"So, that's how we launch," he beamed, "Now, let's close everything up before we head off."

Ian reversed the sequence of pulling levers, flicking switches and turning knobs. From their vantage point in the bay, they watched the water stop flowing down the channel, the doors of the boathouse close up and the channel seal itself up. After only a minute or two, the process was complete, and Billy realised that the boathouse looked like any other seaside shed, and the channel from the boathouse to the ocean was completely invisible.

"Would you like to stay here in the wheelhouse," Ian asked, "or would you prefer to retire to the saloon for the journey?"

"There's no question in my mind," Jane enthused, "I'm staying right here."

Billy nodded in agreement. He couldn't imagine not watching Mouse drive the *Gypsie* through Pumicestone Passage.

"Excellent," Ian agreed, "If you each press one of the small green buttons on the wall behind you, two quite comfortable jump seats will slide up from the floor."

Jane and Billy pressed their green buttons, and two panels in the floor slid silently back under the rear wall. With a small hiss of escaping gas, a brass pole with a flat panel on top rose up out of the floor on either side of the wheelhouse. When the poles reached the correct height, they stopped and a clunk indicated they had locked into place.

The panel on top of each pole then began to unfold, turning into a padded seat cushion with a matching padded backrest, all held in place by thin metal rods. At the same time, a separate set of floor panels slid in from the sides, with a cut-out to accommodate each of the brass poles. When these panels locked into place with a soft click, it looked as if the jump seats had been built into the deck of the wheelhouse.

"The *Sea Gypsie* is just full of surprises, isn't she?" Billy observed.

—

"We've only just scratched the surface, old chap," Ian chuckled, as he turned the wheel and pushed up the throttle, sending the *Gypsie* out of the bay and south into Pumicestone Passage.

Chapter 19

Caloundra, Colony of Queensland, Australia
Sunday 13 September 1942

For the next hour, Ian steered the *Gypsie* down Pumicestone Passage, with the largely pristine coastline below Caloundra on their right, and the spit of Bribie Island to their left. Within ten minutes of leaving the boathouse, all of the trappings of civilisation were left behind them and the trio could easily have been travelling the waterway as if they were the early explorers.

As the spit of Bribie Island started to thicken into the Island proper, Ian slowed the engines of the *Gypsie* to just over idle speed. The boat began to chug gently forward. Ian carefully guided the *Gypsie* through a channel between a large, sandy island and Bribie Island itself, so they would be out of the way of any commercial shipping traffic travelling through the Passage.

Ian turned to his passengers and gave them a small, mock bow.

"Would you care to take a tour of the *Sea Gypsie*?" he enquired with a smile.

"Why Captain," replied Jane, playing along, "We'd be delighted."

Ian stepped through the door of the wheelhouse and walked along the side of the yacht towards the stern. When he reached the rear of the main cabin wall, he jumped down onto the deck of the boat. Jane, then Billy, followed him onto the stern deck.

"This deck is a wonderful place to relax and take in the view," Ian advised them, "and a number of chairs and lounges can be positioned on the deck using the controls set into the panel over there on the wall."

Billy nodded appreciatively, realising the deck was equipped with the same type of furniture system that had deployed the jump seats in the wheelhouse.

"Through here," Ian motioned to the two solid timber doors, with their large glass windows, "is the saloon."

Ian opened one of the doors and invited his friends to enter. As he did so, a gentle puff of cool air pushed out of the saloon and onto the deck. Jane stopped, surprised.

"Ah, the saloon is air conditioned." Ian said, noticing her reaction.

"Air conditioned? What does that mean?"

"One of Grandfather's inventions," Mouse explained, "the steam engines are under the saloon, and even though they are well insulated, they do still generate quite a bit a heat that can make this room quite uncomfortable."

"So, Grandfather devised a way to direct a flow of air into the saloon that has first been chilled, using a clever combination of chemical processes and some ingenious mechanical systems."

"That's incredible!" Billy said, "An invention like that would make our homes so much more comfortable."

"Not to mention our factories," Jane added, "and our schools."

"Grandfather did share all his drawings and devices with the Academy," Ian responded, "but it's up to the government to release the new systems to the public."

"Besides," he continued, "the system for air conditioning is quite complex and expensive. It's rather prone to breaking down, and I must admit, I'm still not completely sure about the complexities of how it actually works."

Billy and Jane nodded, then started looking around the saloon. Along each of the side walls were long padded lounges, and Billy noticed there were several panels in the floor, similar to those in the wheelhouse and on the deck outside.

"The lounges can convert into beds," Ian explained, "and additional chairs can be brought up through the floor panels, and they convert into beds as well."

"In a pinch, the *Gypsie* can sleep 12 people, but with up to four on board, she's very comfortable."

"There are also tables that come up through the floor panels, so you can use the saloon as a dining room if the weather is inclement."

"Through here," Ian said, pointing forward to the doors on either side of the front wall of the saloon, "is the galley on the port side and the equipment locker on the starboard. Beyond the galley is the pantry and chiller, while through the storage locker and down the stairs is the head."

Ian looked up to see the bewildered looks on Jane and Billy's faces.

"Sorry," he said quickly, "Grandfather taught me some nautical terms, and then insisted I use them whenever I came on board. I think I just fell back into the habit when we stepped into the saloon."

"The galley is the kitchen," he explained, "and the port side is the left-hand side when facing forward."

"Forward is the bow, isn't it? And the rear is the stern?"

"Yes, that's right, Billy."

"The starboard side is the right-hand side, and the head," he said, blushing slightly, "is the lavatory."

Jane smiled brightly at Ian and swept her arms around to indicate the whole of the *Sea Gypsie*.

"She's absolutely magnificent, Mouse!"

Ian blushed a little bit more but nodded his thanks to Jane. Then, he glanced at the chronometer mounted to the wall of the saloon.

"I say," he said, clearing his throat, "it's nearly 12. How about a spot of luncheon?"

"But we didn't bring a picnic today."

"Not to worry," Ian smiled, "the *Sea Gypsie* has a fully stocked larder. I'll go see what I can find."

oOo

While Ian rummaged in the larder and the galley, Billy and Jane moved out of the saloon and onto the deck. Billy pressed several buttons on the control panel, and a table with three chairs emerged from the deck.

Billy slumped down into one of the chairs, happy, but a little exhausted from the excitement of the morning.

"Well," he said, "I honestly never expected to end up here when I got up this morning."

"Neither did I," laughed Jane.

"I suppose this changes your plans for exploration. You'll have a lot more freedom to explore now."

"The boat will certainly make things easier, but Mouse and I had always intended to explore the coastline and the islands."

"You weren't planning on inland treks?" Billy asked, surprised.

"We do want to head inland eventually," Jane responded, "but the coast holds the most interest for us."

Billy nodded. Most of the people he knew loved the ocean. One of the main reasons his grandfather had settled in Caloundra was because it was nestled right on the sea.

"Why don't you tell me about your family, Billy," Jane asked, as if reading his mind.

Billy started for a moment, but quickly recovered.

"My grandparents settled here in the late 1890s. The Landsborough and the Leach families, as the first two settlers, secured some large tracts of land, but Grandfather arrived in Caloundra only a couple of years later, and was able to secure one of the smaller parcels.

"My father was born here shortly after they moved into the property, and we're actually still living there today. My grandfather built an extension onto the back of the house, and my grandparents moved into it when my father got married."

"Are your grandparents still with us?"

"Grandfather is, but my grandmother passed not long after my parents got married."

Jane nodded.

81

"My grandparents both passed last year."

"I'm sorry to hear that, Jane."

"Thank you, Billy. It was a bit of a shock at the time, as they both died at the same time - there was an accident on a wet night and their carriage overturned."

"But Mouse helped me through it," Jane added, softly, "he really is such a dear fellow."

After a moment, Jane sat forward a little on her chair, brightening.

"So, tell me Billy, what do your parents do?"

"Mother stays at home, although she picks up a little bit of work with ironing and mending from time to time. Father works for the ginger factory. He's a sales representative, so he travels quite a bit. Mostly it's down to Brisbane, and sometimes it's out to some of the little country towns. But every now and then, he has to travel to Melbourne to report to the big bosses of the company.

"In fact, he left for Melbourne this morning, and has to give some sort of presentation to the Chief of Operations tomorrow morning."

"Tomorrow morning? Will he make it in time?"

"The company wants him there urgently this time, so they've spared no expense. He's on the train to Brisbane now, and will be on an airship for Melbourne by mid-afternoon."

"An airship! How exciting!"

"It is! But now," Billy said, smiling, "tell me about your family? Are they as famous as Mouse's ancestors?"

Jane laughed, and her eyes sparkled with what Billy thought might have been mischief. She seemed to be about to answer Billy's question, when she was interrupted as Ian came out through the door of the saloon and out onto the deck, carrying a tray of drinks and sandwiches.

"I thought a light repast might be in order."

The trio settled back to enjoy their lunch in companionable silence. The only sounds were the gentle lapping of waves against the hull, and the occasional squawk of a seagull.

After a few minutes, the sandwiches were finished - none of them had realised quite how hungry they were - and Ian turned his attention to discussing his plans for the *Sea Gypsie*.

"There are an enormous number of shipwrecks here in Pumicestone Passage. These waters have not been kind to vessels over the years.

"Some of the more significant ones, like the boat from the *Queen of the Colonies* or the *SS Dickie*, have a short description in *The History*, but the vast majority have never been mentioned. You can only find out about them by trawling through the newspaper archives in the library.

"Barely a handful of the vessels that have been lost in this area have had their wrecks located, and I think we should do something about.

"After all," he continued, "a great many sailors and passengers lost their lives in these wrecks, and it just seems wrong that we don't know where they ended up."

"Here, here," Jane exclaimed.

"So, where do you want to begin?" Billy asked.

"And how do you want to go about it?" Jane added.

"Now that we can travel whenever we wish, I suggest we divide up the Passage into a series of grid squares, and conduct a thorough, meticulous search in each grid. That way, if there's anything to find, we'll find it.

"And," he added quickly, "more importantly, we'll be able to document exactly where each wreck lies."

"Excellent," enthused Jane, "I think that's a splendid plan. And we certainly know our way around the library archives, now."

Billy had become quiet, thinking hard.

"Mouse, Jane," Billy asked, "how will you locate the wrecks?"

"From the newspapers, mostly, old bean."

"No, I mean, how will you know if you're over a wreck when we're out here on the ocean? We could be anchored over a wreck right now, and we wouldn't even realise it was down there, let alone what ship it might have been."

"Ah," Ian said, snapping his fingers in realisation, "I see the problem you're alluding to.

"Once again," Ian continued, "it's Grandfather and his connection to the Science Academy that comes to the rescue.

"The *Sea Gypsie* is fitted with a rather cutting-edge version of sonar and some largely experimental seabed mapping equipment. The wheelhouse has a large display readout that actually plots the sea floor in great detail. When we pass over a wreck, the equipment will capture an image of it."

"Like an undersea photograph?" Billy asked, incredulously.

"Yes, I suppose it is. There's a repeater for the image in the saloon, so the sea floor can be monitored from there as well. And I can even set the equipment to sound an alarm if we travel over, say, something metal on the seabed."

Billy shook his head in amazement.

"So, when do we start?"

"We'll need to do some preparation and research first," Ian said thoughtfully, before turning to Jane.

"What do you think? Start of the Term holiday?"

Jane thought for a moment, then nodded.

"Yes, I think that should be just about right. That way, we can be well prepared, and spend most of the Christmas holiday working on the search."

Ian, Jane and Billy all grinned excitedly.

Ian held up his glass in front of the others.

"To the search", he toasted.

They all clinked their glasses together.

"The search!" they all chimed in unison.

"Now then," Ian said, "I rather hate to be the bearer of bad news, but I'm afraid we really must begin making our way back to the boathouse. We travelled with the current to get here, but it'll take quite a bit longer to get back, since we'll be fighting the current."

"Of course," Billy responded, "what can we do to help?"

"You're both welcome to keep me company in the wheelhouse."

"Lead the way, Mouse, lead the way."

Chapter 20

Caloundra, Colony of Queensland, Australia
Monday 21 September 1942

In the week since their trip in the *Sea Gypsie*, Ian and Jane had made a start on their research for the shipwreck search. They had managed to obtain an old Admiralty chart for Pumicestone Passage and had carefully marked out a grid pattern.

The grid started at the northern end of the Caloundra township, and extended east just far enough to include Bribie Island. The grid extended south as far as the southern edge of Bribie.

"We must take particular care when we go to the eastern side of Bribie," Ian had explained, "The *Sea Gypsie* isn't really designed for open water travel. I think she can handle the ocean on a reasonably calm day, but I'm not certain how she'll go in a squall, or even if there's a decent wind blowing.

"Grandfather took me out in her many times, teaching me how to sail her, but we only ever went to the far side of Bribie Island once."

Ian shivered involuntarily at the memory.

"Let's just say, I was more than a little worried that day."

Billy and Jane waited patiently for Ian to continue the story, but after a few moments they realised he had said all he was going to say about it.

oOo

As much as they were excited about the exploration of the Passage, Ian and Jane's main focus for the past week had been preparing for the mathematics examination Mr Gibson had announced on their first day at the College.

Even though they had only been at the school for two weeks now, it was clear to everyone, including the Masters, that Jane and Ian were academically gifted. Even without their exploits as researchers and explorers, it was clear that the two students were well suited to mathematics and the sciences.

While Ian had a clear preference - almost a gift - for the Science of Mechanisms, Jane was equally adept at the Science of Organisms. Both students were at the top of the class for the Science of Compositions and for Mathematics.

It was, therefore, a matter of principle that they excel in the mathematics examination, and gain entry into the Advanced Placement course.

Actually, Billy thought, it's more a matter of pride than principle, although he kept this observation to himself.

Now that the day of the examination had arrived, Billy noticed his friends were filled with excited energy.

When they met at the eucalyptus tree at recess, Ian and Jane huddled together, quizzing and prompting each other on various mathematical formulae and theories. Much of what they were discussing was far ahead of Billy's current knowledge, so he sat back and observed, rather than trying to participate.

Some students might have felt left out or abandoned by their friends in a situation like this, but Billy was perfectly content to let his friends focus on their upcoming exam. He didn't need to feel like he was the centre of attention.

It always impressed Billy when he saw how people rose to embrace their strengths. Billy knew he was a very capable student, but he also recognised that Ian and Jane were far more advanced than he was in Mathematics and the Sciences. For Billy, this was not a cause for rivalry or petty jealousy. He was happy for his friends and proud of their achievements.

By comparison, in the study of History, Billy was perhaps slightly ahead of Ian and Jane, although that was mostly because of his ability to tell the stories of *The History* with such passion and energy that the audience would be swept up into the moment. Billy always quietly thanked his father for teaching him how to read *The History* is such a passionate and lively way.

The one area where Billy was far ahead of his Ian and Jane was in sport. Even though it was only the third week of the term, Billy had already earned a place on the rowing squad. He was yet to make one of the crews, but for now, he was content to be on the squad and learning how to row.

After all, he mused, a month ago he'd never touched an oar. However, with his natural talent for all things physical, Billy was very quickly becoming adept at the sport.

Rowing was a year-round sport at the College, and students who made the squad needed to attend training twice a week after school, as well as carnivals and competitions each month. The Sports Master, Mr Roberts, had also made it very clear that they were expected to maintain at least a passing grade in every academic subject if they wished to remain on the squad.

"Under no circumstances," he had growled at them, "are you to let rowing interfere with your studies.

"Nor," he continued, "are you to let your studies interfere with your rowing."

When the students looked at him with confusion, Mr Roberts softened his glower, ever so slightly.

"You must find balance," he clarified, "You will, throughout your lives, have many responsibilities - to family, to work, to the Empire. If you put all of your energy into any one of these responsibilities, your other obligations will suffer.

"While you're here at the College, the other Masters and I will help you and guide you. We'll get you to practice meeting more than one responsibility at a time, starting with balancing your academics with being on the rowing squad.

"If you start to find one of your responsibilities is suffering, do not ignore the problem. I assure you, it will not resolve itself. Do not hesitate to talk to me or one of the other Masters about your situation and obtain our assistance.

"Are we clear on this matter?"

"Yes, Sir," the students all responded in unison.

The sound of the warning bell to mark the end of recess brought Billy back to the present.

Ian and Jane got up quickly, ready to head to the Mathematics building and sit the first half of the examination.

"Good luck," Billy said to them, as they quickly packed their things back into their satchels.

"Thanks Billy," Jane replied, smiling, "I appreciate that."

"Cheers, Old Bean," Ian said, taking a moment to look Billy in the eye before returning to ensuring all his equipment was in his bag.

"Will I see you at luncheon?"

"Probably not," Ian responded, "I believe the candidates only get a 20-minute break before going into the second part of the exam, and the break doesn't line up with lunch."

Ian and Jane started to move quickly towards the Mathematics building.

"Perhaps after school, then?" Billy called after them, "I'll be frightfully keen by then to hear how you both went."

Jane laughed, delightedly.

"Of course, Billy," she called back over her shoulder, "we wouldn't dream of keeping you in suspense a moment longer than we have to."

Billy found himself standing alone under the eucalyptus tree. Smiling, he quickly put his things into his satchel and hurried off to the English building for his next class.

oOo

Billy waited by the gate for half an hour after school finished, but there was no sign of Ian or Jane.

He was almost ready to go back into the grounds to see if they'd headed to the eucalyptus tree, when he saw the two students coming around the corner of College House.

Both of his friends looked drained, as if they had just undergone some form of trauma. Clearly the examination had been an ordeal.

"Jane, Mouse," Billy called out excitedly.

Both students looked up at hearing their names and raised their hands in a feeble wave. They seemed almost incapable of responding beyond that meagre gesture.

As they got closer, Ian and Jane smiled weakly at Billy.

"Don't ask." Jane said, exhausted, "I don't think I have the energy to answer."

Billy must have looked disappointed at not being able to find out how the exam went, as Ian took a deep breath, as if mustering his strength.

"There were a lot of questions," he explained, "far more than you might normally see in an exam.

"Most of them were quite straightforward," he looked at Jane for confirmation, and she nodded weakly, "but there were just so many of them."

"When will you get the results?"

"Mr Gibson said he'd let us know by Friday."

"I think I'm going to sleep until Friday," Jane murmured.

Billy laughed gently.

"How about I escort you two home?" he suggested, "I'd hate to see you collapsed in the gutter somewhere from exhaustion."

Ian and Jane smiled and shuffled to stand either side of Billy.

"Home, James," Ian joked, as Billy started to walk them away from the College.

Chapter 21

Noosa, Colony of Queensland, Australia
Wednesday 7 October 1942

"It's almost time," the cell leader said, "take up your positions."

The sun had set hours ago, and the Noosa beach was completely deserted.

Two men, dressed head to toe in black, nodded at this order and moved up the beach towards the dunes. They stopped a few feet away from the cell leader, crossed their arms over their barrel chests, and began to scan the area for any interlopers.

The cell leader didn't expect to be interrupted at this late hour, but if some hapless local decided they couldn't sleep and went for a walk along the beach, his men would alert him to abort the mission.

Facing the ocean, the cell leader was pleased that the moon was hidden behind the clouds tonight. The darkness added to his sense of destiny, although he couldn't really explain why. He just knew this was a precipitous moment.

He also knew it almost certainly wouldn't rain tonight, and he was glad he didn't have to deal with that complication. This was the most dangerous part of the mission, and he would only relax when the agent had arrived and they were all safely away from the beach.

The cell leader struck a match and lit the kerosene lantern he held in his hand. Raising his arm above his head, he began to swing the lantern gently from side to side, tracing three wide arcs of light across the ocean in front of him.

He lowered the lantern, counted slowly to three, then raised the lantern and gave two more slow, wide swings. When he had finished, he lowered the lantern to the sand, and turned down the wick until the flame was extinguished.

This was the precise signal he had been instructed to give, at this hour, on this night, on this beach. If he received no response to the signal, his instructions were to repeat the pattern every 15 minutes, until an hour had elapsed. If there was still no response after that, he was to go home, and repeat the signal each night until he received a response or was given different orders.

—

Within a minute of giving the signal, two brief flashes of light came from several hundred yards off the coast, followed by the sound of oars dragging through the water. The operative was on his way, and the cell leader felt a flush of excitement at finally meeting him.

The cell leader knew only that this codename meant 'wolf' in Russian, and that according to his reputation, this name was well deserved. He was known as an agitator, spreading sedition and unrest into pockets of disillusioned citizens all across the Empire. He was an agent of the Bolsheviks, who had overthrown their Imperial masters, the Romanov family, in the 1917 revolution.

As Volkov stepped off the small boat onto the beach, the cell leader rushed forward to greet him, trying to hide his surprise at how young the Russian looked.

"He's not even 30 years old," the cell leader thought, "so young to have seen so many battles."

"Comrade Volkov," he enthused, in hushed tones, "I am honoured to meet you."

Volkov stared at the cell leader with his pale blue eyes. The cell leader caught himself staring at the broad scar that ran across the left side of Volkov's face, from chin to ear. He quickly looked away. Everyone knew how Volkov had earned that scar, and he did not want to be caught staring at it.

"Da," Volkov responded, continuing to stare at the leader.

The cell leader knew very little Russian, but he knew this meant 'yes'.

Without another word, Volkov looked up towards the dunes, and began striding off the beach.

The cell leader scrambled to catch up and lead Volkov to the carriages.

The Wolf had arrived in the Colony.

oOo

Brisbane, Colony of Queensland, Australia
Monday 12 October 1942

"Commander," called Lieutenant Leslie Simons, from across the crowded floor of the operations room, "I think you should take a look at this, Sir."

Patrick Bowman looked up from his desk, crowded with papers and maps, to see the young Navy Lieutenant holding a message pad. Patrick stood up, taking the opportunity to stretch the muscles in his back, which had gotten stiff from too many hours sitting in his uncomfortable wooden chair.

As he walked over to the Lieutenant, Patrick surveyed the team he had put together. Every single man and woman in this room was an expert in at least one discipline.

Some were code breakers, people who were so mathematically adept they could spot patterns in hundreds of encrypted characters, and then decipher coded messages. Others were experts in one or more of the Sciences. All were combat trained and weapons certified.

Since the Saturday sitting of Parliament last month, and his subsequent meeting with the Chief, Patrick had been tasked with creating a special operations hub for counter-terrorism operations within the borders of the Colony of Queensland.

He had moved quickly, but discreetly, and had formed the core of his team within two days of returning to Queensland. Within a week, he had secured premises in the sub-basement of an office building in George Street, and had the necessary monitoring and analysis equipment installed.

On a whim, he had nicknamed the operations centre 'The Bunker', and the name had quickly been adopted by his team. Someone had even carved the name into a wooden sign and hung it over the secure door to the facility.

His wife, Mary, was aware of his role in the security forces for the Colony, and that his sales job at the ginger factory was only a cover. The Chief had long ago implemented a policy where operatives, such as Patrick, were able to confide in their spouse. He believed it made his people more efficient if they didn't have to lie to their beloved.

"Tell your spouse, by all means," the Chief had directed, "but no one else. Your parents, grandparents, children, other relatives and friends must all believe your cover story."

This policy had certainly helped when Patrick needed to tell Mary he would be spending the next few weeks, and possibly even months, in Brisbane, running the operation.

"What have you got for me Lieutenant?" Patrick asked.

"We've just decoded a signal from Moscow. It reads:

Volkov arriving 7/10 at 2230

Signal: 3, wait 3, 2

Response 2 quick

ACK

"Volkov," Patrick grimaced, "the Wolf. Yes, we know about him. Do we know where the signal was being sent to, Lieutenant?"

"We don't have a precise address," she replied, "but we know it's somewhere in the vicinity of Noosa."

Patrick considered his options for a moment, then turned to one of the Army Officers on his team.

"Captain Calvin, advise the Noosa operatives to begin Level 2 observation of known and suspected sympathisers. Remind them they must be thorough but discreet. Volkov is a highly experienced agent. If he's in Noosa, the slightest mistake will send him underground."

"Yes, Sir," the Captain replied, before turning to her desk to begin composing the encrypted message for the Noosa team.

"Warrant Officer Higgs," Patrick called across the room.

The Warrant Officer shot to his feet before responding.

"Aye, Sir."

"Prep your team. We may need to do a little break and enter in Noosa."

"Aye, Sir," Warrant Officer Higgs replied, with a devilish glint in his eyes.

Chapter 22

Noosa, Colony of Queensland, Australia
Wednesday 14 October 1942

Over the last seven days, Volkov had been setting up his operation, using the house of the cell leader as his base.

"Comrade Volkov," the cell leader announced, officiously, "the preparations are complete."

Volkov had quickly decided that the cell leader was a simpleton, and that his allegiance to the revolutionary cause was not fuelled by anything other than his own dreams of power and prestige.

Fortunately, Volkov did not require zealots at this stage of his operation. That requirement would come later. But for now, the subservient cell leader was useful for his contacts and his home, in fulfilling this part of Volkov's mission.

"Nyet," Volkov replied, before switching to heavily accented English, "No, the preparations are never complete. There is always more to be done."

The cell leader nodded and scurried away to find something else to do.

Volkov looked around the room, taking in all of the details.

The dining table had been placed in the middle of the living room, and the other furniture either removed or pushed to the side. Maps of the Colony had been hung on the walls, and the small red pins marked buildings of significance. Photographs of prominent members of society and the government, all cut from newspapers, were also pinned to the walls.

Papers covered the table, including diagrams and plans of buildings and carriage routes. There were pamphlets as well, calling for the people to rise up against their cruel imperial monarch and to cast off the chains of oppression. Boxes of pamphlets, roughly printed on cheap paper, were stacked in the corner of the room.

"No," Volkov decided, "we are not ready yet."

"But we are close."

oOo

—

Brisbane, Colony of Queensland, Australia
Wednesday 14 October 1942

Commander Bowman stared at the large map of Noosa that had been pinned to the wall of The Bunker. His eyes moved along the streets marked on the map, looking for inspiration about the headquarters of the terrorists.

"Where are you hiding?" he muttered under his breath.

Behind him, in the centre of the operations room, a quiet buzz of voices told him that his team were busy analysing all of the data, trying to answer the same question.

A Corporal appeared at his shoulder, with a decoded message in his hand.

"Sir," Corporal Ramirez said, handing over the slip of paper.

Patrick unfolded it, already knowing what it would say.

"Progress Update," was the simple message, signed "Chief."

Patrick refolded the paper and handed it back to Corporal Ramirez. He turned to face the group working busily around the large table in the centre of the room.

"Where are we, people?"

The team stopped working for a moment, turned and looked at the Commander.

"We've narrowed down the possible locations for the cell to three locations on the southern end of the township," summarised the Captain Calvin.

"Good," replied Patrick, "on what basis?"

"Based on Volkov's previous history," the Captain continued smoothly, "we believe he's setting up a fairly substantial base of operations. This is his first foray into Queensland, so he'll set up a headquarters first, followed by multiple small units spread throughout the Colony."

Patrick nodded.

"Noosa makes sense as a headquarters. It's relatively small compared to Brisbane, and is far enough away that it doesn't get anywhere near as much attention as the capital.

"It's also close enough to provide relatively easy access to Brisbane and the major routes from there to the regional centres and the other Colonies.

"Very good, Captain," Patrick congratulated her on her analysis of the situation so far, while nodding to indicate she should continue.

"The type of headquarters Volkov will likely set up will require a certain degree of isolation. There will be quite a bit of traffic into and out of the site in the first seven to ten days, as Volkov brings in people and equipment.

"In addition, he will require supplies for a team of people, and will likely create a stockpile of food and water, should he find himself surrounded and in a siege situation. This has allowed us to narrow down the options to just three properties on the southern edge of Noosa."

Again, Patrick nodded.

"So, the problem then is to identify which of the properties is Volkov's headquarters?"

"Yes, Sir," the Captain concluded, "that's our current sticking-point."

"Excuse me, Sir?" Lieutenant Simons spoke up, from the back of the room.

"Yes, Lieutenant," Patrick responded, encouragingly.

"My last posting was to the Directorate's Statistics unit. Our task was to monitor purchases of items by Citizens across the Colony. We were looking for spikes in spending, and purchases of unusual items."

"Yes, Lieutenant, I'm aware of the Statistics Unit."

"The Unit also tracks purchases of unusual quantities of everyday items," she continued, "If Volkov's headquarters is being stocked with food and water for a large number of people, more than a normal household, the Statistics Unit will have data on those purchases."

"Including who made the purchases?"

"Yes, Sir, in most cases."

"Well done, Lieutenant," Patrick said, giving the young woman a smile, "That could be the breakthrough we're looking for."

Patrick turned to his Executive Officer, Squadron Leader Peale.

"Squadron Leader, contact the Statistics Unit and have them send over their data on Noosa for the last 12 months."

"Yes, Sir."

"Time is short people," Patrick told his team, "let's get that data in and analysed. I want a specific location identified within the next 24 hours."

Patrick walked to his desk to compose his update for the Chief.

oOo

Brisbane, Colony of Queensland, Australia
Thursday 15 October 1942

"We have it, Sir," Captain Calvin said quietly.

"Verified?" Patrick asked, working hard to keep his tone neutral.

"Yes Sir, two independent analyses."

"Very well, brief the team."

"Gather round, people," Captain Calvin called out.

Everyone stopped talking, and moved towards the front of the room, where Captain Calvin and Commander Bowman stood in front of the large map of Noosa township.

"We have been able to ascertain," began Captain Calvin, "that a rather unusually high quantity of water and tinned food have been purchased, over the last six weeks, by the owner of this property on the southern edge of Noosa."

The Captain used a pointer to mark a house that backed onto virgin forest at the very edge of the town.

"On its own, this data is suspicious," she continued, "but not conclusive. However, there have also been a number of deliveries of some rather specialised equipment and parts that could be used to construct surveillance mechanisms and, potentially, weapons.

"There is little doubt that this property," the Captain again tapped the map, "is the location of a terrorist cell."

For a moment, there was silence in the Bunker. Then, Warrant Officer Higgs spoke up, looking directly at Commander Bowman.

"Sir, your orders?"

"Warrant Officer," said Patrick gravely, "the order is 'Go'."

Chapter 23

Noosa, Colony of Queensland, Australia
Friday 16 October 1942

Dawn was still an hour away when the hull of the launch crunched against the sand on the southern end of the beach at Noosa. The assault team were almost silent as they slipped over the side of the boat and raced up the beach into the cover of the dunes.

As the launch turned away and headed back out to sea, Patrick Bowman signalled his team to fan out and begin moving towards the target. He and Warrant Officer Higgs needed to move the team into a position to surround the isolated house within 30 minutes. The attack was scheduled to begin 10 minutes before dawn.

Patrick and Warrant Officer Higgs had spent most of the trip from Brisbane to Noosa planning the assault. Normally, he would have preferred at least a day of careful planning before executing an action like this, but Patrick knew that he simply didn't have that much time. Volkov had arrived in Noosa nine days earlier, and if he stayed true to his usual methods, the first terrorist attacks were perhaps only a day or two away.

The Royal Navy Cruiser he had commandeered to take them to Noosa was state-of-the-art. The cruiser, *HMS Cooktown*, had been built with two hulls in parallel, with the deck suspended between them and the superstructure built on top of the deck. The engineers called it a 'catamaran', and according to her Captain, she was the fastest thing in the Navy.

She had two enormous steam engines, one built into each hull, driving high-efficiency screws sitting under the water line. Her twin hulls meant she virtually skipped over the water, instead of ploughing through it like a traditional single-hull ship. This combination meant that the *Cooktown* was capable of phenomenal speed, and virtually guaranteed Commander Bowman and his team would arrive at Noosa in time to execute their mission.

Leslie Simons eased in beside Patrick at the top of the sand dunes, and he could hear her breathing, fast and a little ragged.

"Steady, Lieutenant," he advised her in a whisper, "remember your training. Channel your fear and nervousness into controlled bursts of energy."

"Aye, Sir," she replied, drawing a deep breath and letting it out slowly to regain control.

Patrick waved his arm to the left, then to the right, signalling his team to move towards the target.

oOo

Patrick had taken up position at the front of the property, about 30 yards from the front door. To his right, near the corner of the building crouched Captain Calvin. The Captain could see Warrant Officer Higgs, who was at the rear of the building and would coordinate the team securing the rear of the property.

To his left was Lieutenant Simons. Even though Simons was on her first mission, Patrick had given her command of the team attacking from the left.

When Patrick gave the signal to go, both Lieutenant Simons and Captain Calvin would see it immediately. The Captain would pass the signal on to Warrant Officer Higgs, and the attack would begin on all sides of the building within a few seconds.

Patrick hoped this would give his team the elements of surprise and coordination, letting them take the building and its occupants without serious resistance. The intelligence reports they had received suggested that only Volkov was truly dangerous, and the local cell members were likely to surrender once they realised they were being attacked by His Majesty's forces.

Unfortunately, Patrick knew from bitter experience that sometimes the information he was given before an operation wasn't complete or accurate. He also knew that sometimes, when people were backed into a corner, they would behave in unpredictable ways. Ways that, in the heat of the moment and the confusion of battle, they might wrongly believe would allow them to survive.

Patrick held up his gloved hand, showing Lieutenant Simons and Captain Calvin his five extended fingers. The Captain mirrored his gesture, and Patrick knew that the Warrant Officer would be repeating the signal to his team.

Patrick lowered one finger, then another, then another. He could feel multiple sets of eyes watching his signal.

Patrick lowered another finger, so that he only held one finger in the air. When he lowered that finger, so that his hand formed a fist, his entire team, spread all around the building would silently creep up to the walls before charging in through the doors.

Just as Patrick lowered his final finger, and his team stood up to advance, one of the cell members strolled around the corner of a small woodshed over to the left.

She was tying up her overalls as she walked back towards the house. It seemed she had gone behind the woodshed to relieve herself.

Patrick cursed silently, willing his people to stop, hoping the woman wouldn't notice the lines of operatives stealthily approaching the house. If they were very, very lucky, she'd make it the last 10 yards to the house and his team would be safe.

The woman turned her head towards the approaching agents. She must have seen movement out of the corner of her eye. She screamed, grabbing at the rifle she had slung over her shoulder.

One of Patrick's team raced towards her, aiming to silence her before the alarm was raised. The operative tackled the woman to the ground, cutting off the scream.

But the agent was just a fraction too slow. The woman swung her rifle around and even as she was falling under the weight of the agent, she managed to squeeze the trigger.

The weapon was one of the newer automatic rifles, and five bullets shot from the barrel with a series of bright flashes and a deafening roar. Patrick knew they had seconds now before the cell members inside the house would begin firing through the windows and doors, trying to take out his team.

"GO, GO, GO!" Patrick roared, and began sprinting for the door of the house. He didn't look back. His team was so well trained, he knew they would respond instantly to his order to attack and would be converging on the house.

One way or another, this was going to be over in the next few minutes.

oOo

Inside the building, everyone froze when they heard the scream. When a moment later the sound of rifle fire was heard just outside, the cell leader quickly counted his people.

"Kelly," he thought, "Kelly is missing."

In a matter of moments, the cell leader had worked out what had happened. The roar of an agent outside telling his team to 'Go' was all the confirmation he needed.

Volkov didn't need anywhere near that many seconds to process what was going on. He was already moving away from the doors and windows, and bracing himself to repel the attack, before the rifle outside had even finished firing.

Suddenly, he felt a hand grab his arm and spin him away from the living room toward one of the bedrooms at the rear of the house.

Volkov was about to knock the hand away and deliver a vicious blow to the owner, when he realised it was the cell leader pushing him into the other room.

"Quickly, Comrade Volkov," the man hissed, "through here."

As they entered the room, the cell leader quickly closed the door, then pulled on a heavy wooden chest of drawers. The drawers slid easily, moving on hidden wheels, revealing a rectangular opening in the floor.

"Through here, Comrade," the cell leader gestured at the opening, "this tunnel was dug as an escape route, in case of an attack by the authorities.

"There is no light in the tunnel, and it is only just big enough for a man to crawl through. But it will take you to safety at the edge of the forest.

"Go Comrade. Go now. We will hold them off for as long as we can, to give you time to escape."

Volkov looked at the cell leader. For the first time, he felt respect for the man.

"Da," Volkov said, "good luck."

He shook the cell leader's hand and dropped soundlessly into the tunnel. The cell leader quickly pushed the drawers back into place, and Volkov was plunged into inky blackness.

Volkov reached into his coat pocket in the tight confines of tunnel and pulled out his goggles. Awkwardly placing them on his head, he pulled the green glass lenses over his eyes and fumbled slightly in the cramped space to flick the switch and activate the device.

With a faint whine from the mechanism, Volkov's vision began to clear. The goggles were working. He could see the walls of the tunnel, and the empty space ahead of him where he needed to crawl. Everything had a green tinge to it, no doubt from the effect of the mechanism and the tinted glass in the lenses, but Volkov didn't care. These goggles were going to help him escape.

Volkov began to crawl silently down the tunnel.

Chapter 24

Noosa, Colony of Queensland, Australia
Friday 16 October 1942

"Warrant Officer, secure the prisoners in the back bedroom," Patrick ordered, while standing in the centre of what had once been the living room of the house.

The entire fight had lasted a little less than the three minutes Patrick had estimated. The cell members were poorly organised, and when Patrick's team burst through the doors of the house, shouting for them to surrender and brandishing their weapons, most of the terrorists quickly complied.

Three or four cell members had tried to stage a rear-guard action, holding Patrick's team back for a short while with pistols and knives. But, after the terrorists had been allowed a few moments to make a show of being brave, Patrick's team advanced on them. That was when they decided to lay down their weapons and sink to their knees with their hands on their heads. Patrick was pleased that, apart from the initial, accidental burst of gunfire from the woman outside, not a single shot had been fired.

"Captain Calvin, any sign of Volkov?"

"No, Sir. Either he wasn't here when we attacked, or somehow he slipped the noose while we were moving in."

Patrick felt his jaw tighten in frustration at having missed their quarry.

"Very well," he said, making sure to keep his voice even, "I want a complete inventory of every piece of evidence in this room, Captain. Every scrap of paper, Every push pin.

It looks like we have every detail of his entire operation here. I don't want to miss a single clue that might lead us to any other cells, or to Volkov."

"Understood, Commander," she replied briskly, before turning to task her senior staff with the painstaking work.

"Excuse me, Sir," Corporal Ramirez had again appeared at Patrick's side.

Patrick was so distracted by the plans pinned up around the room and strewn all over the table, that he didn't even notice the airman come into the house. Patrick looked up and saw the distressed look on the woman's face, although she was making a good show of trying to hide it.

"I think you'd best come outside, Sir," the Corporal said quietly.

Patrick glanced over at Captain Calvin, nodding for her to accompany them out to the front of the house.

Corporal Ramirez led the two officers towards a shape lying on the ground, near where their assault had started. With a sinking feeling in his stomach, Patrick realised this was just a few paces to his left at the time he'd given the order to advance on the house.

The shape on the ground was Lieutenant Simons, with a corpsman kneeling over her.

As the officers approached, they could see that the corpsman had stripped the combat webbing off the Lieutenant, and applied several field dressings to her belly, her left arm and the left side of her head. Blood was seeping through the bandages, but the Lieutenant was conscious, if heavily medicated for the pain.

"The Lieutenant was hit by three of the rounds discharged by the terrorist when we tackled her, Sir," the corpsman explained.

"I'm sorry, Sir," Lieutenant Simons croaked, "I think I missed your party."

The corpsman injected her with an additional dose of sedative, and the Lieutenant fell back into unconsciousness.

"If we can get her back to the *Cooktown* quickly," the corpsman continued, "the Lieutenant should recover fully from the belly wound."

"The wounds to her arm and head are not life-threatening," the corpsman looked at the Lieutenant to make sure she wasn't awake, "but I don't believe we'll be able to save her arm, and her left eye has been completely destroyed."

"Call in an evac," Patrick ordered, without a moment's hesitation, "I want her on the *Cooktown* within the next 20 minutes."

Patrick stalked away from the prone form of the Lieutenant, heading out of earshot of the corpsman. Captain Calvin followed him as Patrick continued walking down the side of the house and around to the rear of the building.

When Patrick stopped, Captain Calvin came to stand close, allowing him to talk to her in a quiet whisper. The Captain knew that he would need to vent, and with Squadron Leader Peale coordinating things from The Bunker, she was his next most senior officer.

Captain Calvin placed a hand on his arm, a reassuring touch she hoped would help keep him grounded and in control.

"What can I do to help, Patrick?" she asked, wanting to take some of the burden away from him.

Patrick ignored her efforts, consumed in the moment with rage at the situation.

"I don't care what it takes," Patrick whispered through gritted teeth, "I want Volkov found. I want him hunted down. I will not stop until he is in custody. The Wolf is now the prey."

oOo

Volkov emerged from the tunnel at the rear of the house, just behind the first line of the forest.

He knew he needed to escape, but for the first time, Volkov found himself paralysed with indecision.

Everything he had worked for was gone. The entire mission was compromised. The mission that Moscow believed would make the Empire quake, and perhaps even crumble and break apart, was over before it had begun.

He had almost completed the planning for this audacious set of acts. Now, all of that planning, all of the information about his mission was in the hands of the Empire.

They also had the cell members in custody. Once they worked out who the cell leader was, they would have confirmation. The cell leader didn't know everything, but he knew enough to be able to corroborate the plans laid out on the dining room table.

"What now?" he thought, feeling enormous tension from the stress of the situation, like a rubber band in his mind being twisted tighter and tighter.

"I can't go back to Russia," he realised, "With a failure of this magnitude, the best I could hope for would be to be stripped of rank and privileges and sent to the salt mines for the rest of my miserable life".

He felt like the rubber band of stress in his head would never stop twisting.

Movement near the house caught Volkov's eye, and he looked up to see two of the officers coming around the side of the building. They stopped at the back of the building.

Volkov quickly positioned the receiving antenna on the top of his goggles and tapped the activation button. He focussed his attention on the audio signal being fed from the antenna into his earpiece.

"...I do to help, Patrick?"

The voice was tinny, the circuits in his goggles working hard to pick up the sounds and amplify them for Volkov.

He saw that it was the woman who asked, and the man next to her was breathing hard. Judging by the body language the man was displaying, Volkov suspected he was trying to compose himself.

Volkov took a moment to use the binocular function of the goggles to zoom in on the two officers.

The woman, judging from the rank insignia, was a Captain in their Army, while the man was a Navy Commander. That probably made him the team leader. Volkov zoomed in a little tighter and could just make out the name patch on the man's combat webbing.

"Bowman," he whispered, "Patrick Bowman."

It always amazed Volkov how the Empire forces felt the need to use embellishments to show their rank and authority, and he found it utterly bizarre why they needed to put their names so prominently on their military clothing. With hardly any effort at all, Volkov had learnt the name and rank of the team leader.

Now, the man, this Commander Patrick Bowman, was speaking. Volkov turned his full attention to discovering what he would say next.

"I don't care what it takes, I want Volkov found. I want him hunted down. I will not stop until he is in custody. The Wolf is now the prey."

Volkov felt the tension in his head tighten again, but this time it was like the rubber band had been twisted to the breaking point. With a final, painful, flash of white-hot light and pain in his mind, he felt the rubber band snap.

A sudden, cold calm descended on Volkov. Every stress faded away. His mission was forgotten, Moscow was an irrelevance to him now. Every fibre of his being was now focused on this Commander Bowman.

"So, you want to hunt, Commander?" Volkov asked himself, "Do you not realise that If you try to corner a wolf, you should expect that he will bite.

"Da, you have taken everything from me, Comrade Commander Bowman. Now I shall return the favour and take everything from you.

"But not today. Not today," Volkov mused, "My revenge will be slow and precise, a work of Machiavellian art.

He turned away from his new quarry and began moving silently and stealthily through the forest, leaving the house, and his former life, behind.

Chapter 25

Caloundra, Colony of Queensland, Australia
Tuesday 3 November 1942

After the excitement of the first two weeks of school, culminating with the Advanced Placement examination, Ian, Jane and Billy found themselves settling into a routine. Each week followed the same schedule, and all three students were becoming adept at judging the time without being totally reliant on the bells.

Each Monday was an academic day, starting with Mathematics before recess, then English until luncheon, and Science in the afternoon. The students were not permitted to train for any sports teams on Mondays, although if they wished to play a friendly game of football at luncheon, it was allowed.

Tuesday and Thursday were devoted to History in the mornings, Mathematics after recess, and sport in the afternoon. For the boys, the sport was boxing, while the girls attended gymnastics training.

"Fit and flexible!" was the mantra of Mr Roberts, as he alternated between the boxing and gymnastics classes, so that each group had him as their coach once each week.

Wednesday and Friday were again focussed on the academic subjects. English was always scheduled for the morning session on these days, followed by Science after recess. Mathematics class was held after luncheon on Wednesday and History class was conducted in the afternoon on Fridays.

As Friday after school was the parade for the Empire Service Scheme, all of the students wore their cadet uniforms for the whole day. This meant that the students were able to move straight into their cadet training after school finished, without needing to rush home to change or to store their uniforms in their cramped gym locker.

As Billy was on the rowing squad, he had practice after school on Wednesday each week, so he needed to bring his rowing kit to school that day and store it in his locker until after class. Billy was pleased that the College provided the special uniform for sport teams if you made the squad. He wanted to try out as many sports as he could, and he didn't want his parents to have to keep buying him boots, jerseys and all the other kit.

He was growing taller and broader as the year progressed, and some of the clothes he'd been given at the start of the school year, just a couple of months ago, were now getting too small for him. His mother was able to make some adjustments, but eventually she told Billy he needed to apply to the school for a larger size.

Billy noticed that Ian was also getting taller, although he didn't seem to get any stockier, despite all the hard training in the boxing ring and in the field with the cadets. Billy's mother assured him that Ian would 'fill out' one day, and it was just a matter of time.

Jane too growing taller, and she seemed to be growing her hair longer, although the natural curls were always present, no matter how tight she braided or plaited her hair. Billy would even, occasionally, tell her how stylish her hair looked, although this often earned him a strange look from Jane that he could never quite fathom.

Along with the rest of the girls in First Form, Jane was also growing into a young lady. The students had already covered gender and reproduction in their Science of Organisms class and had been told by Mr Isaacs of the sorts of changes they should expect to see in their bodies over the coming months and years. Billy found, however, that seeing the changes happening to one of his closest friends was perhaps a little too realistic.

Billy also began to notice that Jane was developing strong, well defined muscles, particularly in her calves, thighs and arms.

"You're not secretly boxing, are you Jane?" Billy asked jokingly one day, knowing full well that Jane's fitness was coming from her hard work twice a week at gymnastics.

"Hardly," Jane had harrumphed, making it very clear that she did not wish to discuss the matter any further.

oOo

Billy had tried out for the cricket team, and even though he was only in First Form, he had been placed in the second reserve squad. Although this meant he wouldn't be representing the College in the cricket competition that was about to start, it did mean he'd get to train each Thursday afternoon, throughout the summer season, with the older, more experienced students in the team.

Ian and Billy continued with their weekly boxing sessions, developing their skills and stamina in the ring as the term progressed. Both boys enjoyed boxing, as they had been brought up with the notion that all gentlemen of breeding and good manners must be able to box whenever a situation demanded it.

There was little doubt that Billy's natural athleticism made him a graceful and effective boxer. While Ian lacked some of this grace, he more than made up for it with bravado and dedication. No matter how many times Ian got knocked to the canvas, he would always get back up again, eager to continue the bout. In the boxing ring, Ian did not live up to his nickname - he most definitely did not act like a mouse.

Sometimes when they met at the College gate on Tuesday afternoon, Billy and Ian would be talking excitedly about their boxing session that afternoon. After his teasing Jane about boxing a few weeks ago, Billy began to notice that she would become quite withdrawn when the boys were talking about the sport.

On this particular Tuesday, he saw that Jane looked quite glum as he and Ian were chatting about their session in the ring.

"What's wrong, Jane," Billy asked gently.

"It's boxing." she said, "It frustrates me."

"Frustrates you?" Ian asked, puzzled, "what's wrong with boxing?"

"Nothing's wrong with boxing! You just don't understand!"

Ian and Billy looked at each other, concerned about Jane's outburst. Billy couldn't remember a time when Jane had been flustered about anything.

Jane took a deep breath, trying to calm herself.

"Don't worry about it," Jane breathed, with an effort to make her tone sound light, "It's nothing, really, I'm just being a bit silly, that's all."

"All right, if you say so," Ian shrugged.

Billy tried to hold Jane's gaze, but she turned her head away. Billy could see Jane didn't want to explain, but he realised that this was something that was important to her, and that if she didn't let it out, it was only going to fester. Billy valued his friendship with Jane too much to let it be soured by something that Jane was holding inside.

"I can tell you don't really want to talk about it," Billy began.

"That's right," Jane snapped, then stopped herself and looked sheepishly at the ground.

"I'm sorry," she said, "it's not your fault.

"Or Mouse's," she sighed.

"Don't worry about it," Billy reassured her, "we all get a little snappy sometimes.

"Don't we, Mouse?" he added, jabbing Ian in the ribs.

"Hmm? What? Oh, oh yes, quite right."

Billy rolled his eyes a little while shaking his head slightly, bemused by Ian's inability to sometimes read social cues.

Jane saw the eye roll and giggled. Billy smiled at her reaction to his reaction, pleased that Jane had relaxed a little.

"So," he prodded gently, "what's the matter?"

Jane looked at Billy earnestly before responding.

"I like gymnastics, but..." she said, haltingly.

"Uh-hm. But?" Billy nodded his encouragement for her to go on.

"But I don't like how only girls can do gymnastics and only boys can do boxing." Jane blurted out in a rush.

Jane had Ian's full attention now.

"We're all required to participate in the Empire Service Scheme," Jane continued, looking from Ian to Billy and back again, "which is training us to defend the Empire."

The boys nodded, encouragingly.

"So why is it that I can carry a rifle and learn how to use a bayonet, yet when it comes to sport outside the Cadets, I'm only allowed to do gymnastics. Why can't I do boxing, or cricket, or even rugby?"

Ian opened his mouth to respond, then paused for a moment before closing it again. Then he chuckled a little.

"You know," he said, "I was just about to say that that's just how it is. And then I realised that I would have sounded just like my grandfather.

"I loved Grandfather deeply, but he was far too old-fashioned in his attitude to women. I'm sure that he would have followed that statement up with a quip about women needing to know their place."

Ian turned to face Jane, becoming serious.

"I'm sorry," he said, "I didn't really think about how unfair it is that you can bear arms for the Empire, but that only boys can box."

"Thanks Mouse. I appreciate that."

Billy considered this for a moment.

"Do you think we can get the rules changed?"

Jane's mouth set in a firm line. Billy could see she had made up her mind.

"Let's find out."

Chapter 26

Caloundra, Colony of Queensland, Australia
Thursday 19 November 1942

Jane had been busy since her revelation about the unfairness of girls being excluded from boxing.

Quietly, Jane began asking the girls in the gymnastics class about how they felt about not being able to participate in some of the other sports offered by the College. Very few of the First Form students were interested in boxing, let alone any of the other 'boys sports' as they kept calling them.

Jane marvelled at how these girls could simply accept that their role in society was exactly the same as their mothers and grandmothers had been. This was such a modern age, a new era.

There had never been such a long period of peace in the Empire. There were so many wonderful new inventions being released by the Science Academy, it almost seemed like a new device or mechanism was made available to the people every week.

And yet, the traditional social roles seemed to be fixed within the College. Jane knew, from her own observations, that this was not the case in the rest of the town, and she suspected it was not like this in the rest of the Empire.

The more Jane pondered the problem, the more she realised that the issue was one of College, not Empire, policy. If the issue was isolated to the College, it would explain why girls were required to participate in the Empire Service Scheme, and why so many women, across the entire Empire, were able to work at a host of different jobs. The Empire had long had women who were captains of ships, both civilian and military. Jane had recently discovered that some of the bravest and most capable people in the Empire, the airship pilots, were women - a fact she found thrilling.

With this realisation, Jane felt far less overwhelmed by the unfairness of the situation. She was no longer facing the challenge of trying to change the Empire, or the Colony, or even the town. All she needed to do, to redress this gap, was to change the policy of the Caloundra Colonial College.

Although Jane was surprised that none of the other First Year students seemed interested in boxing, she didn't even consider that she might be wrong about this issue. Just because the idea of opening up boxing to girls wasn't popular with her classmates didn't mean that she should stop her campaign for change.

Jane's first thought had been to raise a petition and to get as many girls as she could to sign. Then, when the petition had circulated through the whole College, she would present it to the Headmaster with a polite but firm demand for a change in the policy.

Now, it seemed that a petition wouldn't be effective. If the First Form girls, who knew her well and liked her, wouldn't get behind her push for change, it was unlikely the older girls would come on board.

Jane realised she needed to take a different approach, but what that approach should be wasn't clear.

oOo

Every now and then, the schedules for the different Forms at the College would need to be changed. Sometimes this was because one of the Masters became ill. At other times, one of the staff would need to attend a conference, or to deal with some urgent family matter. When this happened, the College would often combine classes together.

That was why, on this hot and sunny November afternoon, Jane's First Form class was doing gymnastics alongside the Third Form girls.

Initially, the two Forms were kept separate by the Instructor, Miss Mayweather. As she only worked part-time at the College, and only in the gymnastics classes, none of the students knew her as well as their Masters. Although she liked to keep herself very professional, she was always encouraging the students, especially when they tried new movements.

About half-way through the session, Miss Mayweather blew the whistle that hung around her neck.

"Thank you, Ladies," she informed them loudly, "good work this afternoon. After the break, we're going to do some combined work. First Form, you'll be paired up with Third Form students for the next session.

"Ten minute break, please, then back here in two lines, by Form, facing each other."

Jane and the other students quickly moved off for their break, as soon as Miss Mayweather blew her whistle for the second time.

At the side of the gymnasium, Jane was re-tying her shoelaces when a blonde student approached her.

"Are you Jane?"

Jane looked up, to see that the girl was older, but not very tall, and had long blonde hair. Her most striking feature, though, was her deep blue eyes, which were shining with intent.

"Yes, that's right."

"Jane Everington-Smyth?"

Jane nodded, curious.

The girl leaned down towards Jane, dropping her voice to a hoarse whisper.

"I believe you might be trying to change the rules that prevent girls from participating in certain sports."

"That's right," Jane replied, making no attempt to lower her voice from her normal speaking level.

The other girl looked around, quickly, as if trying to make sure no one was looking at them.

"My name is Ann, Ann Roberts."

"Hello Ann," Jane smiled, then paused for a moment.

"You wouldn't happen to be related to our Sports Master, would you?"

Ann blushed a little, again looking furtively around.

"Yes, he's my uncle."

"How curious," Jane thought, "I wonder if she's been sent over here to try to talk me out of pursuing this change."

She tried to keep a neutral expression on her face, but Ann's seemed to detect the thought running through Jane's head.

"It's all right," she said, smiling a little but still whispering conspiratorially, "I'm on your side."

"I'm very glad to hear that, Ann," Jane admitted, "I was beginning to think I was the only one who wanted to box."

"That could very well be true. I have no interest in getting into a boxing ring."

Jane looked at Ann, a little confused, but Ann continued speaking without waiting for Jane to voice her confusion.

"My position has nothing to do with the sport itself. I'm neither for nor against boxing.

"What I do object to, is the automatic disregard for the wishes of those girls," she indicated towards Jane with a slender hand, "who do wish to box, or play some other sport."

"And," she continued with a mischievous grin on her face, "those boys who wish to learn gymnastics."

Jane looked at Ann with a mix of surprise and awe. She had been so focussed on how the girls were being treated unfairly that she had never even considered that there might boys who felt the same way about the restrictions and expectations placed on them.

"So, how do I go forward from here? I've been feeling that since there's no popular support for the change I'm proposing, it might not be worth pursuing."

"Nonsense," Ann responded, without a moment's hesitation, "even if you're the only female student in the entire College who wants to do boxing, that is reason enough to bring the matter to the attention of the Masters and the Head."

Hearing the conviction Ann brought to the problem, Jane felt her spirits lift. It was clear that Ann had great strength of character and was just as determined as Jane to see the right thing done.

"Let's work together on a proposal," Ann suggested, "If we put our minds to it, I'm sure we can come up with a list of reasons why the College should change this old-fashioned rule."

"That's sounds wonderful, Ann! Thank you!"

The gym was suddenly full of the echoing trill of Miss Mayweather's whistle.

"Quickly, now, ladies," the Instructor called, "it's time to get on with our class."

Jane and Ann began moving toward their respective lines in the centre of the gym. As they parted, Ann leaned in towards Jane.

"Let's meet after school," she whispered.

"At the front gate," Jane whispered back, smiling broadly at her new friend.

Chapter 27

Caloundra, Colony of Queensland, Australia
Friday 26 November 1942

"Landsborough!" the voice shouted, somewhere very close to Ian's head.

He knew why the Instructor was yelling at him, but knowing why didn't change the fact that it was actually happening.

Marching around was not one of Mouse's strong points, and this particular drill practice was not going well. Ian kept tripping over his own feet, or turning left when he should turn right, or making a mess of some of the more intricate drill movements.

"Yes, Corporal!" Ian responded, almost instinctively.

"Is there something wrong with your feet?"

Ian knew he was supposed to be standing at attention, but he couldn't help himself. He looked down at his boots.

"Stand up straight, man!" Cadet Corporal Byrne barked.

Ian shot back up to attention.

"Yes, Corporal."

Sean Byrne raised an eyebrow. He wasn't sure if Ian had said 'yes' to standing up straight or 'yes' to there being something wrong with his feet.

"Cadet Johnson!" he snapped, to the cadet at the far end of the front rank, "Fall out and take the squad for drill practice."

"Yes, Corporal," responded Johnson, before moving out of his position in the rank of cadets, using the fancy sequence of movements that Ian always found baffling.

Sean looked back at Ian.

"Cadet Landsborough, fall out. With me."

Ian attempted to do the fancy steps that he was supposed to use to leave the rank, and this time got fairly close to getting it right.

Sean groaned inwardly and tried to stop his eyes rolling at Ian's attempt at the drill movement.

All of the cadets had been training in the drill movements for a few months now. For most of them, it was just a controlled form of walking, with someone else telling you, loudly, which way to go and when to change direction. The cadets had all been told how the discipline required for precision marching as a group was an important skill, that could be translated into coordinated movement on the battlefield if the Empire ever needed to go to war again.

Sean moved away from the rest of the squad, with Ian following behind him, until they were out of earshot of all the cadets.

"Are you trying to get back at me for the incident on the first day of school?" Sean asked quietly, his voice cracking slightly with tension.

"Is this your way of getting revenge for when I punched you on your way to your first class?"

Ian looked at Sean, dumbfounded.

"Corporal," he said quietly, "you gave your word that you would never behave like that again. I could not hope for a better outcome than that from the incident.

"I have no desire for revenge. The matter was dealt with like gentlemen, and that is the end of it, as far as I'm concerned."

"Then why," Sean persisted, "are you constantly embarrassing me in front of the entire squad, not to mention the senior cadets, with your awful marching? Are you looking for cheap laughs by playing the fool during drill practice?"

"Absolutely not! I take all the aspects of Cadet training very seriously. I'm not trying to be funny, or to embarrass you. I struggle with most things that are physical in nature."

"Don't mess with me! I've seen you box. You can handle yourself!"

"The only reason that I can box is that my father started teaching me when I was four years old. I can do physical things, it just takes me longer to learn them than most people.

"Trust me," Ian added, "I'm no better at dancing than I am at drill!"

Sean looked hard at Ian, trying to judge if the younger boy was lying to him, or worse, playing him.

Finally, he sighed, satisfied that Ian was telling the truth.

"We have to fix this. The Officers are always watching, and if you can't do the drill movements, I'll be held accountable. I'd like to be promoted to Cadet Sergeant next year. And if you don't pass the drill assessment in January, you may be discharged from the Scheme"

"I understand," Ian said quietly, "I don't want to be the cause of you missing out on your promotion. And I certainly don't want to explain to my father why I'm unable to do my duty to the Empire. What do you need me to do?"

"You mean apart from actually being able to perform the drill movements?" Sean said with a half-smile.

Ian nodded, and Sean considered their options.

"All right," he said eventually, "the only way I can see to fix this is for you to do extra drill practice.

"Every Friday lunchtime, and Saturday mornings, we'll do drill practice. Here at the College. I'll give you one-on-one coaching, and we'll see if that can hurry you along with your learning.

"Once we break for the Term holidays, we'll increase the coaching to four times a week. We'll do Mondays, Wednesdays, Fridays and Saturdays, for at least four hours each day. With three weeks of holidays, that gives us an extra twelve sessions."

Ian thought for a moment about their plans to go searching for shipwrecks during the Term holidays. He, Jane and Billy had been planning to take the *Sea Gypsie* out for a week at a time, sleeping on board, and only coming back to shore on Sundays to refuel and restock the larder.

Now, all those plans would have to be scrapped. All because he couldn't make his arms and legs do what they were supposed to on the parade ground.

Ian nodded at Sean.

"Thank you," he said simply.

Sean nodded, then turned his head slightly to see where the squad had marched to in his absence. Seeing they were fairly close by, Sean turned back to Ian.

"Fall in with the squad."

"Yes, Corporal," Ian responded, squaring his shoulders before making his best effort to march back to the squad.

Sean watched him march the short distance, furrowing his brow at the valiant but futile effort Ian made at marching.

"We really have our work cut out for us," he muttered, before marching briskly onto the parade ground to take over the squad for the rest of the drill session.

oOo

After the cadet parade had finished, Billy and Jane waited at the front gate of the College for Ian. They had both seen Ian get taken out of the squad and be given what looked like a very serious talking to by Sean on the side of the parade ground. They knew Ian was struggling with many of the physical aspects of the training, and they were concerned that Sean may have been bullying Ian.

Eventually, Ian joined them at the front gate. Billy noticed he was dragging his shoes a little and was looking quite downcast.

"What happened, Mouse?" Jane was quick to ask.

Even though she was keen to give him a hug, she had to restrain herself, as such physical contact was not permitted while they were wearing their uniforms.

"I'm afraid I must impart bad news," Ian said glumly.

Jane gasped, trying to keep her mind from whirling into terrible thoughts of military discipline.

"We're going to have to cancel our exploration of Pumicestone Passage in the Term holidays," he said, with a slight crack in his voice and a tear welling in his eye.

"What? Why?" asked Jane incredulously, "Sean has no right to take your boat away from you! That's not within his authority!"

"Jane, it's all right," Ian said gently, "Sean didn't do anything like that."

"Really?"

"Yes, really. Sean's offered to give up his Saturdays and half of his holidays, to give me remedial drill coaching. We only have a few weeks until the drill exam in January, and I have a great deal still to master if I'm going to have any hope of passing the test and staying in the Scheme."

Billy and Jane looked at each other and nodded. They both knew that Ian was largely hopeless at the drill movements, and even though they'd both tried to help him in the weeks gone by, he was still far below the standard.

"Seems to me that getting someone as experienced as Sean to help, is a great way to get your ready, Mouse," Billy commented, supportively.

Jane nodded her agreement.

"That's very generous of Sean," she said, "but that does still leave you some time during the holidays to go exploring."

"Sadly, no, Jane. The least I can do to repay Sean is to spend the other half of my time practicing what he's teaching me. If I fail the drill test, it will reflect very badly on him, and that isn't fair."

Jane was touched by Ian's selflessness, and his consideration for others. She could see how strongly he felt his obligation to Sean, and how badly he felt about disappointing his closest friends.

Jane felt her heart swell with pride for Mouse, and she looked around quickly to see if anyone was nearby. When she saw the coast was clear, she grabbed Mouse and gave him a huge hug.

Mouse resisted for a moment, then gave in to the wonderful feeling of being in Jane's arms.

Chapter 28

Caloundra, Colony of Queensland, Australia
Monday 29 November 1942

Ann and Jane had been working furiously on their proposal since their conversation in the gymnasium. They had met after school most days for the past week, and had spent quite a bit of time together this last weekend, drafting and re-drafting the document until they were now satisfied that the language and the tone was perfect.

The had debated whether to keep the title simple, or to make it sound more legal and complex. Jane took the view that if their proposal sounded like a formal document, then it would be taken more seriously by the College staff. Ann felt that a simple title would convey their intent more clearly, and this would help the Masters to see that it wasn't such an overwhelming change after all.

In the end, they found a compromise. 'Proposal for Inclusive Sports Programs at Caloundra Colonial College'.

The proposal was a little over two pages long, highlighting how the College was not in line with the policies of the township or the Colony in terms of the roles of women. Ann and Jane had spent a great deal of time researching women who were successful in their chosen field, including some who played competitive or representative sports, and had written short accounts of the roles of those women in their proposal.

Jane and Ann were particularly pleased with the conclusion, which they had spent several hours crafting.

'We do not make this proposal for a change to policy in order to allow any individual student to participate in any particular sport from which they are currently excluded. This proposal is submitted on the basis that each and every student has the capacity to decide for him or herself the sport or sports in which they might care to participate.'

'The change outlined in and requested by this proposal, is one of principle. If this change is adopted, there is unlikely to be a flood of girls joining up for boxing, or boys enrolling in gymnastics. Instead, only the barest handful of students who feel so inclined may change sports.'

'But every student in the College will have been afforded the opportunity to make a choice based on their individual aptitude and inclination, regardless of whether or not they exercise that choice.'

"There," breathed Jane, "it's finally finished."

Ann reached over and gave Jane a hug.

"You've done a great job."

"No," Jane corrected her, "we've done a great job."

After a moment longer, Jane gently pulled out of the hug, smiling at their achievement. Ann looked into her eyes, smiling back.

"She's so pretty," Ann thought, "and it's been wonderful spending all this time with her. I don't want it to end."

Ann cleared her throat, not quite trusting that her voice wouldn't betray her innermost thoughts.

"So," she said instead, "now we need to present this to the Masters. Starting with my Uncle."

"Are you sure he'll see us?"

"Yes, but that's about as far as my influence will stretch. Even though he's family, he tries very hard to keep a professional distance when we're at school."

The two girls hurried across the College grounds, towards College House. They knew Mr Roberts would be in his office during the luncheon break today.

As they reached the steps of the House, Ann reached out and held Jane's hand.

"Good luck," she whispered, giving Jane's hand a gentle squeeze and feeling an electric tingle run down her spine from the touch.

Ann and Jane climbed the steps together, turned into the corridor that lead to the offices, and arrived moments later outside the door to Mr Roberts' office. Ann knocked on the door, firmly but politely.

"Enter," came the gruff voice from inside the room.

Ann pushed open the door and stepped through, with Jane following close behind.

The office had a small desk near the centre of the room, with a few papers, pens and pencils scattered about. The desk chair Mr Roberts was sitting in looked like it was two sizes too small for his muscular frame. The wall of the room was covered with shelves. There were numerous sporting trophies and pictures of Mr Roberts with various teams and players. Everything looked very clean and well looked after. Jane couldn't see a speck of dust on any of the trophies.

"Is this a social visit, Ann?" he enquired, looking quizzically at Jane.

"No, I'm afraid not. Jane has something she needs to present to you."

"I see," the Sports Master said, before sitting up even straighter in his chair.

"Very well, Roberts," he said formally, nodding his head at Ann before turning his full attention to Jane.

"Proceed, Everington-Smyth."

Jane momentarily forgot her carefully prepared speech, under the watchful eye of the Sports Master.

Then, she took a deep breath, composed herself, and began to present their proposal.

As Jane spoke, Mr Roberts listened patiently, but Ann noticed the tension in his hands and his jaw.

"Oh, poor Jane," she thought, "he's going to tell her off."

When Jane had finished the presentation, it was Mr Roberts' turn to draw a deep breath.

"Everington-Smyth," he began, "that was a very good oral presentation. I shall inform Mrs Franklin, when next I see her, of your performance."

"Thank you, Sir," Jane nodded graciously, "but what of our proposal?"

"Yes, your proposal," he said, looking rather pointedly at Ann, "did my niece inform you that this notion had been presented previously? By her?"

"No, Sir," admitted Jane, glancing at Ann.

"So," the Master continued, "I can reasonably conclude that she didn't tell you the outcome of her previous attempt?"

"No, Sir."

"I see," Mr Roberts said, with a slight shake of his head before looking at Ann.

"Ann, would you care to enlighten Everington-Smyth?" he said gently.

"I thought it would be different this time," Ann said to her Uncle, "because the idea wasn't coming from a family member.

"I'm sorry," she said, turning to Jane, "I thought Uncle would listen to you, as you're so passionate about wanting to do boxing."

"Why didn't you tell me you'd presented this before?" Jane demanded, unable to keep the hurt from her voice.

"I didn't want to discourage you from trying," Ann replied simply, "just because I'd failed before."

"Failing in the past wouldn't have discouraged me. Knowing about it would have helped me to not make the same mistakes a second time." Jane said, with more than a hint of bitterness in her voice.

"Jane," Mr Roberts said quietly, shocking Jane by his use of her first name.

Jane looked over at the Master, who was looking at her kindly.

"Ann didn't withhold any vital information from you. When she came in here, two years ago, to talk to me about this matter, there wasn't any logic or structure in her argument.

"She rambled on about 'doing what was right', but couldn't explain why she thought this was important. When it became clear that she didn't want to participate in boxing herself, her entire argument fell apart."

Jane nodded, most of the anger fading away, but she still retained some of the hurt.

"And now?" Jane asked.

"This is an entirely different attempt," the Sports Master intoned, "this is well written and cleverly crafted."

Jane smiled, and Ann almost grinned.

"So you'll present it to the Headmaster?" Jane asked.

"Yes, I will. But I need to tell you now that it will not be accepted by the Head."

"What? Why not?" Ann interjected.

Mr Roberts sighed.

"I have known Headmaster Carpenter for close to 20 years. He is an excellent educator, and a great supporter of students. I have never seen him not beaming with pride at every graduation ceremony or sporting triumph."

"But?" asked Jane.

"But," Mr Roberts nodded, "he is a very old-fashioned gentleman, who has managed to ignore certain modern trends. He is a traditionalist, and he will not entertain a non-traditional policy, no matter how well argued or passionately presented.

"I'm sorry, girls," he added softly, "I'm afraid that's just how it is."

"I see," Jane said, defeated.

Then, she straightened her shoulders and looked directly at Mr Roberts.

"Thank you for listening to our presentation. We appreciate your time, Sir."

Mr Roberts nodded, a little proud that Jane was displaying the strength of character to take this rejection so stoically.

Jane turned and quietly left the office. Ann hesitated a moment longer.

"Go work it out with her," Mr Roberts said, "you make a good team."

Ann smiled lovingly at her uncle, then hurried out the door after Jane.

Chapter 29

Melbourne, Colony of Victoria, Australia
Wednesday 23 December 1942

The room was dimly lit from the light of several oil lamps placed strategically on side tables. The flickering lights cast dancing shadows on the leather-bound volumes that filled the grand mahogany bookshelves running from floor to ceiling on each wall.

Patrick Bowman stood perfectly still, just inside the doorway to the opulent reading room. He could see the overstuffed high-back leather chairs dotted around the room, creating small enclaves where powerful and well-connected people could trade secrets and call in favours.

He knew he was not welcome here, that he would never sit on one those leather chairs. But that didn't concern Patrick. He had a job to do, and that job put him in the field, not in this place of privilege and power. However, even though he'd prefer to receive his briefings in the Directorate office on Collins Street, sometimes it was necessary for him to see the Chief at his Club.

After a few moments, Patrick's eyes adjusted to the gloom in the reading room, and he was able to work out where the Chief was sitting.

Quietly, taking care not to disturb any of the other club members, Patrick moved towards the Chief. Despite his stealth, the Chief must have worked out Patrick was nearby.

"Bowman," the Chief called out quietly, "come here, man."

"He has eyes in the back of his head," Patrick thought, "as well as eyes and ears everywhere else in the Colonies."

"Good evening, Sir," Patrick said, making a small bow as he stepped closer.

The Chief waved away the courtesy.

"Good work on the Noosa problem, Bowman. You did well capturing the cell leadership. Those Bolshevik revolutionaries will think twice before setting up camp in our backyard again."

"Thank you, Sir."

The Chief seemed to sense Patrick's hesitation.

"Don't concern yourself with Volkov," the Chief said, emphatically, "we've broken the back of the wolf.

"We have all of the plans for his intended operations. Volkov will not be warmly received when he returns to Russia," the Chief allowed himself a wry smile, "with his tail between his legs.

"You and your team have done an excellent job analysing the documents you seized in the raid."

"Thank you, Chief," Patrick nodded, "although we've just barely scratched the surface in the last two months. There is perhaps another six months' worth of analysis before we have a complete picture of what he was planning.

"This was a very complex, very comprehensive operation, crossing borders between the Colonies, and," Patrick hesitated.

"Indeed," the Chief replied, leaning in close to Patrick, "even suggesting some very powerful figures in our governments may have been targets."

"Chief, may I ask about Lieutenant Simons?"

"Simons, yes. I read your report Commander. Threw herself in front of the bullets, to protect one of the NCOs, who was in the line of fire."

"Yes, Sir."

"I've submitted your recommendation for the Lieutenant to be awarded a gallantry commendation."

"Thank you, Chief, but I was hoping for an update on her medical status. I've made some enquiries, but I've been unable to obtain any useful information."

"Yes, that doesn't surprise me Commander. I've taken charge of her case, and she's now in one of my programs."

Patrick raised an eyebrow. As a senior officer in the Directorate, he knew that the Chief ran a number of 'special programs', mostly developing cutting edge technology for the defence of the Realm.

The details of these programs, though, were only known to the staff assigned to their particular program, and the people on one program had no idea about the other ventures. Only the Chief was aware of the full extent of this part of the Directorate.

"As you are aware, Commander," the Chief continued without pausing, "when an operative suffers injuries as severe as Lieutenant Simons, they are discharged from further service once they have been treated. Of course, they receive a generous pension from His Majesty, and their medical treatment is provided at no cost for the rest of their life.

"But they cannot continue to serve in His Majesty's armed forces. And I have always felt that this approach was a waste.

"After all," he chuckled mirthlessly, "Lord Nelson lost an arm, and later an eye, and yet he continued to serve, as did many others who had lost an arm or a leg.

"I have an Advanced Cybernetics program, based in Sydney, which has been developing prosthetic limbs for patients like Lieutenant Simons. I have two types of scientists working on this team.

Stephen Archer

"The engineers are among the best in the field of automatons. They have been extending and applying their knowledge to the development of complex prosthetic limbs. Arms and legs that are capable of mimicking a full range of motion.

"The second group of scientists on this team are the specialists in Organisms. And it is this second group who have made the most significant breakthrough in this program.

"These scientists believe they have managed to find a way to tap into the nerve impulses of the human brain, and to use those impulses to control the artificial limb."

Patrick barely managed to hide his gasp of astonishment.

"You mean the prosthetic arm or leg moves under the control of the person's mind, just like their flesh and blood limb?'

"Yes, quite," said the Chief, "although it's still very early stages. Lieutenant Simons will be our guinea pig, so to speak.

"The boffins in the lab have also been working on a little something for her left eye. Since the Lieutenant will need to wear a skull cap to house the wires leading from her brain to the arm, they thought they might be able to attach an eyepiece to the cap.

"The lead scientist tells me it will act a little like a film camera, capturing moving images and transmitting them through the wires in the cap directly into her brain. It won't give her 20-20 vision, mind, but once she gets used to interpreting the signals, she'll have more than enough sight to remain an agent."

Patrick was delighted with this news. Mind controlled prosthetic limbs and artificially generated vision! What an amazing Empire!

"When can I see her, Sir?"

"Not for a few months, I'm afraid, Commander. There is still a great deal of work to be done."

"Thank you, Chief," Patrick looked fondly at the man sitting in the plush leather chair, trying to convey his gratitude for the wonderful ray of hope for Lieutenant Simons.

The Chief nodded slightly, in acknowledgement, before continuing.

"Now, I have another job for you, Commander."

"Of course, Sir," Patrick agreed quickly, hoping this would be an easier job than his last assignment.

"Go home and spend Christmas with your family."

"But Sir," Patrick protested, "there's still so much information to be analysed."

The Chief held up a hand, silencing him.

"You have your orders, Commander. I have already sent instructions to Squadron Leader Peale that he is to stand down the entire team, himself included, until 11 January."

The Chief drew a breath before continuing, more gently.

"You've worked hard and achieved a great deal. But there is a cost for that achievement, and your questions about Lieutenant Simons prove to me that you are paying that cost.

"You cannot continue to pay forever. From time to time, you must put the burden down, and spend time with those who so often are neglected when we are focussed on doing our duty.

"For now, The Bunker is sealed, Patrick, and you are to go home."

"Thank you Chief," Patrick nodded, before turning to leave the club.

On his way to the front door, Patrick wondered if he'd have time to buy William a Christmas present from one of the big Melbourne stores, before he had to catch the train back to Brisbane.

Chapter 30

Caloundra, Colony of Queensland, Australia
Tuesday 12 January 1943

"William, hurry up, you'll be late for school!"

Billy's mother was standing in the doorway of his room, watching him practice with his new fountain pen.

The pen had been a gift from his father for Christmas, something he picked up for Billy when he was in Melbourne on one of his business trips for the ginger factory. Billy had been ecstatic when he opened it on Christmas morning, and had vowed to practice using it every day. He wanted the writing in his notebook to be perfect.

"Thanks, I'm nearly done."

Billy made a swooping letter 'y', then completed his practice with a final flourish on the letter 'z'. He stood up from the desk, admiring his workmanship.

"You've come a long way in just a couple of weeks," he thought, "another week or so and you'll be able to start using the pen in your notebook."

Quickly putting his things into his satchel, Billy raced for the front door of the house, kissing his slightly bewildered mother on the cheek as he went by.

"Life is good," Billy thought.

His father had come home for Christmas and stayed until yesterday. He'd spent so much time away in the last few months, Billy was thrilled to have him home for such an extended stay.

But even before his father had arrived home on Christmas Eve, Billy had discovered some interesting new things over the Term holidays.

With Ian tied up in his additional drill practice, Billy had at first imagined that he'd spend most of the holiday alone. He was comfortable enough with being on his own, but he enjoyed the company of his close friends.

When Jane had knocked on his door on the first day of the holidays, asking to spend the day with him, Billy was very happy to oblige. He liked Jane as much as he liked Ian, and he found her to be very pleasant company.

Jane was very quick-witted and could find something funny in most situations. He and Jane would wander the shopping areas of Caloundra, or spend hours watching the ocean from the sand dunes at the top of the beach. Once, they even went to visit the wreck of the SS Dickie, washed up on the shore of the beach that had been named after the stricken vessel.

A few days into the holiday, Jane arrived at his door with another girl in tow.

"Hello Ann," Billy said, smiling broadly at the attractive girl with the piercing blue eyes.

"Hello William," Ann replied, "I'm surprised you remember me!"

"Of course," Billy said gallantly, "you're very hard to forget."

"Ah," Jane said, a little confused, "you two know each other?"

"We met on the first day of school," Billy replied, "but how do you two know each other?"

"Ann helped me craft the proposal for equality in sport."

The trio spent the rest of the holidays together, laughing and joking, spending time at the beach and even visiting the cinema towards the end of the holiday.

Over the course of the holiday, Billy had become increasingly aware that he was becoming smitten with Ann. Even though she was older than Billy, he found himself wanting to be standing near her, and he found her deep blue eyes mesmerising.

Billy had also noticed that Ann, while friendly towards him, was far more attentive to Jane. At first he thought that Ann simply wasn't interested in him.

"Perhaps there's already a boy in her life," Billy thought, a fact which would hardly surprise him, given how attractive she was.

But then things started to get confusing.

As the days passed by, Billy began to notice how Ann would lean forward and brush a stray lock of hair out of Jane's face when they were in the middle of a conversation.

Ann seemed to hang on every word Jane said, and was always the first to start laughing at one of Jane's jokes. Jane didn't seem to respond to this attention from Ann, but she didn't do anything to stop it either.

Meanwhile, Billy began to realise that Jane seemed to be paying particular attention to him. The occasional touch, the quick laugh, was all very friendly, but Billy was sensing something more meaningful in the way Jane was behaving towards him.

He had always imagined Jane and Ian to be a couple, even if they didn't hold hands. Their shared bond through academics and exploring seemed to make them a natural 'fit' for each other. Billy just couldn't quite figure out what was happening.

His greatest fear was that he would say or do something that would upset or offend one of his friends. With each passing day, Billy realised, the risk that he would unintentionally cause offence increased.

In the end, he decided to seek advice from his mother, the only other person he knew who was able to read the emotional clues of the people around her.

The next afternoon, when the girls wanted to go shopping in the Main Street, Billy decided it was the ideal opportunity to discuss the situation with his mother. He begged off going to the shops and sought out his mother in the kitchen.

After explaining his observations, his mother paused her baking and considered her response.

"Throughout your life," she explained, "you'll meet many people. A small number you will dislike, but you will like most of the people you meet.

"That's a gift, Billy. Most people have trouble liking and being liked. For you, it comes naturally, and has done since you were four or five years old."

Billy nodded.

"Now that you're getting older," she went on, "you'll begin to develop more intense feelings towards a very small number of people. These people will become your closest friends."

"Like Ian and Jane?"

"Yes, that's exactly what I mean. And I imagine those feelings you have towards Ian and Jane will only get stronger over time.

"And your friends are feeling much the same way you do. Perhaps to a different degree than you, but in a very fundamental way, they are having the same feelings. Would you agree with that?"

For a moment, Billy considered the behaviour he had seen, and done, realising that his mother was correct.

"Yes," he said, "I can see that we all are in the same boat, so to speak."

Mary Bowman nodded, pleased that her son understood.

"Now, the thing to remember Billy," she continued, "is that your friends are not so perceptive as you. They do not have your gift for sensing the emotions of those around them.

"This is not a criticism, of course. Very few people are as perceptive as you. But this means that your friends are much more likely to struggle with their emotions and may even try to form closer bonds with people who don't feel the same way towards them."

Billy pondered this for a full minute. His mother watched his face, waiting to see if he would grasp her meaning.

"So," he said, trying to put his thoughts into words, but still unsure if his thinking was correct, "the way I feel towards Ann isn't being returned, but that doesn't mean Ann doesn't like me. It just means that I want a closer relationship than Ann does."

"Good, go on." Billy's mother nodded.

"And Ann wants a closer relationship with Jane, but Jane is more interested in building a closer relationship with me."

"Yes, that seems about right."

"So, how do I deal with this? And what about Ian? I always thought Ian and Jane were a couple!"

Mary Bowman laughed.

"Those are excellent questions, William," she smiled lovingly at him, "and if you ever find the answer, please let the rest of us know!"

Chapter 31

Caloundra, Colony of Queensland, Australia
Tuesday 12 January 1943

"I see you, little man," Volkov said to himself, from the shadow under the eucalyptus tree across the street.

He watched the boy race out of the house, heading towards the College. The boy was wearing his cadet field uniform, his slouch hat pushed down firmly on his head.

"Ah, yes," Volkov mused, "the drill test this afternoon."

It had taken Volkov almost a month to find out where Commander Patrick Bowman lived. This would have been a very simple task for one of his team back in Moscow, but now that he was cut off from these resources, he had very little access to information.

Volkov had departed Noosa the night of the raid, moving quickly into the hills to avoid detection. After three days, the team sent to track him down had given up the search, apparently deciding he had fled.

"They probably believe I've gone back to Russia," Volkov thought.

He began working his way down the coast, travelling by train under a false name. He stopped at every township along the way, and went to the town hall as soon as they opened.

Once, a town clerk had been hesitant to allow Volkov to access the records.

"I'm sorry, Sir, these records are only available to government officials, or people conducting research for *The History*."

"Very good, young man," Volkov replied, turning on his practiced upper-class English accent, "that is the answer we expect our staff to deliver to such an enquiry."

"Sir?" the young man responded, confused.

"It's quite all right, young man. I am one of the senior aides to Sir Leslie Wilson."

"The Governor of the Colony?"

"Yes, quite." Volkov continued smoothly, raising his nose a little higher, as the British aristocrats were prone to do when dealing with underlings.

"Now, as I've established my role as a government official, might I have access to the records?"

"Of course, Sir! Right this way, Sir."

Volkov despised using this approach, as it utterly devalued the records clerk. But the Empire had maintained the class system to ensure that those with power and privilege were never denied anything they wanted. Volkov's need for information was so desperate, that he was willing to stoop to exploiting that system, even though his original mission was to destroy it and free the people from this insidious form of slavery.

Trolling through the public records in each town hall, he finally located the details of the Bowman family from the census data held in Caloundra. From that information, he was able to find their home address from the Lands Titles Register.

Armed with these details, Volkov began his surveillance.

Over the weeks since arriving in Caloundra, he had closely observed the comings and goings from the house. He had perused their mail, and even gone through their garbage looking for insights into their patterns of behaviour.

For such a senior member of the Directorate, Volkov was surprised to discover there was no security surrounding Commander Bowman, his family or their friends.

A plan began to form in Volkov's mind.

He would start with the outermost circle of friends, then work his way inwards towards the Commander's wife and son. Volkov would exact his revenge layer by layer, watching the Commander suffer with each blow. Finally, the Commander would be left as broken and defeated as Volkov had been in the forest after the raid in Noosa.

Making sure he stayed well back and out of sight, Volkov followed the boy down the street.

oOo

"Squad," barked Corporal Byrne, "Atten-shun!"

The cadets snapped their feet together and whipped their arms around from behind their backs to rigidly by their sides. The movement was swift and coordinated, with every cadet moving as one.

"By the right, quick march!" came the next command.

Every student, including Ian Landsborough in the front rank, stepped off together with their left foot. Each cadet took a stride of the same length, staying in line with the person to their right.

Seated on the side of the oval were the drill assessors for this test. Cadet Sergeant O'Meara and Company Sergeant Major Golding sat ramrod straight in their wooden chairs, clipboards balanced on their laps, pencils in hand ready to score each cadet - and Cadet Corporal Byrne - as the set of drill movements were performed.

"I'll assess Corporal Byrne and the front rank," the CSM said, "while you assess the middle and rear ranks."

"Yes Ma'am." came the quiet reply from the Sergeant.

After the squad had marched 30 paces across the oval, Corporal Byrne issued a new command.

"Squad," he bellowed, "Halt!"

As one, the squad took one more step before coming to a complete stop and driving their heel into the ground with a resounding thud.

"Right in threes, right turn!"

Every cadet swivelled their body to the right, pivoting on the heel of their right foot and the ball of their left. When they had all turned ninety degrees, they all brought their back foot up and again, slammed their heel into the ground as one.

"A-bout turn!"

Again, the cadets moved as a single unit, every person in time with the others.

The assessors made notes on their clipboards, their faces inscrutable.

oOo

For the next fifteen minutes, Sean Byrne gave command after command, and the squad followed every instruction.

On more than one occasion, Sean frowned deeply when a member of the squad lost their concentration and failed to complete a drill movement properly. Ian Landsborough was one of those cadets.

Despite the hours of tuition Sean had given Ian over the last few weeks, Ian still struggled with his drill movements. His performance had vastly improved, there was no doubt about that, but still Sean was concerned.

Improving was good, but Sean knew that just an improvement would not be enough. Ian needed to reach the minimum standard in drill, or run the risk of being discharged from the Empire Service Scheme.

"Corporal Byrne," CSM Golding called out across the parade ground, summoning him to join her and Sergeant O'Meara.

"Ma'am," Sean responded, before turning to the squad of cadets.

"Squad, stand-at ease," he ordered.

The cadets obeyed instantly, moving their feet to stand shoulder-width apart, while placing their hands behind their backs.

"Cadet Bowman, fall out and take the squad."

Billy snapped to attention.

"Yes, Corporal," he said smartly, before making the fancy movement with his feet to leave the ranks.

Billy took up the position in front of the first rank, facing the squad, while Sean marched over to the CSM.

"How do you think that went, Corporal?" the CSM asked, her face set like a mask, giving nothing away.

"Overall," Sean replied, "very well. The cadets have come a long way in just a few weeks."

CSM Golding nodded.

"How would you assess your performance, as a drill instructor and as the squad commander this afternoon?"

"I gave the entire sequence of commands without error or hesitation," Sean responded, "and believe I have shown significant dedication to my role as their instructor, Ma'am."

"Yes, I'm aware of the extra hours you've put in Corporal."

Sean was surprised to hear that the CSM knew about his coaching sessions with Ian, but he kept his face neutral.

"You've done very well," CSM Golding continued, "I intend to recommend you for a commendation from our Commanding Officer, Major Stanley."

"Thank you, Ma'am."

"I'm also pleased to inform you that Sergeant O'Meara and I have agreed that all the members of your squad have met the minimum standard for drill movements for this level of their training."

Sean's relief was almost overwhelming. He couldn't wait to congratulate Ian on his success.

"Thank you, Ma'am, thank you Sergeant."

"Sergeant O'Meara," the CSM said, turning to the Sergeant standing next to her, "will you let the squad know their result. I'm sure they're very keen to find out how they went."

"Certainly, Ma'am."

"Corporal Byrne, stay for a moment. There's another matter I wish to discuss with you. Carry on, Sergeant."

As Sergeant O'Meara marched towards the squad, the CSM turned back to Sean.

"Corporal," she began, in a quiet voice, "I am very impressed with how you've performed your role."

"However, I'm not convinced that you are ready to take on the responsibilities of the next rank. I've discussed this with Cadet Lieutenant Hodges, who agrees that you are an excellent Corporal, but need a little more time in that role before being elevated to Sergeant."

Sean nodded ever so slightly at this devastating news.

"Yes, Ma'am," Sean replied, trying to keep the disappointment out of his voice, "I understand."

"I wish to be very clear, Sean," the CSM said, supportively, "this has nothing to do with the work you have done to get Cadet Landsborough up to speed with his drill. We all recognise what an amazing effort you put in to achieve that outcome, and your commendation from the CO will be well-deserved.

"You worked extremely hard with Cadet Landsborough, but your motivation to do so was based on how you would look if he performed poorly.

"The hard work you put in was as much about helping you to get promoted as it was about helping the Cadet stay in the Scheme.

"And that, I'm afraid, is the difference between how a Corporal sees such a situation, and how a Sergeant would view it."

Sean nodded, a little morosely.

The CSM looked at Sean closely, as if deciding whether or not to share some key insight.

"Sean," she said eventually, leaning very close and whispering, "I was in the same situation when I was a Corporal, and I did exactly what you did, with the same motivation. I helped a cadet because I wanted to look good for promotion.

"And for exactly the same reason that I've just given to you, I was passed over for promotion to Sergeant."

Sean looked at the CSM in shock.

"It made me realise that I needed to work hard for the benefit of others. Not selfishly, but for the sole motivation of making my team into their best. I learned about the difference between helping others to make me look good and helping others so they become good.

"It's about being responsible, not just 'in charge'. Once I had learned that very tough lesson, and started putting it into practice, my subsequent promotion to Sergeant, Staff Sergeant, Warrant Officer and ultimately, CSM, was incredibly fast, and more than made up for the extra time I spent as a Corporal.

"Learn from this, Sean. It will make you a better Sergeant, and a better citizen."

"Thank you, Ma'am," Sean nodded, "I appreciate what you've shared with me."

"You're welcome, Corporal." the CSM said, once again standing straighter, "Now, take over your squad."

Chapter 32

Caloundra, Colony of Queensland, Australia
Tuesday 12 January 1943

After they had been dismissed from the drill assessment, Jane and Billy had gone to the Explorers Club, under the eucalyptus tree in the quadrangle. Ann, who had been watching the assessment from the side of the oval, had joined them there.

All three students were lying on the mat Ian had set up last year, relaxing. Jane and Billy were reviewing their performance in the drill test, with Ann offering an opinion from time to time.

"I think you did very well," Ann enthused, "I don't think my drill was anywhere near your standard when I was in first year."

"Thanks, Ann," Jane responded, realising Ann was directing the praise to her, "But I think Billy is the true drill guru."

"Don't be so modest," Ann chided gently, "you were a picture of precision out there!"

Jane blushed a little, and Ann reached out her hand to gently stroke Jane's arm. Jane reached her hand around, placing it on top of Ann's, before patting her hand. To Billy it looked like a friendly gesture, but he suspected Ann was reading more into it.

Moving her hand away from Ann's, Jane reached out towards Billy. She gave him a playful punch in the shoulder, smiling broadly.

"So, I'm expecting you'll be on the list when they announce the promotions next week."

"I'm not so sure about that," Billy replied. "We've only been in the cadets for a few months."

"Others have been promoted that quickly before." Jane responded, "Apparently our CSM made Corporal before she finished First Form.

"Besides, with all the hard work Sean put in to help Ian pass, he's bound to be promoted to Sergeant. And that leaves a vacant Corporal position for you to step into.

"I think you'll make a wonderful Corporal," Jane purred at Billy, gently rubbing her hand along his bicep.

Billy put his hand on Jane's, just as he'd seen Jane do to Ann a few moments ago, hoping to express his gratitude for her complement.

As Billy's hand touched hers, Jane arched her fingers slightly, spreading them so that Billy's fingers slipped between hers. It looked very much as though they were holding hands against Billy's arm.

At that moment, Ian came around the corner of the path that led to the Explorers Club.

"Thank goodness that's over," Ian said, before he noticed Billy and Jane holding hands.

Billy saw Ian go pale, and quickly removed his hand from Jane's. He started to get up, but Ian waved him away.

"Sorry, old bean," he said quietly, "I didn't realise you and Jane were..."

Ian stopped talking, taking a moment to compose himself.

"I can't really say I'm all that surprised," he said, forlornly, "it was rather predictable, I suppose."

"Mouse," Billy protested, "I can only imagine what you think is going on, but..."

"I think I'll take a break from the Explorers Club for a while," Ian said, turning away from the group and walking back along the path that led to one of the exits to the quadrangle.

"You don't have to leave, Ian," Jane called after him.

Billy started, staring at Jane. In all the time he had known them, Jane had never before used Ian's name. She had always, always, called him 'Mouse'.

Billy felt his stomach tie into knots. His closest friends were breaking apart, and Billy felt powerless to do anything to stop the destruction.

oOo

None of the cadets or their instructors could see Volkov. He was perched high in a tree, more than 100 metres from the edge of the Caloundra Colonial College grounds. The natural bushland surrounding the College was a perfect hiding place, and his goggles allowed him to see the faces of the individual cadets as they marched around the drill square.

"Foolish Empire," Volkov thought, "thinking you can make children into soldiers by getting them to walk together in lines."

Over the weeks he had been observing them, Volkov had identified the key targets.

William, the one they called Billy, was the son of Commander Bowman, and would be the last target attacked.

Volkov was having trouble deciding which of the two closest friends of William should be his first target. He was uncertain whether attacking Ian or Jane first would yield the better result for his plan to break the spirit of the Commander.

But, Volkov had become aware that something had changed in the group dynamic in recent weeks.

With the Landsborough boy spending all his time with the drill instructor, an opening existed in the group. Into this space, a new girl had entered the circle of friends. Some investigating revealed her name was Ann, and she was the niece of the Sports Master at the College.

Fascinated, Volkov continued to observe the group.

Volkov chuckled when he realised that William was captivated by Ann, while Ann had taken a fancy to Jane, and Jane was smitten with William.

"Quite the little 'love triangle' you have there," he thought, as he pondered how their feelings for each other might be exploited to achieve his goal.

oOo

After the drill assessment, Volkov had quickly moved to one of his alternate observation posts.

Volkov could almost guarantee that the group would head to their so-called 'Explorers Club' once they were dismissed from the parade.

"They are so predictable," he mused.

Using his goggles and the audio amplifier, Volkov watched the group interaction with detachment. There was nothing new to see, they were all behaving as predicted.

And then Volkov saw movement out of the corner of his vision. He turned his head slightly to the right and focussed the goggles on the path that led to their little spot under the tree.

The Landsborough boy, Ian, was walking briskly along the path, heading straight for the group.

Volkov began tracking the boy closely. He was suddenly very curious about how he would react when he saw William and Jane apparently holding hands.

Of course, Volkov knew that this was a one-sided relationship, and that as far as William was concerned, the handholding was completely innocent. But current appearances suggested something far more than simple friendship, and Volkov suspected that Ian harboured deep feelings for Jane. He was intrigued to see how this would play out.

"Sorry, old bean," he heard Ian say, through the audio amplifier in his goggles, "I didn't realise you and Jane were…"

Volkov watched the sadness creep over the face of the boy, fascinated.

"I can't really say I'm all that surprised, it was rather predictable, I suppose."

"Mouse, I can only imagine what you think is going on, but…"

"I think I'll take a break from the Explorers Club for a while."

Volkov watched Ian turn away from the group and begin walking back along the path. With the enhanced vision that the goggles provided, Volkov could see his shoulders shaking from his sobbing.

Volkov realised he needed to adjust his plan. If something happened to Ian Landsborough now, it would unite the group, as they tried to support each other through the crisis.

No, the Landsborough boy, and the girl Jane, would need to wait for their turn. And so, Volkov realised, the decision as to who would be the first target had been made for him.

Ann Roberts would soon suffer a terrible accident.

Chapter 33

Caloundra, Colony of Queensland, Australia
Thursday 18 February 1943

"I really wish you'd let me talk to you, Mouse."

"I don't believe there's anything much to say," Ian replied, before walking into the history classroom and sitting at one of the desks in the front row.

For more than a month, Billy had been trying to sit down with Ian, hoping to find a way to bridge the gap that had grown between the friends.

They had become so close as a group over the course of the school year, but now, they just seemed to be fractured, broken.

Ian no longer sat with Jane or Billy during any of their classes. Where once they were an inseparable trio, now Ian was on his own, not engaging with Billy and Jane, and barely even looking at them.

"Just leave him, Billy," Jane had insisted, "when he's ready to stop pouting, he's welcome to come spend time with us again."

Billy was becoming increasingly upset by the situation. He was, of course, very fond of Jane, but only as a friend. But with Ian's rather dramatic departure from their group, Jane's affectionate behaviour towards Billy had only increased.

Every now and then, Billy would notice Ian staring at Jane, bewildered and hurt, as she hung onto Billy's arm as they walked to class, or laughing loudly at something he said. Billy tried to make it clear that he didn't feel towards Jane the same way Jane felt towards him, but Ian didn't seem convinced.

Billy and Jane still met at the eucalyptus tree each recess and luncheon, and Ann was often already there when they arrived. But Ian hadn't joined them. Billy didn't know where Ian spent his breaks, just that it wasn't at the Explorers Club.

The mat was still in place under the tree, but Billy noticed about a week after Ian had stormed off that the Explorers Club sign was now missing from the fork in the trunk of the tree where Ian had wedged it on the first day of school.

Billy wasn't sure if the removal of the sign, most likely by Ian, was the most devastating thing about this whole affair, or if it was seeing Ian in their classes each day, but being unable to talk to him.

Even during the boxing training sessions, Ian and Billy remained separated. The Sports Master had divided the class up according to weight. This enabled the students to practice their skills without being partnered with someone heavier, who would be able to throw a more powerful punch.

Mr Roberts blew his whistle, stopping all of the activity in the gymnasium.

"Gather round, everyone," Mr Roberts called, "You too, girls."

All of the First Form students formed a semi-circle in front of Mr Roberts.

"As we are now only a couple of months away from the end of the school year," he informed the students, "we're going to have a selection trial of everything you've learned so far.

"The selection trial will be held today, for the boys, and next Thursday for the girls. At the end of the trial, the most talented and capable students in each of the sports will be selected. These students will then receive additional coaching, and will perform an exhibition on graduation day in May.

"This is a First Form tradition, and your only opportunity to be selected. The higher Forms do not have exhibitions on graduation day.

"Girls, please take a seat in the bleachers. Boys, line up in front of the ring.

"As you know, boys, we normally train in our weight divisions. However, we don't have the time on graduation day to run an exhibition of each weight class.

"So, for the selection trial today, every student will spar with every other student in the class, regardless of weight."

The boys looked at Mr Roberts in surprise. Some of the bigger boys, in the higher weight classes, grinned and laughed quietly at this news.

"Now, for those of you who think this is going to give you an advantage," Mr Roberts said, glaring at the bigger boys, "you'll need to think again.

"The Assistant Coaches and I will be scoring you on the 10-Point system, over three rounds, with a handicap for those who are in the higher weight divisions. The handicap will be two points for each weight division between the fighters.

"For example, there are two weight divisions between welterweight and featherweight classes. When one of you bigger welterweight lads fights a featherweight," he said, indicating the smaller students in the class, "the welterweight will start each round four points down.

"To win the round, the welterweight fighter will need to overcome the points gap from the handicap."

Some of the bigger boys groaned quietly. The handicap system meant that they'd have to work much harder to win their bouts, and their additional reach and power would not be enough to guarantee them a win against the smaller boys.

"Are there any questions?" Mr Roberts asked, pausing for just a moment.

"Good," he said, knowing he hadn't left enough time for anyone to raise their hand, "let's begin."

oOo

While waiting for their turn, Billy kept glancing over at Ian. Every time he looked, Ian was staring straight ahead. He wasn't even watching the matches going on in the ring. He was simply staring into space.

Each time Billy would spar with another student, he could hear Jane cheering him on. Billy noticed, however, that Jane remained silent when Ian was in the ring.

Finally, the moment arrived that Billy had been dreading since this selection trial was announced.

"Bowman, Landsborough," Mr Roberts called, "into the ring."

Billy climbed through the ropes at one corner of the boxing ring. Ian entered the ring at the diagonally opposite corner.

Ian's face was a mask of anger and resentment. Billy could see that Ian was intending to use this sparring session to vent some of his emotions.

He wasn't completely sure that he blamed Ian for feeling that way. Even though Billy knew he hadn't done anything wrong, from Ian's perspective, he appeared to have acted like a cad.

The two boxers moved to the centre of the ring. Ian stared into Billy's eyes as they briefly touched gloves. He didn't say anything, but the cold look in his eyes was enough to tell Billy that Ian would come out aggressively from the very start of the first round.

As the bell for the start of the first round was rung, Ian shot out of his corner, moving faster than Billy had ever seen him move before. Billy wasn't even halfway to the centre of the ring when Ian came up to him, swinging his fists into a strong left-right-left combination at Billy's torso.

Billy was barely able to deflect the blows, and his forearms stung from the hits from Ian's gloves.

Ian danced away, moving out of Billy's reach. Ian watched Billy's eyes the entire time, never wavering in his stare.

Billy kept his hands in a defensive posture, staying on the balls of his feet. But he did not pursue Ian around the ring. Instead, Billy kept turning on the spot as Ian wove around him.

Billy knew he had the skill to defeat Ian in the boxing ring, even with a handicap of four points per round. Billy was also aware that he was in the running for one of the spots in the exhibition team.

But Ian was his best friend. Billy felt torn between his conflicting emotions. On one side was his own competitive nature, and the prestige that went with being selected for the exhibition team. On the other was the realisation that his friend was hurting, and that this fight was the only opportunity Mouse would have to lash out physically at Billy.

Normally so confident in the boxing ring, Billy felt his mind drifting as he looked for a solution to his inner conflict. Ian noticed Billy's concentration drop, and seized the opportunity.

With lightning speed, Ian dashed inside Billy's defences and landed two quick blows to Billy's solar plexus, before delivering a punishing right cross to Billy's jaw.

For a moment, Billy saw nothing but blackness, and he staggered a step or two before dropping to his knees.

Ian danced away, while the referee came over to examine Billy.

Shaking his head to clear it, Billy slowly got back to his feet. He could dimly hear Jane shouting at him, over the ringing in his ears.

"Get up," she was screaming, although her voice sounded quite far away, "Get up and get him."

Ian had heard her too, and he turned his eyes to look at Jane as if she had just ripped his heart out of his chest. It was the most devastated look of pain Billy had ever seen on another human being.

Ian dropped his arms to his sides and turned to walk out of the ring. The referee stopped him, standing between Ian and the ropes.

"You can't leave part way through a round, Landsborough. The match must continue until the final bell."

"For what purpose?" Ian asked, before sighing and turning back to face the centre of the ring.

Ian and Billy both took up their defensive stances, and the referee signalled for the match to continue.

Billy began landing blow after blow on Ian's arms, body and head. Ian kept his guard up, but he refused to go on the attack.

Each time Billy broke through Ian's defences, he'd knock Ian to the mat. And, each time, Ian would slowly get back up, resume his defensive stance, and the bout would continue.

Ian took blow after blow, and once Billy realised that Ian was only going through the motions, he started pulling his punches.

"William," Ian said, lowering his gloves, "this won't do. Box properly, or I'll walk out of the ring right now."

"But Mouse," Billy began.

"Properly!" Ian hissed, bringing his gloves back into position.

Billy resumed his attack, landing blows and knocking Ian down, over and over again. He was having trouble seeing, as tears welled in his eyes at seeing his friend in so much pain, both physically and emotionally.

Finally, the third round was over, and the bell was rung for the last time in the bout. Billy returned to his corner of the ring, to await the decision of the judges.

Ian walked back to his corner, stepped through the ropes and left the ring. Then he kept walking, leaving Billy, the Sports Master and the gym full of stunned students behind.

Chapter 34

Sydney, Colony of New South Wales, Australia
Friday 5 March 1943

"Commander Bowman," the orderly poked his head through the double swinging doors that blocked the corridor, "you can come through now Sir."

Until a few months ago, Patrick had no idea that this facility even existed, buried under the Sydney Botanic Gardens. The entrance was hidden inside one of the pavilions that dotted the gardens, and an armed guard was permanently stationed in the antechamber immediately behind the concealed entrance.

After walking through the double doors, Patrick entered a long corridor, with a series of laboratories along each side. The laboratories had large glass windows, set into the walls of the corridor, and as he strode down the corridor, Patrick could see experiment after experiment being performed in the labs.

The only laboratory that interested Patrick, though, was the one near the end of the corridor. The sign on the laboratory door said 'Advanced Cybernetics'. A much larger sign read 'Authorised Personnel Only'.

As he entered the Cybernetics Laboratory, Patrick's senses were assaulted by the strong smells of both hospital antiseptic and high-grade mechanism oil. This was his third visit to the facility in recent weeks, and he was still a little overwhelmed by that strange combination of odours.

A very prim and proper, grey-haired woman in a lab coat was standing in the middle of the room, leaning over a metal table. At the sound of the door opening, she turned and smiled cheerily at Patrick.

"Welcome back, Commander."

"Thank you, Professor Hamilton. How is the Lieutenant?"

"Always straight to business with you, isn't it Commander?" the Professor noted airily, "Still, I suppose in your line of work, getting quickly to the point is rather important."

Patrick nodded, silently encouraging the Professor to begin the update on her patient.

The term 'patient' probably wasn't the correct term to use any more for Leslie. Her initial injuries had been treated and her condition stabilised, so even though she'd had her left arm amputated and her left eye removed, she was no longer a patient.

If it hadn't been for the intervention of the Chief, she wouldn't be a Royal Navy Lieutenant either. After her treatment, she would have been discharged, to become Miss Leslie Simons, citizen of the British Empire, wounded in the service of His Majesty.

Professor Hamilton referred to the Lieutenant as 'the subject', but Patrick was unwilling to use that term to a woman who was a dedicated member of his team.

"The subject has been making excellent progress," the Professor began, with only the slightest hint of excitement in her otherwise stately tone of voice.

"Her shoulder and stump are supporting the weight of the prosthetic arm very well. The arm itself is quite heavy, as you know. But we've made some adjustments to the attachment straps and provided her with extensive physical training to develop the shoulder muscles.

"She is now able to wear the arm for up to 12 hours at a time, and only requires a two-hour break before it can be refitted. I anticipate that by the end of next month, she will be strong enough to wear the arm permanently."

"Very good, Professor. How is the neurological net progressing?"

"Again, excellent. As you recall, we were able to fit a metal cap over her scalp on the left-hand side of her head, and introduced a number of ultra-thin wires from the cap to the various impulse centres of her brain.

"We've been monitoring and fine-tuning those connections for the past three weeks, and we now believe we've created the correct pathways from the subject's brain to the control mechanisms in the arm."

"Are you ready to conduct a full test?"

"Yes, Commander. That is why I asked you to come to the laboratory today."

Patrick felt his pulse begin to race. Finally, some progress for the Lieutenant.

oOo

Leslie was sitting in a large padded chair, in the centre of the testing area of the laboratory. The chair reminded Patrick of a barber's chair, with its high back, padded footrest and adjustable height and tilt mechanisms.

Resting on a table attached to the left-hand side of the chair was the prosthetic arm. The brass fittings of the arm glinted in the surgical lights mounted in the ceiling of the testing lab, and the technicians were carefully checking the readings on the tiny gauges built into the forearm assembly.

Patrick could see thin pistons connecting the upper and lower parts of the arm, although they were recessed below the surface of the arm in tiny grooves. There were also a number of places, particularly around the inner elbow, where tiny brass cogs could be seen. At the moment, these cogs were still, but Patrick had seen the demonstration where they would spin incredibly quickly when the arm was in motion. Together, the pistons and the cogs gave the arm great strength and speed compared to a human arm.

The prosthetic had already been connected to Leslie's shoulder, with a series of leather straps, secured with strong brass buckles. Patrick doubted the arm could be forcibly removed from her shoulder in any sort of hand-to-hand combat situation.

A black cloth eye patch covered the place where her left eye should be, but it was the metal skull cap which was the most unsettling.

Her head had been shaved, but only on the left-hand side, leaving her straight blonde hair cut short on the right. The brass plating of the cap covered the entire left-hand side of her skull, and the pieces were customised to perfectly follow the contours of her head.

Patrick could see exposed wires traveling across the top of the cap, in a crisscrossing web, before being gathered together and tied in a bundle just above her left ear. The bundle of wires looped down onto her shoulder, before branching out again and connecting at various points along the arm.

"Do not be concerned, Commander," Professor Hamilton said quietly, as if sensing his discomfort at the exposed wires.

Patrick looked hard at her, demanding an explanation.

"We have deliberately left the wiring exposed, to enable us to make all necessary adjustments during the testing phase. Once the prosthetic arm and eye are both fully functional, we'll be able to conceal the wiring and add some protective measures to the mechanisms.

"Good," was Patrick's only reply, before turning back to look at the Lieutenant.

Professor Hamilton walked towards the large chair and stopped in front of Leslie. The Lieutenant stared at her, her eye unblinking.

"Are you ready?"

"Let's do this thing, Doc."

The Professor nodded at the technicians, who took two steps back from the chair.

"The brain functions which control the movement of our limbs are largely unconscious," the Professor explained, for the benefit of both Patrick and Leslie.

"We do not need to say to our arm 'pick up that ball' or 'push on the door handle', as these functions occur without active thought.

"But, we are able to exert control over our bodies when we choose. We are able to suppress a smile, or to stop ourselves from reaching out for something, by applying conscious thought to the muscles, instructing them what to do.

"This is how you learnt to do drill movements when you were in the cadets. The actions you take, for example, to halt or to about face, are not instinctive when you first learn them. These movements require you to consciously direct your limbs. It is only later, when you have mastered the movements, that you are able to execute them without conscious thought.

"Do you understand?"

Leslie nodded, her eye still fixed on the Professor.

"Good," the Professor continued, "as this conscious thought is exactly what is required for you to operate your new arm.

"We believe we have correctly wired the skull cap into your brain, to allow the signals to interact with the mechanisms in the arm. If we have succeeded in this wiring, you will be able, with a little mental effort, to move the arm.

"Let's begin. Raise the arm off the table."

"How high?"

"Ah, you military types are all the same," the Professor chuckled, "You need a precise measurement for everything!

"I don't care if you lift your arm an inch or your raise your hand like you're back in school asking a question. Just raise the arm."

Leslie furrowed her brow, concentrating on sending a signal to the prosthetic arm. Even though the room was cool, the Lieutenant began to sweat. Patrick thought it was as if she was trying to lift a heavy weight with one hand, and was struggling to overcome the force of gravity.

"Stop there," the Professor said gently.

Leslie relaxed.

"You are trying to use muscles that do not exist," the Professor said, tapping a fingernail on the metal casing of the arm to create a hollow ringing sound.

"This task is not about force, as there are no muscles to apply force, nor tendons to contract to create movement. Do not think about the mechanics. Do not strain. Simply think about the arm lifting gently off the table, as if you were just picturing it in your mind."

Leslie nodded, and took a deep breath before closing her eye.

"Whenever you're ready, Leslie," Professor Hamilton said gently.

Patrick was a little startled by the Professor's use of the Lieutenant's first name, but he recovered quickly when he realised she was using it to help her relax.

The arm on the table twitched slightly, then the tiny pistons began to move and the cogs began to turn. Everything about the mechanisms in the prosthetic arm were near silent. Only the tiniest sounds of metal gears engaging could be heard.

As Patrick watched in amazement, Leslie lifted the arm off the table. As she opened her eye, she turned the arm at the shoulder and bent it at the elbow, so the artificial hand was turned towards her face.

With a quizzical look on her face, Leslie waved the hand from left to right, pivoting from the elbow and bending at the wrist. Stopping the movement of the hand, she flexed the fingers, forming a fist before opening her hand and counting down from five to one with her fingers.

She looked up at the Professor, grinning broadly.

"What's next, Doc?"

Chapter 35

Brisbane, Colony of Queensland, Australia
Wednesday 10 March 1943

"Sir, we've received new information about Volkov," Squadron Leader Peale informed Patrick.

Patrick raised an eyebrow, looking up from his desk at the tall pilot.

"Volkov? He scarpered back to Moscow after we thwarted his plans last year."

"Yes, Sir. Or at least, that's what we thought. However, new information coming from Moscow is telling a rather different story."

"Go on," Patrick said, indicating Peale should take a seat.

"These reports have taken months to be smuggled out of the country, at great risk to the few operatives we have in Russia.

"According to this new information, Volkov did not return to Russia after he escaped during our raid. It seems Moscow is in rather a flap about it and has declared him a rogue agent."

Patrick was aghast. If Volkov had gone rogue, he was operating independently of Moscow's control. He could be anywhere, planning anything. When he was being given orders, Volkov was one of the most dangerous men in the world. If he was working to his own agenda, he might just be unstoppable.

"Are the reports reliable?"

"Yes, Sir. All indications are that the intelligence is genuine."

"Are there any indications about his location, his intentions, potential targets?"

"No, Sir. It appears he's gone to ground somewhere, but we can't ascertain where. As for his intentions, our assumption is that he is going to try to complete some form of the mission he was originally assigned."

Patrick considered this for a moment.

"One of the riskiest things we can do, Squadron Leader, is to make assumptions about The Wolf."

oOo

Caloundra, Colony of Queensland, Australia
Wednesday 24 March 1943

"Stroke, Stroke, Stroke!"

Billy fell easily into the rhythm the coxswain called, as they rowed their boat - called a 'shell' Billy had learned - down the river in the afternoon sunlight. The weather was still warm, although autumn was upon them, and the splashes of river water that fell on his arms and legs from the oars of his crew mates had a touch of coldness that was refreshing against the sweat from the effort of rowing.

He had fallen in love with rowing. The physical exertion and the concentration needed to stay in time with his fellow crew members allowed him to forget about every other distraction in his life.

The irony of loving rowing was not lost on Billy. It seems that over the last few months, all of the problems and issues he was dealing with were all caused by the love he and others were experiencing.

Billy really longed for the simple days at the start of First Form, when all he needed to worry about was making sure he got to class on time. Back then, the hardest thing he had to deal with was trying to understand all the terminology in the Organisms classes.

Ian hadn't spoken to any of them since the incident in the boxing ring. It was as if a door had been slammed closed on their friendship.

At first, Billy was concerned his friend was suffering from some kind of depression, and was worried he might hurt himself, or someone else. Then, Billy noticed that Ian was spending his time outside of class with Sean Byrne, and that concern was eased.

It was understandable that Ian would turn to Sean when he was feeling hurt and betrayed. Sean had spent a great deal of time with Ian during the summer, coaching him in drill, and it was clear that Ian respected and admired the older boy.

Billy was glad that Ian had someone to turn to, someone to support him. While he was disappointed that Ian didn't want to be part of their group, Billy was relieved that he wasn't on his own.

So that only left the problem of the two girls.

Normally, Billy would have been able to see both Jane and Ann riding their bicycles along the path beside the river, keeping pace with his shell.

More than once, he'd seen them get tangled up with the Sports Master or the Rowing Coach, who were also on bicycles trying to coach the crew along the river. Billy found it hard to keep the rhythm when he saw, out of the corner of his eye, the girls crashed into the Master and all three fall to the ground in a tangle of limbs, accompanied by shrieks from the girls and barely contained curses from the Master.

The logical part of his brain told him that Jane was only there to follow him as he rowed along the river. He also knew that Ann was only there to spend time with Jane. He knew that he shouldn't encourage either girl in their infatuations, but Billy was so enamoured with Ann, that he didn't want to do anything that might mean he saw less of her and her mesmerising blue eyes.

Jane wasn't on the bicycle path this afternoon. She was working with Mr Gibson, the Mathematics Master, on some advanced problems that she hadn't quite come to grips with. And because Jane wasn't at rowing practice, Ann wasn't there either. Billy found himself wishing he knew where she was and what she was doing.

The rhythm of the oars lulled Billy, and he found himself thinking about his friends as he rowed.

"Stroke!" shouted the coxswain.

"Mouse!" thought Billy.

"Stroke!"

"Jane!"

"Stroke!"

"Ann!"

"Bowman!"

Billy looked up, shaken from his reverie, to see the coxswain glaring at him.

"Get into the rhythm, man! You're in the Engine Room."

"Sorry," Billy said sheepishly.

Even though he was only in First Form, Billy was bigger and stronger than many of the older boys at the College. When he joined the rowing squad, Billy was placed in the centre of the shell, which the Master called the Engine Room, as this was where the greatest power was generated.

Billy shook his head, trying to clear it. Wherever Ann was, he'd be able to see her after practice. Right now, though, he needed to concentrate.

oOo

As Billy was leaving the College grounds after practice, he heard the sirens of the ambulance service a block or two away.

Billy felt a sinking feeling in his stomach, that he couldn't explain. Somehow, he knew something was wrong with one of his friends. He didn't know how he knew - he just knew.

He took off at a run towards the sound of the ambulance.

When he arrived at the scene, a large goods cart had overturned, spilling barrels of grain onto the roadway. The horses that had been pulling the cart were being calmed by the driver, and the ambulance siren had been turned off.

A small crowd had gathered to witness the scene. Some of the men, who had come out of nearby shops when the accident happened, had now been allowed to start to collect the grain barrels, rolling them back towards the cart. Everyone else was being held back by a wooden barricade erected across the street, with a burly policeman on duty.

Billy ran up to the barricade and quickly surveyed the scene. Just beyond the overturned cart, Billy could see the ambulance officers kneeling on the ground, providing treatment to an injured person.

Billy could only see the long blonde hair of the victim, and he gasped in horror. He was about to slip under the barrier, when the policeman spotted him.

"Stop there, son," he called gruffly.

"Is that Ann Roberts?' Billy asked, his voice shaking.

The policeman looked at him quizzically.

"Why?"

"She, she's…" Billy hesitated for a moment, then committed himself to the half-truth, "she's my girlfriend."

The face of the policeman softened. He looked around to see if his Sergeant was nearby.

"Look," he said quietly, "I'm not supposed to release any information, but you seem like a nice kid."

The officer paused, considering his next words carefully.

"It looks like she tripped and fell into the road, just as the goods cart came along. The driver did his best to swing the cart out of the way, which is why it's now overturned. Unfortunately, he wasn't able to swing the cart enough, and the young lady was run over by the back wheels."

Billy frowned for a moment.

"How odd," he thought, "Ann's one of the best gymnasts in the College. I've never seen her trip over anything."

As quickly as that thought entered Billy's mind, he pushed it aside for a more urgent question.

"Is she going to be all right?" He asked the constable.

"I don't know. She's very badly injured."

"Can I go through to see her?"

"No lad," the officer replied, kindly but firmly, "the ambulance officers need to treat her right now.

"And I don't think you want to see her in this condition," the officer thought, "poor thing."

Billy thanked the officer before turning and walking back towards his house.

He didn't notice the man in the dark clothes just on the edge of the scene, with his hat pulled low over his face and a bushy beard concealing the large scar on his left cheek. Billy didn't see Volkov, but Volkov saw and heard Billy.

Volkov smiled to himself, and began to follow Billy home.

Chapter 36

Caloundra, Colony of Queensland, Australia
Monday 15 March 1943

"Quiet please, students," the Headmaster called from the stage at the front of the Assembly Hall.

The students quickly took their seats, hurried along by the Prefects. When everyone had settled, the Headmaster began his address.

"Thank you all for coming along so quickly. We don't often call a whole school assembly, but I wanted to ensure that every student understands what is happening at the moment."

Billy felt numb. In fact, he'd felt numb since the accident. Jane had tried to console him, and had spent as much time with him as she could.

She had visited him at his house after school on Thursday and Friday, and had spent almost the entire day there on Saturday, and again on Sunday. Jane had brought her homework with her, of course, but she had wanted to be there, in the same room, as a reassuring presence for Billy.

Now she was sitting next to him in the Assembly Hall, her hand resting lightly on his arm. Billy looked along the row of First Form students. At the far end of the row, about as far away from Billy and Jane as was possible, sat Ian, staring straight ahead.

"As many of you may know," the Headmaster began, "one of our students, Ann Roberts from Third Form, was involved in a terrible accident last week.

"Ann's parents have asked me to pass on their thanks for all the well-wishes that they have received since the accident. I would like to add to this, by saying how proud I am of all of you who rallied together and offered to help the family with meals, or chores, or some other support over the last few days. It makes me very pleased to see College students banding together to help each other during times of crisis.

"As many of you may not know, Ann's condition is listed as serious, but stable. Our little hospital here in Caloundra is not able to provide the care that Ann needs. Therefore, Ann has been transferred to the Brisbane Hospital this morning."

A murmur spread around the students at this news. It was rare for someone to be taken to Brisbane for medical care, and it indicated how serious Ann's injuries must be. Billy looked ashen at the news, and Jane reached down to hold his hand.

The Headmaster allowed the students a moment to react before continuing.

"I have been informed that Ann's prognosis is good, but that she may take upwards of six months to recuperate from her injuries. We should not expect Ann to return to the College before the beginning of the new school year in September.

"Ann's parents will, of course, travel to Brisbane to be with Ann during her treatment. Ann's uncle, our Sports Master, Mr Roberts, has requested a leave of absence from the College, to look after his brother's small farm on the outskirts of the township.

"I have approved his leave, and Mr James, the Senior Assistant Coach, will take over the duties of Sports Master for at least the remainder of this school year."

"We will be conducting interviews this afternoon for the position of temporary Junior Assistant Coach, to ensure we have sufficient staff to run our sports programs."

"Thank you everyone," the Headmaster concluded, "now, please return to your normal classes."

oOo

"You certainly seem well qualified, Mr Loup," the Acting Sports Master, Mr James, informed the applicant, "and your letter of reference is exceptional."

"Merci," replied the trim man seated across the Sports Master's desk, his black moustache waxed to the point where it didn't even quiver when he spoke.

"Oh, I didn't realise you're from France, Monsieur Loup."

"Non," he said dismissively, "I am from Belgium, not France."

"Ah, I see," Mr James paused for a moment, "Forgive me, my French is a little rusty. 'Loup' is French for 'Wolf', is it not?"

"Oui. It is a somewhat unusual name, but," he shrugged, "some names are chosen for us, non?"

"Indeed they are Monsieur Loup, indeed they are," Mr James smiled warmly, "Are you aware that the position is temporary, for just over two months, until the end of the school year?"

"Oui. That suits my plans perfectly. I wish to be in Melbourne before the end of the year."

"Excellent. I will need to confer with the Headmaster, of course, but I believe you are our most suitable candidate Monsieur and I intend to recommend you for the position."

"Merci," Monsieur Loup bowed slightly, then shook hands with Mr James, before turning to leave the Master's office.

oOo

Once he was outside College House and making his way towards the front gate of the College, Volkov smiled and twisted the end of his waxed moustache.

When he had heard that the College required a new Junior Assistant Coach, Volkov had forged a letter of reference and shaved his beard into a thin moustache. With the addition of some moustache wax and a French accent, he was transformed into Monsieur Loup.

He had also prepared an explanation for the large, distracting scar on his left cheek.

"A hunting accident, from when I was a young boy," he had planned to say.

The citizens of the British Empire, however, considered themselves far too polite to even mention it, although Volkov was certain it would be a topic of conversation behind his back, by both the Masters and the students.

Volkov was also a little concerned that using the French word for 'Wolf' might have given away his identity before he had the chance to complete his reconnaissance. But the thought of flaunting his codename so openly gave him such a delicious thrill that he decided to take the risk.

Besides, in the aftermath of the chaos he intended to cause, the investigators would no doubt eventually work out who he was. Volkov couldn't help but chuckle when he thought about how aghast the Directorate would be when they discovered how close he had come to the Bowman family, completely undetected.

With the success of the goods cart accident, the girl Ann was now out of the picture for several months. This left Volkov free to plan for his next course of action. His new position as Junior Assistant Coach would make that task even easier.

He now had direct access to all of his remaining targets five days a week at the school. And, should the students see him outside the College grounds, they wouldn't even think twice about why he was there.

Volkov would now be able to make far more detailed observations of Billy and his friends. And that would help him determine his next target.

oOo

Caloundra, Colony of Queensland, Australia
Thursday 1 April 1943

For the first two weeks following his appointment to the College, Volkov, posing as Monsieur Loup, had taken a number of sports classes for the Second and Third Form students. Frustratingly, he had not been given the chance to take any of the First Form classes.

He would also have liked to observe the Bowman boy in his rowing practice, but he was considered too junior among the staff to be allowed to become involved in that particular sport. His junior position didn't stop him from asking, of course, but the denial was as swift and final as it was polite. Inwardly, Volkov bridled at being told no, but outwardly, he let his Belgian persona show aloofness.

Finally, today, he was going to assist with a First Form class.

"Take up your positions, please, mademoiselles," Volkov instructed, pointing to a line along the floor of the gymnasium.

"My name is Monsieur Loup, and I will be taking your gymnastics class today.

"We will begin with a simple demonstration of your floor exercises. You may perform any combination you wish, although," he paused, looking along the line of students, "I encourage you to perform movements that will demonstrate your skill."

"Anderson," he called, looking from his clipboard to the students.

"Here, Sir," responded a tall thin girl with curly brown hair, stepping forward.

"You will be first. The rest of you, please take your seats on the bleachers."

Volkov moved himself into a position where he could both see the gymnasts and clearly hear what the Everington-Smythe girl was saying. He hoped that by having the girls perform individually while pretending to ignore the remaining students, he might hear something useful as Jane was talking to her friends.

He did not have long to wait.

"I don't understand why he's so distant." Jane pouted, "I mean, I'm doing everything I can to get his attention, but it just doesn't seem to be working."

"Clearly, he's still pining for Ann," the girl sitting next to Jane said, in a sing-song voice, swishing her head and making googly eyes at Jane.

"Shut up, Olivia!"

"Well, he is!" another girl nearby replied, "and you can't really blame him. Her eyes are so blue! It makes her hard to resist."

The girl stood up, glancing over to check that Monsieur Loup wasn't watching, then began an over-dramatic swoon.

"Oh Ann! You are such a delight!"

"Isabel," Jane laughed, "stop it! You are incorrigible!"

"Absolutely," the girl grinned.

Jane looked earnestly at the two girls.

"Thank you for making me laugh."

"You're welcome." Olivia responded, "but, honestly, you need to be patient with Billy. Be there for him, let him know you're around, and he'll begin to appreciate you even more."

"If you know what she means!" Isabel chimed in, winking lasciviously at Jane.

"Stop it!" Jane hissed, as all three girls burst into fits of giggles.

"Interesting," Volkov thought.

He had imagined that making the Everington-Smythe girl his next target would cause the most hurt for the Bowman boy. Now, it seemed that he was indifferent towards the girl.

She was a friend, yes, even a close friend to William. But he did not hold her as dearly as she held him, and this was not what Volkov had hoped for when he was planning his attacks.

No, he decided, the girl Jane was not the best choice for his next target.

Chapter 37

Caloundra, Colony of Queensland, Australia
Saturday 3 April 1943

Over the two months since the drill assessment, Ian had been spending a good deal of his free time in the library, conducting research for the shipwreck mapping expedition in Pumicestone Passage.

At first, Ian had been numb, almost paralysed, by what he called 'The Betrayal'. He had always assumed that he and Jane would be together forever, but clearly that wasn't what Jane felt.

His initial reaction was to cancel the Pumicestone Passage exploration, as that was something they had begun planning together. He didn't want those painful memories to keep surfacing.

As time went by, though, Ian began to realise that the search for the lost ships was something bigger and more important than his feelings towards Billy and Jane. And so, he had resumed his research and had begun preparing the *Sea Gypsie* for extended exploration voyages.

Ian's intent was to take the *Gypsie* out in the long holiday at the end of the school year. That break from school would give him three months to explore, and with careful planning, he didn't see why he couldn't be on the ocean for two, or even three weeks at a time, before needing to come ashore for fresh supplies.

Three months onboard the *Gypsie*. Ian could already feel the relief of escaping his problems and the constant reminders of his pain that would come from such an extended time away. He hoped he might even come back from the trip a little better able to cope with the loss of Jane, and Billy, from his life.

As angry and as hurt as he was, Ian still regretted not sharing in Jane and Billy's company. They had been a good team, and Ian missed having them call him 'Mouse'.

Surprisingly, Sean Byrne had continued to spend time with Ian after the drill assessment. Ian had expected that once the assessment was completed, Sean would return to his friends and Ian would only see him at the parades, or occasionally in the College grounds.

But Sean had continued to meet with him, and had even begun to ask questions about his research. Ian wasn't sure if Sean was interested in exploration, or if he had heard about 'The Betrayal' and wanted to provide support.

Whatever the motivation, Ian was actually glad to have Sean around. He was relaxed and jovial, even though he had been passed over for promotion to Sergeant. Ian had asked him about it when the promotion list was posted on the bulletin board, but Sean had simply shrugged.

Now, the two boys spent a good deal of their time in the library.

"Ian," Sean asked, a little hesitantly.

"Shh!" came a voice from nearby.

It would have been the librarian no doubt, an ancient lady with grey haired tied in a bun that was as tight as her personality. The librarian was insistent on silence in her library, and not even the somewhat soft spot she had for Ian and Jane - her *studenti prima* - would allow for an exception to that rule.

Ian nodded his head towards the nearby door. Leaving his notebooks, pencils and the various newspapers he was researching scattered on the reading table, Ian led Sean through the door and into the small courtyard built onto the side of the town library.

Once they were outside, Ian sat in one of the cafe-style chairs and waited patiently for Sean to gather his thoughts.

"Or his courage." Ian thought, "I'm not sure which."

Sean didn't sit down, but instead paced a little, backwards and forwards, nervously. Finally, Ian couldn't stand to watch Sean struggle any longer, and decided to put him out of his obvious misery.

"Out with it, old bean," Ian said encouragingly, "what is it?"

"I wanted to know," Sean began, "that is, if you don't mind,"

Sean paused again, as if searching for the most appropriate way to ask his question. Ian nodded encouragingly, hoping his friend would get to the point.

"Would you let me come on the *Sea Gypsie* in the holidays?"

Sean's body sagged slightly, as if he'd just managed to ask for one of the most elusive prizes in the entire Empire. Then, he stiffened, gathering himself to try to remain stoic if Ian denied his request.

Ian grinned broadly, letting Sean off the hook.

"Of course you can, old bean! You didn't actually need to ask. All my planning for the last few weeks has been based around both of us being on board."

"Thank you!" Sean gushed, "I've never been exploring before, and I thought you might only want an experienced person on the voyage."

"For all things, there is a first time." Ian said sagely, with a wink at Sean.

Sean grinned and sat down in the chair opposite Ian.

"What do you need me to do, Captain?"

Ian laughed.

"Can you take charge of the stores, please. Work out what we'll need for the trip, then inventory what we have on board the *Gypsie*. Give me a list of the gaps, and I'll see what I can do to get the items we're missing."

"Aye, aye, Captain."

"Carry on, Quartermaster."

They grinned at each other and shook hands, before Ian returned to the library to continue his research, and Sean went to compile his lists.

oOo

Caloundra, Colony of Queensland, Australia
Tuesday 13 April 1943

After realising that he needed to shift his target away from Jane, Volkov had spent two weeks trying to manipulate his way into the boxing sessions with the boys. He had finally managed to convince one of the other Junior Coaches to swap roles for the final weeks of the school year.

Volkov, or Monsieur Loup as he was known by the staff and students, was now the assistant coach for the lightweight division of the First Form boxing sessions. And this new role brought him into close proximity with the Landsborough boy, his next target.

By all observations, the boy was academically gifted, but he lacked much of the grace of the other boys in his division. However, Volkov noted the spirit of the young man. He was never afraid to enter the ring and would always get up after being knocked down.

The other trait Volkov noted was his quite incredible speed in the ring. The boy was fast. Very fast. If he could be trained to utilise his speed, he would become a very competitive boxer in his weight class.

Volkov wasn't even slightly interested in making Ian Landsborough into a better fighter. If, however, Volkov offered to train the boy, give him some additional coaching, he would likely be able to gain his trust. And if the boy trusted him, then that would give Volkov some more creative options for his attack.

oOo

"Very good, very good, merci," Monsieur Loup called to the students gathered around him, "class dismissed.

"Landsborough, un moment, s'il vous plaît," the Junior Coach called, "a moment, if you please."

Ian looked around, surprised, wondering if something was wrong.

"I have noticed," Monsieur Loup began, "that you have great courage and tenacity."

"Thank you, Sir."

"You also have great speed in the ring, but you do not fully use this to your advantage."

"I only do what comes naturally."

"Oui, oui, this I can see. But I think you can do more with this. Would you like to learn how to harness your speed?"

"Yes, please," Ian replied earnestly.

"I cannot provide extra coaching during class time. Are you willing to do coaching after school?"

Ian thought for a moment. After class he had the Empire Service Scheme parade each Friday, and his advanced mathematics classes each Monday and Wednesday. There was always homework from the mathematics classes, which needed to be completed before the next session. If he trained with Monsieur Loup on Thursday, though, he'd still have time on the weekend to complete his homework before the Monday class.

"Would Thursday be acceptable, Sir?"

"Excellent! We will start the day after tomorrow."

Chapter 38

Caloundra, Colony of Queensland, Australia
Sunday 25 April 1943

"Wake up, William," his father whispered, "It's 4:30 in the morning."

Billy's eyes shot open. He looked up at his father.

"Were you only pretending to be asleep?" Patrick Bowman asked with a grin.

"I was only resting," Billy replied, smiling, "ANZAC Day is a very special day, and I didn't want to sleep through the Dawn Service."

Patrick nodded, understanding.

"Come into the kitchen for some breakfast. Your mother is still asleep, so we're just having toast this morning."

Billy padded down the hallway to the kitchen, trying hard not to wake his mother. The smell of warm toast and hot tea drifted towards him, making Billy realise how hungry he was.

When he entered the kitchen, his grandfather was seated in the nook, wearing his Navy uniform, even though he had officially retired almost ten years ago. His white Captain's hat sat on the sideboard, the gold oak leaf braid glowing softly against the deep black of the hat's peak in the flickering lantern light.

"Good morning, Grandfather," Billy greeted his grandfather with love and respect.

"Good morning, William," his grandfather replied, turning in his seat to look at Billy.

As he turned the light caught the medals pinned to Mark Bowman's uniform. Billy could see there were five medals in a row across his grandfather's left breast. Billy knew that medals worn on the left were won by the wearer, while if medals were worn on the right-hand side, they belonged to a relative.

As part of his training in the Empire Service Scheme, Billy had been studying the medals issued by the Monarchs for the various campaigns fought by the soldiers, sailors and airmen of the Empire.

Billy leaned forward slightly to see if he could identify his grandfather's medals. Mark Bowman realised what he was doing and turned a little more to make it easier for Billy to see.

"Go ahead, William. See how many you can identify."

"But first, can you tell me what the order of the medals means?"

"The ones on the outside were issued first," Billy said confidently.

"Good, but not quite correct."

Billy looked a little puzzled, and Mark Bowman chuckled.

"Campaign medals, issued for fighting in the various conflicts, follow that rule." Mark explained, "but medals awarded for specific acts by an individual are given higher status and are always placed closest to the centre of the chest."

Billy nodded.

Mark Bowman pointed to the outermost medal, the one closest to his arm.

"Let's start with this one, William."

The medal was a silver disk suspended from a ribbon made with a wide vertical orange stripe in the centre, a narrow red stripe down each of the outside edges, and a thin blue stripe sandwiched between the red and the orange on each side.

"That's the Queen's South Africa Medal." Billy said, "issued by Queen Victoria for service in the Second Boer War."

"Very good, William. Now let's move on. I'll give you a hint this time. The next three medals are a set."

Billy looked closely at the three medals. The outermost was a bronze star, suspended from a ribbon with red, white and blue vertical stripes. The one next to it was a silver medal, featuring the profile of King George V, with a ribbon made up of a broad orange stripe in the centre, bordered by blue and white stripes with a thin black stripe running between them. The third medal in the set was a bronze medal with a rainbow coloured ribbon of vertical stripes. When Billy looked closely, he could see the colours radiating out from the centre, starting with red, then yellow, green, blue and violet.

"That's Pip, Squeak and Wilfred!" Billy exclaimed excitedly.

Mark Bowman grinned.

"Well done, William. That's the nickname for these medals, but what are their proper names?"

"The first is the 1914 Star, the middle one is the British War Medal, and the third is the Victory Medal."

"Excellent! Now, can you identify this last medal here?" Mark asked, pointing to the innermost medal.

Billy again looked closely, studying the medal. The ribbon design was simple, with a vertical stripe of purple down the centre, and a white stripe on either side. A bright silver bar extended across the face of the ribbon.

The medal itself, though wasn't a disk. This time, the medal was in the form of a burnished silver cross. Billy could see that the vertical and horizontal arms were almost exactly the same length, and each arm ended with a crown embossed into the metal.

Billy gasped.

"That's the Military Cross!" Billy exclaimed, "Awarded for exemplary gallantry.

"And the silver bar on the ribbon means the King awarded the medal to you for a second act of gallantry!"

Mark Bowman nodded.

"Along with my notebook, these medals will pass to your father when I die, William. Eventually, they will pass to you."

Mark Bowman looked earnestly at his son and his grandson.

"I want you both to promise me that when the medals have passed to you, each of you will wear them on the ceremonial days, in remembrance of me and my comrades-in-arms, who fought to defend and extend our Empire."

Mark Bowman reached out his hand. Patrick, and then Billy, shook the offered hand.

"We will." Patrick and Billy said together.

"Good," replied Mark Bowman, "Now Patrick, do you think you could get your father a nice hot cup of tea before we leave for the Dawn Service?"

oOo

By the time the Bowman's arrived at the Cenotaph in ANZAC Park, off the Esplanade at Caloundra, a small crowd had already gathered. A volunteer from the Returned and Services League was handing out candles to people as they arrived. Mark Bowman took the candle, on behalf of their family, and allowed the volunteer to light it for him.

The three Bowman men started to make their way towards the Cenotaph, with Mark Bowman leading the way carrying their candle. They were quite a striking group, with Mark in his Navy Captain's uniform, Patrick in his best suit and Billy in his Empire Service Scheme dress uniform.

Billy was secretly pleased that his promotion had come through just a few days before, and that he was able to attend the Dawn Service with his Cadet Corporal stripes newly sewn onto the sleeves of his uniform.

Billy noticed that when people saw his grandfather approaching, they stepped aside, allowing the group to pass to the front of the crowd. Billy wasn't sure if it was his grandfather's uniform, or his medals, or something else that gave them access. He made a mental note to ask his grandfather after the commemoration service.

When they arrived at the front, an usher wearing a Royal Navy Australia Fleet dress uniform, was waiting for them.

"Good morning, Captain Bowman," the man said, snapping to attention and saluting Mark.

"Good morning, Petty Officer Dalkeith," Mark replied, returning the salute.

"Your seats are this way, Sir," the Petty Officer indicated three seats with 'Reserved' signs on them, in the front row.

"Thank you, Petty Officer."

The Petty Officer quickly whipped the signs off the seats as they arrived at their assigned places.

Mark Bowman turned to his grandson.

"Here William," he said kindly, passing the candle to Billy, "this is your first dawn service in uniform, so I want you to hold the candle for us today."

Billy nodded solemnly, accepting the honour. In a way, he felt like his grandfather was passing on the torch of service to the Empire.

oOo

The dawn service itself was very moving, and Billy noticed more than once his grandfather dabbing at a tear in his eyes.

The Chaplain leading the service was from the Royal Air Force Australia Corps, and his white cassock was draped with a sky blue stole with the Air Force insignia embroidered on both sides.

"On the 25th of April 1915, the Australian and New Zealand forces - the ANZACs - landed on the beaches of the Gallipoli peninsula," began the Chaplain, recounting the story of the Dardanelles Campaign.

"The ANZACs faced overwhelming forces, entrenched on the high ground overlooking the beach. They faced machine gun fire and deadly snipers from the moment of arrival.

"But they did not flinch, though men were being shot left and right. They advanced and dug in, even though the campaign was hopeless. Their bravery and fortitude, their perseverance and their courage are an example to us all.

"Almost 9,000 soldiers died in that campaign, and nearly 18,000 were wounded. These men, and the thousands who survived, are honoured today as Australian Citizens of the Empire who protected us all."

Just as the sun was rising, the Padre led the congregation in The Ode.

"They shall grow not old, as we that are left grow old;

Age shall not weary them, nor the years condemn.

At the going down of the sun and in the morning

We will remember them.

Lest we forget."

As the Chaplain finished reading The Ode, a bugle began to play The Last Post. All of the uniformed members in the gathering, including Mark and Billy Bowman, stood rigidly to attention and saluted.

When these sad notes were finished, the uniformed members lowered their salutes, and two minutes of silence ensued, after which the bugler played Reveille.

The commemoration ceremony ended shortly afterwards, and Mark Bowman turned to his son.

"I'm going to spend some time with my fellow veterans this morning."

Patrick knew his father needed time alone with his war-time friends, to remember their fallen mates as only those who had experienced war could understand.

"Of course, Father. We'll see you for dinner."

"Yes, most likely," Mark agreed.

"Grandfather," Billy called.

Mark Bowman turned towards his grandson. Billy stood rigidly to attention in his Empire Service Scheme uniform and snapped a brisk salute to his grandfather.

With fresh tears in his eyes, Mark Bowman drew himself up to his full height and returned the salute.

"Carry on Cadet Corporal."

As Billy lowered his salute and turned to leave, his father put his arm around his shoulder.

"Well done, William," he said as they walked slowly away, "I think you've made your grandfather very proud today. I know that I'm very proud of the man you're becoming."

Billy didn't reply, but he felt his heart swell with gratitude for his grandfather and his father. He vowed to continue to follow their example in everything he did.

Chapter 39

Caloundra, Colony of Queensland, Australia
Thursday 13 May 1943

"Good, Landsborough, good."

Ian was sweating as he danced around the ring, with Monsieur Loup calling directions as he moved.

"Left arm up! Up! Good.

"Keep moving, don't stay still.

"Get ready to strike…

"Un, deux, trois, NOW!"

On the command, Ian leapt forward, swinging strong punches with his left, then right, then left hands. His arms were moving so fast that they almost appeared to blur. If you were to blink, you'd likely miss one of the punches.

"Good. Again."

oOo

Ian had spent weeks under the tutelage of Monsieur Loup, gaining confidence and skill in the use of his speed to the boxing ring. All the hard work of the training sessions was beginning to pay off. For the first time in his life, Ian felt that he had achieved something in the sports arena.

Now that the session was over for the day, Ian was breathing hard, but was happy. He was standing at the side of the ring, using a fluffy white towel to wipe the sweat from his eyes.

Monsieur Loup was standing a short distance away, watching him.

"You are making good progress, Landsborough. You have come a long way in a short time."

"Thank you, Sir."

"But now, our time is coming to an end. I am only here until the end of term."

"I don't know how to thank you, Monsieur Loup. I'm a much better boxer now, but that is only down to your time and patience in training me."

"Non, non, it is you who has done the hard work. That is what has improved your boxing. I merely opened the door. It was you who stepped through it."

"Even so, is there anything I can do to repay you for your generosity."

"That is very kind, Landsborough. I do have a small favour to ask, if I may."

Ian nodded his head, encouraging the Junior Coach to continue.

"I am led to believe that you have a steam yacht, oui?"

Again, Ian nodded.

"Oui. I will be leaving your Caloundra very soon. I would like, if I may, to ask for a tour of your beautiful coast from your boat. I have only seen the countryside from the shore."

Ian laughed delightedly, as he continued to wipe the sweat from his brow.

"That is a splendid idea! Shall we say, Saturday morning at 10am? We can meet at the rotunda at the far end of Leach Park."

"Merci, that is excellent!" Volkov smiled, but the smile never reached his eyes, "I look forward to it."

oOo

Brisbane, Colony of Queensland, Australia
Friday 14 May 1943

"He's more like a ghost than a wolf!" Commander Patrick Bowman muttered under his breath, repeatedly rapping his knuckles onto his desk in frustration.

The Chief had given Patrick permission to use the entire resources of his team to track down Volkov. And now, after weeks of meticulous research, combing through mountains of intelligence reports, they had virtually nothing to show for their efforts.

"Sir, you have a visitor," Corporal Ramirez said quietly.

"Corporal, you really must stop sneaking up on me like this."

"Certainly, Sir," Ramirez replied, with an evil grin on her face.

Patrick realised she had no intention of ceasing to use her talent at every opportunity, and he sighed good-naturedly.

"Lead the way, Corporal."

As Patrick approached the secure door to The Bunker, he could see a woman in a Royal Navy Australian Fleet uniform, waiting just in the doorway. Her uniform was neatly pressed, and she was looking out across the operations centre, waiting for the Commander.

Pinned above the left pocket of her tunic was a brand-new medal ribbon, the Distinguished Service Order. The ribbon was red, with narrow blue stripes at the edges. The award of this medal entitled the wearer to include the post-nominal 'DSO' after their name in official correspondence.

While the ribbon for the Distinguished Service Order was eye-catching, it was the prosthetic arm and brass half-face mask with optical implant that garnered the most attention.

Patrick grinned when he recognised her.

"Permission to come aboard, Sir," she said formally, offering Patrick a sharp salute.

"Permission granted, Lieutenant Simons," Patrick replied as he returned the salute, "and welcome back."

"Thank you, Sir," Leslie Simons said, stepping from the doorway into The Bunker.

"Congratulations on the award of the DSO, Lieutenant. It was well deserved."

"Thank you for recommending me, Sir."

"How are you adjusting to the prosthetics?"

"Very good, Sir. I'm fully cleared for operations in the field."

"Excellent." Patrick nodded, "Do you have the enhanced capabilities the scientists were discussing?"

"Yes, Sir. I have speed and power in the artificial arm equivalent to three times normal. The neural network coming from the skull cap gives full control over the arm and hand. The wiring, gears and pistons are now all armour plated for protection.

"The armour plating extends over the left side of my face and houses the optical implant. The implant provides a continuous video feed through the neural network directly into my brain, enabling depth perception as if I had two organic eyes.

"The implant can also provide an infra-red view, that can be used for heat detection, a night vision mode, and an enhanced zoom mode that is the equivalent of placing a telescope to my eye."

"I'm certain those capabilities will come in handy in the field, Lieutenant, but right now, I need your not insignificant analytical skills to review all of the intelligence reports. We're having a devil of a time trying to locate Volkov."

"Shall I take up my previous station?"

"Absolutely, Lieutenant, absolutely."

Without another word, Lieutenant Simons strode over to her station in the ops room and began to get to work on the intelligence reports.

oOo

Caloundra, Colony of Queensland, Australia
Saturday 15 May 1943

Ian arrived at the rotunda at the end of Leach Park at the stroke of 10am, to find Monsieur Loup already there.

"Good morning, Monsieur Loup, are you ready for your cruise?"

"Oui, Mon Capitaine."

Ian grinned at the accolade. He quite liked being called 'Captain'.

"This way," he said, guiding Volkov onto the path through the Golden Wattles.

Ian quickly led his passenger to the boathouse and deftly released the padlock. Once inside, he quickly turned on the lighting system and ushered Volkov aboard the *Sea Gypsie*.

"This is the saloon," Ian said, bringing his passenger into the cabin, "You can make yourself comfortable in here while I take the *Gypsie* out of the boathouse."

Ian began pointing out the features in the saloon that his guest might need to access.

"There are a number of tables and chairs under the floor, which can be brought up to deck level. You can control the furnishings from the panel on the wall.

"The galley is through this door," Ian indicated the door at the rear of the saloon on the left-hand side, "and the head is through the equipment locker on the other side."

Ian looked at his passenger, so see if he understood the maritime terminology. Volkov nodded at Ian, making clear that he had heard the terms before.

"Did you meet Sean Byrne, from Third Form?" Ian enquired.

"Oui."

"Sean is the Quartermaster and Mate of the *Sea Gypsie*," Ian said proudly. "He'll be here momentarily, then we'll take the boat out into the bay.

"Until then, please make yourself comfortable. I'll be in the wheelhouse, and if you need anything, you can contact me through the intercom on the control panel."

After Ian had left the saloon, Volkov began to explore the *Sea Gypsie*. He needed to get to know the layout of the boat, and the equipment she carried.

"Interesting," he thought, as he examined some of the specialised equipment in the locker, "the boy's grandfather was quite the inventor."

As he moved below decks, Volkov found the hatchway into the engine room. He pushed it open, and held his breath, waiting to see if an alarm would sound in the wheelhouse. When no response came to his intrusion, he walked into the space.

It was cramped, and the heat from the twin steam engines made the room uncomfortable. Volkov worked his way around the engines, following the pipes that lead up to the funnel. Then, he followed the large drive shafts that ran to the twin propellers at the stern of the vessel.

When he heard the rush of water outside the boat, Volkov realised that they were about to get underway. He quickly backed out of the engine room and returned to the saloon through the equipment locker.

Sean Byrne was standing in the doorway of the saloon, looking concerned. He was clearly wondering where their passenger had gone.

"Is everything all right, Monsieur Loup?"

"Oui," Volkov said evenly, "I needed to use the lavatory."

He watched the young man carefully, looking for any signs of mistrust or suspicion.

Sean's expression relaxed.

"Of course," he said smiling, "we're about to launch. If you like, you can watch from the rear deck, but please take care not to get too close to the edge, as sometimes the passage to the ocean can get a little bumpy."

"Merci," Volkov replied.

With that, Sean ducked out of the saloon and returned to the wheelhouse to assist Ian with the launch.

Volkov had seen that the boy Sean had spent quite a bit of time with Ian, but he hadn't anticipated that would extend to time on board the boat.

As he explored, a plan for attacking the Landsborough boy was beginning to form in his mind. The presence of Sean Byrne was a complication, but only a minor one.

All Volkov needed now was to be vigilant, as he waited for the right opportunity to present itself.

Chapter 40

Caloundra, Colony of Queensland, Australia
Monday 24 May 1943

"This is perhaps my favourite day of the year!" the Headmaster enthused, beaming out at the students gathered in the Assembly Hall.

"As you all know, today is Empire Day, the day we celebrate the achievements of our dear, departed Queen Victoria and her 63-year reign as Monarch of the British Empire.

"Because today is such a special day, we always use the morning session to have our graduation ceremony for the students of both Fifth and Upper Sixth Forms. We'll also have some displays from our sporting teams, and be presenting the academic and sports awards for the other Forms."

The Headmaster paused and looked around the Hall.

"And, of course, I know you're all looking forward to the half-day holiday," he said with a smile.

"Please remember, though," the Headmaster continued, "that only the Fifth and Upper Sixth Form students are completing their school year today. The rest of the College will have the half-holiday today for Empire Day celebrations, but are expected to be at normal classes for the remainder of this week."

"Now, to begin proceedings, I'll hand over to Mr James, our Acting Sports Master, who will introduce the sporting demonstrations."

oOo

Billy was lost in thought during the boxing demonstration. After the bout with Ian during the selection training, he wasn't chosen for the demonstration team. At first, his competitive nature had trouble accepting that decision, as he knew he was one of the best boxers in First Form.

But then he realised that if he had been selected, he would have needed to perform in the demonstration bout with Ian in the audience. Billy could imagine how uncomfortable that would have made Ian feel. If he was truly honest with himself, Billy realised that he would feel very uncomfortable too, standing in the ring in front of the entire school, showing off how much better at boxing he was than Ian.

Despite the distance that had grown between them over the last few months, Billy still thought of Ian as his best friend. He wished there was a way to convince Ian that his feelings for Jane were nothing more than friendship, and that he didn't return Jane's affections.

Jane had actually started spending a little less time with Billy in recent weeks. He still caught her gazing at him from time to time, but she was no longer quite so overt. Certainly, she had stopped hanging off his arm when they walked together between classes, which Billy was rather pleased about.

Right now, Jane was sitting in the row behind Billy, instead of next to him. She had been spending more time with the other girls in First Form, as well as a couple of the older girls in Second and Third Form, and seemed to be quite popular.

Ian was still opting for the place in the row furthest from Billy and Jane. Billy could just see him, sitting in the last chair of his row of seats, staring morosely forward, ignoring the boxing demonstration.

"What should I do?" he kept asking himself, "I don't want this to continue, but I don't know how to make things go back to normal."

Suddenly, Billy's thoughts were interrupted by a loud round of applause from the students sitting around him. Billy looked up, surprised to see that the boxing demonstration was completed, and the students were packing away the temporary ring that had been set up on the stage.

Mr James had moved to the front of the stage and was addressing the assembly.

"Thank you, First Form boys," he said, clearly pleased with the quality of the demonstration, "We'll now take a moment to set up for the gymnastics demonstration from the First Form girls."

Billy wondered whether Jane had been selected for the gymnastics demonstration. He looked around, to see if she'd left her seat to go prepare for the stage. However, Jane was still sitting in her place, chatting quietly to the students either side of her.

Jane looked up, and saw Billy looking at her. She smiled and gave him a wave. Billy smiled and waved back. He felt good that they seemed to be able to remain friends.

The gymnastics demonstration was enthralling, and Billy was so engaged with the performance that he didn't slip back into his contemplation of the issues with his friends.

There were two different demonstrations of floor exercises, involving ribbons, balls and tumbling. The girls moved with fluidity and a grace that only served to highlight the great strength it took to deliver their performances.

After the final routine was completed, there was a moment of silence across the auditorium. Then, spontaneously, the entire student body burst into applause, making a noise so loud that Billy could barely hear himself think. He found himself standing, grinning broadly and clapping his hands so hard they were starting to sting.

Billy looked down the row of chairs towards Ian. He was still in his seat, looking forward as if he hadn't seen any of the gymnastics demonstration or heard the response from the students around him.

"Oh, Mouse," Billy thought, with a pang of sympathy for his friend, "you must be hurting so much."

oOo

After the thunderous applause had died down and the students had resumed their seats, the Headmaster again took to the stage.

"Thank you, Mr James," he said grinning, "for that marvellous demonstration of boxing and gymnastics. I am very proud of the effort you students have put in to be able to perform to this wonderful standard this morning.

"And now," he continued more solemnly, "we will present the graduation certificates to our Upper Sixth Form students.

"These students have completed all seven years of secondary schooling and have successfully passed all examinations for their subjects. Each of these students has been accepted into one of our fine universities for further study in medicine, law or teaching."

The Headmaster began calling out the names of the individual students from Upper Sixth Form. As their names were called, each student rose from their seat, walked to one side of the stage, and climbed the three steps to the stage itself. They then walked forward to the Headmaster, shook hands with him and accepted their graduation certificate, before exiting the stage on the opposite side. Once off the stage, the students walked back to their seats by going all the way around the outside of the students seated in the Assembly Hall.

Finally, there was only one Upper Sixth Form student left to announce.

"While all of our graduating students applied for university placement," the Headmaster said with barely concealed pride, "one of our students has been selected by the Academy of Science for advanced engineering training in the field of Mechanisms.

"Students and Masters, please congratulate the Dux of Caloundra Colonial College for 1942-43, Timothy Horn."

Billy watched Timothy cross the stage and shake the hand of the Headmaster.

"He looks just like an older version of Mouse," Billy thought as he looked at the tall, gangly student with the wire-framed glasses.

"And now, for the Fifth Form graduates," the Headmaster announced after Timothy had left the stage.

"These students have completed five years of study at the College, and have either been accepted into one of the arms of His Majesty's military, or into a trade where they will be apprenticed to a Guild Master for training as bakers, plumbers, carpenters or one of a host of other trades.

"The Fifth Form graduates will join the ranks of those who keep our Empire safe and those who help us all live happy and productive lives."

The Headmaster then read out the names of each Fifth Form student, who in turn left their seat and climbed onto the stage to accept their graduation certificate, before returning to their seat once again by walking around the inside of the Hall.

"We now have a series of awards for our students in the lower Forms," the Headmaster informed the Assembly, once the last of the Fifth Form students had received their graduation certificate.

Mr James stood up to announce the sports awards.

There were awards called 'Full Blues', given to students who had been selected for representative teams in rugby, rowing and cricket. The College also offered a 'Half Blue' award, for students who had shown particular skill in a sport but had not yet made a representative team.

The awards themselves were medallions, mounted on long sky-blue ribbon that would hang around the neck of the recipient. The medallion was a large disk with an embossed picture of College House and the words 'Caloundra Colonial College' underneath, surrounded by a wreath of wattle. The medallion was gold for a Full Blue, and silver for a Half Blue.

"William Bowman," Mr James called from the front of the stage.

Billy looked surprised. He hadn't expected to hear his name called, as he was only in First Form.

"Get up there," the student sitting next to Billy whispered, grinning.

"Half Blue for rowing, Half Blue for cricket," Mr James announced.

Billy quickly mounted the stage and shook hands with Mr James.

"Congratulations, Bowman," the Acting Sports Master said quietly, as he hung two silver medallions around Billy's neck.

"Keep up the hard work and we'll see you with some Full Blues next year."

"Thank you, Sir."

The Headmaster again took to the stage.

"We now have the academic awards," he announced, "for the student who achieves the highest academic results in all of their subjects for each Form."

"While we can only have one Dux of the College, and that student will always be the Upper Sixth Form graduate with the highest academic score, we want to recognise the student in each Form who has shown the dedication to their studies to be ranked first in their year level."

The Headmaster began with Fourth Form, calling out the name of the student with the highest academic results and asking that student to come up to the stage to accept a Certificate of Achievement.

Finally, the Headmaster was ready to announce the First Form winner.

Billy saw a small movement out of the corner of his eye, and glanced down the row of seats. Ian had leaned forward in his seat, paying close attention to this announcement. Billy realised it was the first time he'd seen Ian move during the entire assembly.

"I hope you win, Mouse," Billy thought, "you need this."

"The winner of the First Form academic prize," the Headmaster announced, "by a rather narrow margin, is Jane Everington-Smyth."

Billy heard the squeal from Jane's friends sitting behind him, and he felt Jane brush past him as she stood to go to the stage. But Billy's eyes were locked on Ian at the end of the row, watching his friend's shoulders slump at the announcement. It was as if the life had drained out of Ian's body in that moment.

"Oh, Mouse," Billy breathed, "I'm so sorry."

Chapter 41

Caloundra, Colony of Queensland, Australia
Monday 24 May 1943

"Thank you everyone, that concludes the proceedings today," the Headmaster proclaimed, beaming.

"For all our continuing students, classes resume at 9am tomorrow. Please be on time.

"Until then, Happy Empire Day, everyone."

The moment the Headmaster dismissed the assembly, Ian stood and rushed from the Hall. His hands were thrust deep into his pockets and his shoulders were slumped forward.

His face betrayed his mixed emotions - anger, hurt and frustration. He wasn't sure which emotion was strongest, but together they made for an ugly, evil potion that poisoned his heart and his mind.

Sean Byrne met him outside the Assembly Hall, but Ian barely noticed as the older boy came up beside him.

"Are you taking out the *Gypsie* this afternoon?"

"Yes," Ian grunted.

"That's good. The fireworks tonight will look amazing from out on the ocean."

Ian looked up at Sean, ready to tell him in no uncertain terms that he was taking the boat out on his own. He simply wasn't in the mood to have anyone join him aboard the vessel.

As he looked at Sean's eager, helpful face, though, Ian realised that he would crush the friendship they had formed if he acted so selfishly. Even though Ian wanted to be alone, to wallow in his feelings of self-pity, he just couldn't bring himself to leave Sean ashore.

"Very good, Quartermaster," Ian said with a weak smile, "let's go to the boathouse."

oOo

Billy started looking for Ian as soon as the Headmaster dismissed the assembly. He saw his friend stand up quickly, looking incredibly upset, and almost storm out of the Assembly Hall.

He tried to catch up with Ian, but he was surrounded by his classmates, who all wanted to look at his Half Blue medallions.

"You're so talented, Billy!"

"Well done, old chap!"

"Jolly good show!"

"I don't think they've ever awarded a Half Blue to a First Former before!"

In the end, Billy realised he was never going to catch up to Ian outside the Assembly Hall.

"He'll probably head to the boathouse," Billy thought, "I'll try to catch him there."

oOo

From his vantage point on the stage, sitting with the Masters, Volkov observed the proceedings with great interest.

As a Junior Sports Coach, Monsieur Loup had been placed on the far edge of the stage, well away from the podium where the awards were being presented. No one noticed, then, that he paid scant attention to the proceedings, and instead was intently watching the Bowman boy and his friends.

Volkov noticed with keen interest how far the Landsborough boy was sitting from the other two students in their Form.

"It would seem you still wish to keep your distance," he thought.

When he observed Billy, Volkov could see that even though Ian didn't want to connect, Billy was very keen to rebuild the bridge between them.

"Good," Volkov observed, "that suits my purpose well."

When the assembly was dismissed, Volkov watched Ian Landsborough rush towards the exit. His body language made it abundantly clear what he thought about not winning the academic award for the Form.

Volkov realised that this was the ideal time to strike. The Bowman boy would have realised how devastated his friend would be at not winning the award. If anything happened to Ian now, the blow to Billy would be doubly hard-hitting.

Volkov smiled at the prospect, and made his way out of the Assembly Hall as quickly as he could without drawing attention to himself.

He was quite certain he knew where the Landsborough boy would be heading, and he needed to be there in time to execute his plan.

oOo

Ian and Sean had already spent quite some time over the last few weeks preparing the *Sea Gypsie* for extended cruising and exploring in Pumicestone Passage. Although their longer voyages weren't planned to start until the following week, the preparation they had already done enabled them to launch the steam yacht within a few minutes of arriving at the boathouse.

While Ian primed the steam engines, Sean stowed the gangway and ensured that the lines and connections from the boat to the shed were detached and secured.

The two boys passed each other as Ian came up from the engine room and Sean walked around the deck, checking and adjusting. They grinned at each other. The novelty of taking the *Gypsie* out onto the ocean had not worn off, and was a wonderful treatment for Ian's gloomy mood following the graduation ceremony.

"All ship-shape?" Ian asked.

"Aye, aye, Captain," came the response, before Sean continued around the deck, and Ian headed for the wheelhouse.

A few minutes later, Ian was ready to launch.

"Prepare for launch!" He called over the intercom system, his voice coming through the speakers dotted throughout the vessel and echoing off the walls of the boathouse.

Ian began flipping switches, pulling levers and pressing buttons on the console in the wheelhouse. The giant doors of the boathouse began to open, and the sound of water rushing under the keel of the *Gypsie* got louder and louder.

In front of the boathouse, Ian could see the channel starting to open. The tide was on the way in, so their trip from boathouse to open water would be short.

Ian was pleased about the short run out to the bay. He loved being onboard the *Gypsie*, but he always found the launch to be a little stressful. He knew he needed to monitor the launch systems very closely, or he ran the risk of damaging the yacht on her way to the water.

Quietly, Sean slipped into the wheelhouse. Ian was aware Sean had entered the space, but his face was set in concentration, and he didn't acknowledge the other boy.

Sean quickly settled into his place in the wheelhouse, acting as the Mate by monitoring some of the systems for Ian. Over the months since they had been taking the *Gypsie* out together, they had developed a routine for launches that left very little to chance.

The *Sea Gypsie* moved down the channel towards the ocean, picking up pace as she went.

Neither Sean nor Ian noticed the shadowy figure dart out from the far side of the boathouse and begin sprinting across the sand towards the yacht. The boys didn't see the figure stretch out his hand to grab a rail mounted onto the side of the vessel and use his momentum to swing himself up onto the transom of the boat.

With a further cat-like leap, the figure flipped over the stern and landed on the rear deck, completely hidden from the view of the wheelhouse.

Volkov grinned as he made his way from the deck, through the saloon, and into the bowels of the *Sea Gypsie*.

oOo

Billy arrived at the boathouse completely breathless, having run all the way from the College to Leach Park, and then down the sandy path to the clearing. As he burst out of the grove of Golden Wattle trees, Billy saw the *Sea Gypsie* gliding down the channel towards the ocean.

"Oh no," he thought, "I'm too late."

Billy put his hands on his hips and tipped his head back slightly, sucking in big gulps of air. For a moment, he thought about calling out to Ian, but he knew that he was still too winded from running to shout loudly enough to be heard above the waves and the engines of the steam yacht.

As Billy was about to turn away and head back to the College, he saw someone run out from the far side of the boathouse and sprint towards the *Sea Gypsie*.

"Who on earth could that be?" Billy asked himself, squinting in the bright sun of the early afternoon, trying to make out the identity of the figure.

Billy watched the figure grab a handrail and swing effortlessly up to the transom, then over onto the rear deck. As the man swung over the stern of the boat, Billy caught sight of a thin moustache with the waxed tips.

"Monsieur Loup!" Billy gasped in surprise, "What are you doing?"

Something was dreadfully wrong.

Billy turned and raced back up the path as fast as he'd ever run before.

Chapter 42

Caloundra, Colony of Queensland, Australia
Monday 24 May 1943

"Jane!" Billy shouted when he got to the College campus, "Jane!"

He was still breathless, but his sense of foreboding about what it meant that Monsieur Loup had snuck aboard the *Sea Gypsie* outweighed his physical tiredness.

Billy had no idea if Jane was still at the College. It had been some time since the assembly had finished, and she could easily have left by now, either on her own or with some of her friends. He wasn't sure where to look for Jane if she wasn't here, but he felt an urgent need to find her, and tell her what he'd seen.

Jane came around the corner of College House, a curious look on her face even though she was smiling at Billy.

"What is it?" she laughed, "you're making such a racket!"

Then Jane noticed the state of Billy's clothing, and his panting breaths. She must have also felt his unease, as the smile fell away from her face and she looked at him seriously.

"What's going on?" she demanded.

oOo

"Hmm," Jane mused, after Billy had finished describing what he'd seen, "Are you absolutely certain it was him?"

"Yes, that moustache is very easy to distinguish, even from a distance."

"So why would a Junior Sports Master, whose contract has just finished, stow away onboard Ian's boat?"

"There's no reason for it that I can think of," Billy replied emphatically, "and I have a very bad feeling about this."

"Normally, I would be very hesitant to act on the basis of someone's feelings," Jane said, before quickly adding, "even if it's someone I trust as much as you, Billy.

"But there's no doubt that this is suspicious. If you'd simply seen him on the rear deck during the launch, I'd say he'd been invited. The fact that you saw him sneak aboard rules that out completely."

"I agree," Billy replied, "and I think I know what we need to do now."

Jane looked at him quizzically.

"We need to talk to my parents."

oOo

"I really like your parents," Jane said as they made their way towards Billy's house, "but I'm not sure why you think we must bring this to their attention."

"My parents are the wisest people I know," Billy said simply, "I can talk to them about anything, and they will always listen to me, before offering me advice."

"I see. I don't really have that sort of relationship with my parents."

Billy reached across to pat Jane's arm, as they jogged down the street.

"I don't think anyone else does." Billy reassured her, "Everything I've seen and experienced makes me think that the way my family deals with things is quite unique.

"And if there's a crisis," he added, "and I really believe that's what we're facing, I can't think of anyone better than my parents to provide a level head and sage counsel."

Jane nodded, understanding. They continued towards Billy's house as fast as they could.

oOo

Patrick and Mary Bowman were chatting quietly in the living room when Billy and Jane burst into the house.

As the screen door slammed closed behind them, Mary Bowman leapt to her feet.

"William! What's wrong?"

Patrick Bowman carefully folded the newspaper he had in his lap and turned his full attention on his son.

"Mary, perhaps it's best you sit down. William clearly has something important he needs to discuss.

"Go ahead, William," he encouraged.

Billy drew a deep breath.

"Mouse seemed very upset after the graduation ceremony this morning," Billy began.

He glanced at Jane, but decided it was best not to mention that one of the reasons Ian was so upset today was because Jane had beaten him to the academic prize for their form.

"I imagined he would go down to the boathouse and take the *Sea Gypsie* out. I went down there to see if I could talk to him before he set off for the afternoon. When I got there, the *Gypsie* was already in the channel heading for the ocean, with Ian and Sean Byrne in the wheelhouse."

Patrick Bowman nodded, but didn't respond. Billy continued his explanation.

"As the *Gypsie* was launching, I saw someone run up behind the boat and swing themselves up onto the deck."

"Odd," Patrick said, raising an eyebrow.

"Yes, that's what we thought," replied Jane.

"What is it about this that's causing you to be so concerned, William?" his mother asked, "I could understand if you were curious, but you're not, are you? You find something about this very disturbing, don't you?"

Billy nodded, appreciating once again his mother's insightfulness. He noticed that his father had become even more attentive, now that his mother had shared her perception of how Billy was feeling.

"We know the stowaway," Billy explained, "it's Monsieur Loup from the College."

oOo

"Loup?" Patrick Bowman asked, "You are absolutely sure that's his name?"

"Yes, absolutely," Billy and Jane said in unison.

"Is he new at the school?"

"He's been there a couple of months, I suppose," Jane said.

"Ever since Mr Roberts took leave to look after the farm while Ann's family are at the hospital in Brisbane," Billy clarified, "after Ann's accident."

"That is far too much of a coincidence!" Patrick muttered, a grim expression on his face.

Patrick's eyes snapped up to look at Billy and Jane.

"This Loup fellow, describe him please."

"He's from Belgium," Billy said, "although he sounds quite French to us. And he has a pencil-thin moustache, with lots of wax in it, that he twists and twirls when he's thinking."

Billy noticed Patrick begin to relax a little. Whatever it was that Patrick was looking for, Billy's description seemed to have ruled out Monsieur Loup.

"Oh, and he has the most amazing pale blue eyes," Jane added, with a slightly dreamy tone in her voice, "they look like icicles."

Then, she shuddered involuntarily.

"But he also has a large ugly scar on his cheek! All the way from his chin to his ear, the poor man."

Patrick Bowman sat bolt upright in his chair. He looked at Mary, who met his gaze and then nodded ever so slightly.

"You have to, Patrick," she said, "you can't afford to wait for normal channels."

"I know," he replied, grimly.

oOo

"Billy, Jane, sit here on the couch," Mary said firmly.

Patrick Bowman stood and walked briskly to the portrait of the King that hung on the wall of their living room. When he got to the portrait, Patrick glanced back over his shoulder at Mary, Billy and Jane, then turned back to the portrait and pressed firmly one of the corners of the frame.

To Billy, the portrait looked exactly the same as every other portrait of the Monarch he had seen in every home, school and office throughout the Colony. However, when Patrick Bowman pressed on the frame, the entire portrait slid upwards, revealing an alcove that had been recessed into the wall.

Patrick reached into the alcove and pulled out a small brass funnel that was connected to a mechanism inside the alcove by a thick black cable. As Patrick lifted the funnel out of the alcove, Billy could hear a ringing sound coming through a speaker mounted into the mechanism.

After a moment, the ringing stopped and a voice came through on the speaker.

"Peale," the voice said.

"Squadron Leader," Patrick replied, directing his voice into the funnel "This is Commander Bowman. I've located Volkov.

"He's here in Caloundra and he's hunting my family."

Chapter 43

Brisbane, Colony of Queensland, Australia
Monday 24 May 1943

"Listen up," Squadron Leader Peale called out across the Operations Room of The Bunker, "we have a confirmed sighting of Volkov. He's in Caloundra and he's targeting the friends and family of the Commander."

After less than two minutes on the secure line with Commander Bowman, Squadron Leader Peale was relaying his orders to the teams.

"The Commander wants Captain Calvert and Warrant Officer Higgs to take the assault party to Caloundra on the *HMS Cooktown*. Make all possible speed. He wants you there within 3 hours."

"Lieutenant Simons," Peale continued, "you're not on the assault party for this mission."

"Sir, I'm fully cleared for..."

Squadron Leader Peale held up his hand to silence the protest from the young officer.

"You're not being sidelined, Lieutenant. Quite the opposite. The Commander wants you on point for this mission, and," he added, "quite frankly, so do I."

"Thank you, Sir."

"Get Corporal Ramirez to take you to Eagle Farm Airfield. I'll organise a fast airship to take you to Caloundra, then to remain on duty with you there. Commander Bowman wants you there in under an hour."

"Aye, aye, Sir," Lieutenant Simons replied, before turning toward the exit to The Bunker.

"Let's go Corporal!" she called, as she ran towards the exit.

oOo

Caloundra, Colony of Queensland, Australia
Monday 24 May 1943

Billy stared open-mouthed at his father.

"I'm sorry I couldn't tell you, William," his father began, "I work for an agency that operates in secret to protect the Empire. We track foreign agents and dissidents, stopping them if they try to undermine the authority of the King."

"So," Jane said slowly, "you're not a salesman for the ginger factory?"

Patrick Bowman smiled humourlessly and shook his head.

"You've done this your whole life?" Billy asked.

"After I graduated from Fifth Form." Patrick replied, "I joined the Navy as an officer. I was recruited to the agency about three years into my tour of duty."

"Does Grandfather know?"

Patrick shook his head sadly.

"No. Your grandfather thinks I left the Navy and entered civilian life as a sales representative. He's never said anything to me, but I've always had a sense that he's a little disappointed that when we go to the ANZAC Day ceremony I'm not in uniform and I don't have any medals to wear for service to the Empire."

Billy nodded, then suddenly realised something.

"But you do have a uniform, don't you? I heard you say you're a Commander. That's only one rank below Grandfather's!"

"That's right, Billy," Patrick nodded, "I'm the Commanding Officer for the Directorate unit that monitors the Queensland Colony."

"And Monsieur Loup is really a foreign agent," Jane said, putting the pieces of the puzzle together.

Suddenly, she put her hand to her mouth in horror.

"And you think he pushed Ann under that carriage!"

Patrick nodded.

"But why?" Billy asked.

"I led a raid last year to stop a very dangerous man, codenamed Volkov - 'The Wolf'. I think he's worked out that I stopped his mission and now he's targeting me."

"By attacking Ann?" Billy asked, "And now Ian?"

Patrick waited a moment before replying, to see if Billy or Jane would make the connection.

"Of course!" Jane exclaimed, "if Volkov hurts Billy's friends, that hurts Billy, which in turn hurts you, Mr Bowman."

Patrick nodded.

"Men like Volkov are trained to cause maximum damage. His approach would be to attack those who are close to me, in a slowly closing circle until he finally gets to me at the end.

"I'm afraid your friend Mouse is in grave danger."

oOo

Bribie Island, Colony of Queensland, Australia
Monday 24 May 1943

A little over two hours after leaving the boathouse, the *Sea Gypsie* had arrived at the southern end of Bribie Island.

"I think there's a wreck somewhere near here," Ian explained to Sean, "but it's not marked on any of the maps."

"Do you know what ship it is?"

"No, the records weren't specific at all. The only thing I could find was a reference in a captain's log about sighting a wreck somewhere around the southern tip of the island."

"Sounds a bit vague," Sean observed, "I thought the captain's logs were supposed to be accurate."

Ian laughed.

"Captains are people too. They make mistakes, they leave things out, and sometimes," he added ruefully, "they add things that aren't quite true."

"Do you mean, there may not be a shipwreck here at all?"

"Well, that's certainly possible, Sean. But there's only one way to find out. Shall we go exploring?"

Sean nodded eagerly, and turned to the section of the console that held the equipment for mapping the seabed. As he flipped some switches to activate the mechanism, a slow, steady 'ping' sound started coming from the speaker in the console.

Twenty minutes later, the ping from the mapping equipment turned urgent, getting louder and faster to get their attention. Ian throttled back the engines on the *Gypsie*, bringing her to a gentle stop. The boat began rocking rhythmically in the swell.

"Well, look at that!" Ian exclaimed.

In front of the *Gypsie* was the bow of a large shipwreck, run aground on the rocky shore of the island. She was listing at about a 10-degree angle to the starboard, and only the front of the ship could be seen on the beach. Ian estimated that perhaps only a quarter of the ship could be seen above the waterline.

"She must be laying on a steep drop-off," Ian said, "and from the angle she's on, you'd almost have to be on top of her to spot her."

"No wonder no one's ever found her before," Sean exclaimed, "we didn't even see her until the equipment picked up the underwater traces."

"I'll drop the fenders over the side, Sean. Can you cast a line over to the wreck, so we can haul ourselves in?"

Sean nodded, and headed out to the locker to get some heavy rope to tie the *Gypsie* to the wreck.

oOo

Caloundra, Colony of Queensland, Australia
Monday 24 May 1943

Patrick stood still on the edge of the small airfield, but every muscle in his body was tense.

Time was critical in this mission, and Volkov had a massive head start. He also had an enormous waterway, Pumicestone Passage, to hide in, along with all of the tiny inlets and small creeks in the mangroves that could shelter the *Sea Gypsie*.

"Let's go, Lieutenant," Patrick muttered under his breath, as the airship *Antelope* inched closer to the ground.

"You can head out to the ship now, Sir," he heard the ground crew chief say, when his team had secured the mooring lines.

Patrick didn't need to be told twice. He sprinted forward and leapt aboard the *Antelope*.

"How long to complete refuelling," Patrick glanced at the name badge of the young Air Force Officer sitting in the cockpit, "Flying Officer Davies?"

"About 20 minutes, Sir."

"Very well," Patrick fumed.

He needed to get airborne, to begin the search for the *Sea Gypsie*, but he couldn't afford to leave the airfield without full fuel tanks. Patrick knew they needed to stay on the search for as long as possible and didn't have time to return to Caloundra for refuelling.

"What do you need me to do, Sir?" Lieutenant Simons asked.

Patrick looked at her and saw that the Navy officer had realised he needed something concrete to focus on while the refuelling was underway.

He nodded, once again reminded how valuable this officer was to his team.

"We're going to fly low over the Passage, Lieutenant, in a widening search grid. I want you to use your enhanced vision to search for a steam yacht called *Sea Gypsie*. I believe Volkov is on board and is a threat to the crew."

"Understood, Sir."

Patrick glanced at the chronometer mounted in the wall of the gondola, then turned and opened a large map on the table behind the cockpit.

"Flying Officer," he called to the pilot, "show me the search grid."

Chapter 44

Bribie Island, Colony of Queensland, Australia
Monday 24 May 1943

"There," Sean said, grunting, "that should hold her."

It had taken nearly fifteen sweaty minutes to tie up the *Gypsie* so she was bumping gently against the side of the shipwreck. From this position, Ian and Sean only needed to take a large step across and slightly upwards, to be standing on the deck of the wreck.

"We need to try to find out the name of the ship," Ian told Sean, "so I'd like you to search through the bow sections, looking for any logs, journals, orders or other documents that might give us a clue as to her identity."

Sean nodded, reaching into the equipment locker above his head and removing a bundle of clear bags, in which he could seal any books or papers he found. He passed a second bundle of bags to Ian, who tucked them into a pouch on his webbing.

Both boys were wearing webbing, which was similar to the style issued to cadets in the Empire Service Scheme. Unlike the green of the military issue, though, these webbing sets were black and had pouches that could contain exploring equipment instead of ammunition.

"I'm going to head towards the stern." Ian continued, "There's likely to be some identifying information in the engine compartment, or perhaps in the crew quarters."

"Won't that part of the ship be underwater?" Sean asked, looking with concern at Ian.

"No, I think she's run aground, rather than being holed. If that's the case, there won't be any flooding in the compartments below the waterline."

The two boys moved out of the equipment locker, though the saloon and onto the rear deck of the *Gypsie*.

"Are you ready?" Ian asked.

Sean grinned in reply.

"Then let's go!" Ian exclaimed, as they jumped across the small gap and onto the deck of the wrecked ship.

oOo

Volkov had found that he'd been able to move unobserved around the boat throughout their journey so far. When the two boys were in the wheelhouse, Volkov was free to move about in the saloon. While there, he'd quickly found a way to turn on the intercom remotely, so that while he was secreted in the saloon, he could hear what Ian and Sean were discussing in the wheelhouse.

When they moved into the equipment locker, Volkov was able to hide in the crawl space between that room and the head. With the engines of the *Gypsie* turned off, he'd been able to wear his goggles and to tune in to the planning session in the next room.

"So," he thought, "they're going to separate. Good."

Volkov had been wondering how he would go about incapacitating the Byrne boy, so he would be free to attack young Mister Landsborough. Now, they had solved the problem for him.

After they finished their planning and had collected their equipment, Ian and Sean had moved through the saloon and out onto the rear deck. Volkov waited until he heard the soft click of the door to the saloon before he climbed carefully out of his hiding place.

While he waited for the two explorers to leave the *Gypsie* and board the wrecked ship, Volkov looked closely at the contents of the equipment locker.

"Excellent," he said softly, "that's exactly what I'm looking for."

Volkov picked up two small items and slid them into his pockets, where the new additions joined the equipment he'd been issued all those months ago, before he left Moscow.

Silently, he stole out onto the deck. The boys had already gone across to the wreck, and Volkov was alone on the steam yacht. He paused for the briefest moment, then deftly leapt across the narrow gap and began to move towards the stern of the shipwreck.

oOo

Caloundra, Colony of Queensland, Australia
Monday 24 May 1943

Billy was pacing slowly around the living room, his hands thrust deep into his pockets.

He knew he'd done the right thing by confiding in his parents, although at the time he made that decision, he had no idea how much his father would be able to help. He was still stunned about his parent's double-life, but in this moment, Billy couldn't be more grateful for his father's influence and ability to take swift action.

Jane was seated on the couch, her head in her hands. Billy could see her shoulders gently shaking, and he knew she was crying. For the first time he could remember, Billy wasn't sure what to do to comfort Jane, or even if he should try.

With a troubled look on his face, Billy looked at his mother, silently communicating his need for her advice. Mary Bowman caught the look from her son, and slowly stood up.

"I'm going to make a pot of tea," she said simply, then turned and walked into the kitchen.

Jane didn't stir, and Billy followed his mother silently into the other room.

"I feel powerless to help Ian," he began, "but surely I can help Jane!"

"Sometimes," his mother said gently, "the best thing you can do to help someone is to not help them."

"That makes no sense at all!" Billy cried, "How is not helping, helping?"

"Jane needs to process her emotions right now, William.

"She doesn't need you or anyone else trying to give her a solution to her problem, or to try to solve it for her. This is about how she feels, not what she's doing."

"So, what do I do?"

"You wait."

"Really?"

"Yes, William, really.

"Jane is a clever girl. She's been dealing with a lot of different emotions, all mixed up together, over the last few months. This situation with Ian and Volkov has brought all of those feelings to a head.

"Give her time to process them, to reflect and to consider. It's what she needs most right now. If she reaches out to you for a hug, or some sort of reassurance, give it to her. But otherwise, leave her be."

oOo

Pumicestone Passage, Colony of Queensland, Australia
Monday 24 May 1943

The drone from the engines of the *Antelope* reverberated through every muscle and sinew of her body. To Leslie Simons, it felt as though she was being held in the rough calloused hand of a giant, who was shaking her from side to side in his fist.

She had absolutely no intention of complaining, of course. This was a dire situation, with at least one young man's life, and possibly two, hanging in the balance.

Leslie knew she had every right to be bitter. Volkov had stolen her arm, her eye and, for a long time, she thought he'd stolen her career as well. She simply couldn't imagine her life without being in service to the King, and she was grateful beyond words to the Chief and the Directorate for giving her the ability to continue as an agent.

This mission, then, was her first opportunity to repay the debt she owed to the Chief for saving her. There was no way she was going to complain about the rough ride she had to endure.

In order to enable Lieutenant Simons to scan the largest area of ocean in the shortest amount of time, Commander Bowman had ordered her to lie on the loading ramp of the *Antelope*, with her head hanging over the edge of the ramp in the open air.

The ramp itself descended from the rear of the gondola, and was designed to allow trolleys and carts of equipment and supplies to be easily loaded and unloaded from the airship. When raised, the ramp became the rear wall of the gondola. When lowered, the entire rear section of the airship compartment was open to the sky.

"Sir, I must object!" the young pilot had almost shouted at Patrick, when he was told about lowering the ramp during flight, "this is dangerous and highly unorthodox.

"The airship will be incredibly difficult to manoeuvre with the ramp down, not to mention the risk to your officer."

The pilot drew a deep breath.

"I'm sorry, Sir," he asserted, "as airship captain, I cannot allow this course of action."

Patrick fixed the young officer with a glowering stare.

"Flying Officer Davies," Patrick said with a terrifying calmness to his voice, "your objections are noted. Now, you will carry out my orders or you will be relieved of duty."

The pilot held his ground.

"Sir, if you relieve me of duty, you won't have anyone to fly the *Antelope*."

"I do not have time for this, Flying Officer," Patrick said quietly, without taking his eyes off the pilot, "I am a Navy Officer, but I completed pilot training with the RAF in 1931 and have over 200 hours logged on this airship type."

"I am more than qualified and capable of flying the *Antelope* on this mission.

"Now, Flying Officer, I will ask you one last time - will you take your post or will you step aside?"

For a moment, the Flying Officer was speechless. Then, he managed to recover himself.

"Lieutenant Simons," he stammered, "let me show you the override that will allow you to lower the ramp while we're in flight."

Chapter 45

Bribie Island, Colony of Queensland, Australia
Monday 24 May 1943

Ian had struggled for the last few minutes to pull a large watertight door open. The shipwreck was on such an angle that he had to wedge his legs against the bulkhead and pull with all his might to overcome gravity and the weight of the door to get it open.

Once the door reached the point of equilibrium, though, it only took a small additional force to swing it all the way open. The metal handle of the door slammed into the bulkhead with a loud bang that echoed through the adjoining chamber and made this section of the ship quiver slightly.

With the door open, Ian was able to peer into the large cabin beyond. The far corners of the room were shrouded in darkness, but a ventilation shaft pierced the ceiling and Ian could see a sliver of afternoon sunlight coming through the opening.

"That shaft goes up to the top deck," Ian thought, as he swung himself into the room.

The floor of the room was littered with broken metal and pipes, lengths of chain and broken timbers and furnishings. Ian could see that some of the pieces on the floor were once part of the ventilation shaft, and there was a hole in the floor where the shaft had once continued downwards.

"I see," he mused, "the shaft went all the way through the ship, from the deck to probably the engine room."

Ian ran a hand along a thick metal pole that ran from floor to ceiling in the compartment, right next to what was left of the ventilation shaft on this deck.

"Of course," he realised, "this metal pole was the support column for the shaft, to prevent the hollow tube from flexing too much in heavy seas."

Ian began lowering himself carefully along the floor, heading for the far end of the room, when he heard a loud metallic clang above him.

He spun around to see the watertight door, the one he had worked so hard to open, had somehow closed behind him, trapping him in this compartment.

oOo

Pumicestone Passage, Colony of Queensland, Australia
Monday 24 May 1943

"Anything?" Patrick shouted above the noise of the propellers of the *Antelope*.

"Nothing yet, Sir," came the reply.

Leslie had been lying almost motionless on the loading ramp of the airship for over an hour now, the only movement coming from the gentle tilting her head as she carefully scanned left and right on the ocean below her.

Patrick felt a sudden rush of paternal pride in the young Lieutenant. She had gone through so much pain with her treatment and the fitting of the artificial arm and eye. And yet, she had never once given up. When things went badly during the treatment, she simply shrugged it off and tried again.

Now, she was displaying the exact same tenacity for this mission. Not for him, not for his family, but for the estranged friend of his son.

No, he reminded himself, she's not doing this for Ian. She's doing this for a citizen of the Empire, because that's what service means.

"Carry on, Lieutenant," he called.

oOo

Bribie Island, Colony of Queensland, Australia
Monday 24 May 1943

Sean heard the bang, and felt the vibration through the metal decking, even though he was almost all the way to the bow of the wreck.

"Sounds like Ian's found himself a watertight door," he thought.

During his own journey up towards the bow, Sean had come across a couple of watertight doors. He'd needed to push quite hard on them, putting his shoulder into the movement.

"No wonder it's such a loud clang," he said to himself, as he thought of the struggle Ian would have with getting a door open.

Although Sean was stronger, Ian was wiry, and Sean felt confident he'd be able to manage the watertight doors.

He began to whistle his favourite tune, a happy little sea shanty his grandfather had taught him, as he climbed higher towards the bow of the ship.

oOo

As Ian tried to make his way back to the watertight door, a figure emerged from the shadows to his right.

Ian whirled towards the shape, but stopped when he recognised the figure.

"Monsieur Loup?" he exclaimed, "What are you doing here?"

"An excellent question, Landsborough," Volkov growled, losing his Belgian accent and reverting to his Russian intonation.

"I don't understand…"

"Well, then, let me explain."

Volkov rushed forward with incredible speed, holding something that looked like a fountain pen in his right hand.

Ian tried to duck away, but he was off balance and still struggling to comprehend what was going on.

Volkov grabbed Ian's webbing with his left hand and swiftly brought the pen around, stabbing it into Ian's exposed neck. Ian briefly cried out, before the sound was abruptly cut off and every muscle in his body locked rigid.

A moment later, all of his muscles relaxed and he could no longer support his own weight. Volkov took the strain of Ian's collapsing body through his grip on the boy's webbing.

Volkov carefully removed the pen from Ian's neck, and depressed the small lever on the side that retracted the needle. He then lowered Ian to the deck of the compartment and leaned his inert body against the metal support pole.

"You've been injected with a toxin that will paralyse all of your voluntary muscles for the next few hours. Do not worry, your heart will still beat and you will still be able to breath."

"At least, for the moment," Volkov grinned evilly.

"No doubt you are wondering why I am doing this to you. The answer is both simple and complicated.

"The simple part is that I am doing this for revenge. The complicated part is that I am not seeking revenge on you.

"You, young Ian Landsborough, are simply a pawn in this game."

Volkov took a step or two away from Ian and bent down to pick up a length of chain that was laying on the deck. The chain was thick and heavy, and Ian could see from the corner of his eye that the chain was wedged under a huge timber beam that had crashed onto the compartment floor.

Dragging the chain over to Ian, Volkov wrapped it tightly around one of his ankles. He then reached into his pocket and brought out one of the items he'd taken from the equipment store on the *Gypsie*.

"I'd like to thank you for this padlock," Volkov said, "I didn't bring one with me."

With a flourish, Volkov snapped the padlock onto the chain, locking it tightly to Ian's ankle.

"We don't want you getting away," he chuckled, tugging viciously on the chain to make sure it didn't slip off. The chain dug in and a small trickle of blood seeped down towards Ian's foot. The pain must have been severe, but Ian couldn't cry out because of the paralysing toxin.

"I had considered leaving you here to starve," Volkov admitted, "but I think that since we're below the waterline, we can be more … nautical."

Volkov moved down towards one of the lower corners of the compartment. Ian saw him reach into his other pocket and pull out a small tube.

If Ian wasn't paralysed, his eyes would have gone wide when he recognised the tube. It had come from the equipment locker and was one of his grandfather's miniaturised explosive charges.

Volkov planned to blow a hole in the side of the wreck and let the seawater pour in. The toxin meant that Ian wouldn't be able to move to escape, and even if he could move, the chain locked around his ankle only had about 6 feet of length before it was pulled tight.

"I think you have worked out my plan, Landsborough," Volkov chuckled, seeing the fear in Ian's eyes.

With a swift movement, Volkov put his hands over his ears, just as the explosive charge detonated. The roar of the explosive was deafening, and Ian's body rocked from the concussion of the blast.

Most of the shockwave was absorbed by the debris that littered the floor of the compartment, but Ian felt blood running down the side of his face and suspected one of his eardrums had burst. The pain from the wound was unimaginable.

The water poured into the compartment, and Ian sensed he would have perhaps fifteen or twenty minutes before he was fully submerged.

"And now," Volkov said, "I will bid you farewell. Dasvidaniya."

In his hand, Volkov held a small cylinder with a mouthpiece on the top. He quickly bit down on the mouthpiece and turned a small valve on the side of the cylinder. Ian saw his cheeks puff out, as air from the cylinder flowed into Volkov's mouth.

With a mock salute, Volkov turned and dove into the water. Ian could see him swimming under the water, breathing from the cylinder. In a moment, his shadow passed out through the hole the explosive had made in the side of the ship and then he was gone.

Ian sat frozen in the flooding compartment, alone and afraid.

Chapter 46

Bribie Island, Colony of Queensland, Australia
Monday 24 May 1943

"That was not a pressure door!" Sean thought when he heard the enormous boom that echoed through the wreck.

He felt the tremor through the ship, much stronger than the slam from one of the watertight doors. A frown creased his forehead and he stopped whistling the sea shanty.

"Something is definitely not right," he muttered aloud.

For a moment, Sean was torn with indecision. He tried to weigh up the importance of finding the information about the wrecked ship, against the need to investigate the noise in case Ian was in trouble.

In his imagination, Sean pictured bulkheads collapsing, or debris shifting across the sloping deck, trapping Ian under huge timber beams or twisted metal pipes. He saw his friend injured under the rubble, unable to get himself free.

Sean turned away from the bow of the ship, and started making his way aft, towards the area where Ian was exploring.

oOo

Pumicestone Passage, Colony of Queensland, Australia
Monday 24 May 1943

Lieutenant Simons stopped the constant turning of her head and stared directly south. She'd caught sight of movement in that direction, but it was a long way off, down near the southern tip of Bribie Island.

"It's probably just another whale, or a pod of dolphins," she thought, and was about to resume her search, when a tiny red light blinked in the corner of her vision.

Leslie knew the light wasn't really a light, of course. She knew that it was simply the way her optical implant created a warning in her brain when the mechanism detected something, and the programming decided to alert her to it.

She switched to infra-red mode and saw a strong heat plume in the same area as the movement she'd detected a moment earlier. It was far too hot to be a whale. It was almost certainly a vessel.

"Commander," she shouted back into the open rear cabin of the airship.

Patrick was by her side on the ramp in moments, risking the deadly fall into the ocean below by not wasting time securing himself to a safety line.

"Yes, Lieutenant."

"Movement and a heat plume at the far southern edge of the island. I think it's too hot to be an organism, and it's too close to the shore to be a merchant vessel."

"Good work, Lieutenant, we'll check it out. Stay here and direct us to the contact. Do not let it out of your sight!"

"Aye, Sir!"

oOo

Bribie Island, Colony of Queensland, Australia
Monday 24 May 1943

Volkov's dive into the water in the compartment of the wrecked ship came as a shock. Even though he was in a sub-tropical region of the world, the water was cold enough to make his head hurt and his body ache.

Then, Volkov remembered that he was in the southern hemisphere, and it was moving into winter at this time of year. For a moment, he longed for the bright sunshine of summer in his beloved Russia.

Shaking his head to clear it, Volkov began to swim strongly through the hole in the side of the ship, before turning gracefully in the water and heading for the surface. His breathing was slow and steady, the cylinder providing all the air he needed to escape the flooding compartment.

When his head broke the surface of the water, he threw the cylinder away and it sank, unceremoniously, towards the bottom of the ocean. Volkov looked around to get his bearings.

The light from the late afternoon sun was just starting to weaken, and he realised he'd surfaced about 30 meters from the stern of the *Sea Gypsie*.

Once aboard the vessel, he would be able to start the engines and steam back to the mainland. He knew he'd be leaving the Byrne boy stranded on the island, but there was plenty of food and water to allow him to survive until he could attract the attention of a passing ship.

He began to swim towards the steam yacht.

oOo

Sean had slipped more than once on his way to the stern of the ship, scraping his knee on the rough plating of the deck. Finally, though, he reached a large watertight door that barred his way to the lower part of the ship.

He couldn't imagine why Ian would have closed this door behind him.

"Perhaps Ian couldn't open this door," he thought, "in which case, he would have decided to try a different route."

Sean was about to turn away when he heard a strange sound coming from the compartment on the other side of the watertight door. He listened carefully, holding his breath to be able to hear the sound more clearly.

It was a rushing sound, a gurgling sound, and with a sudden, terrifying realisation, Sean worked out what it was. The compartment on the other side of the door was flooding.

"Ian!" he shouted through the thick metal door, "Ian! Are you in there? Can you hear me?"

There was no response, but Sean couldn't afford to take the risk. He grabbed hold of the handle on the watertight door and heaved.

Nothing happened. The door didn't move.

"Must be the pressure on the other side," Sean thought.

He braced himself against the bulkhead, placing both his feet on the wall panel and grabbing the door handle with both hands. Sean took up the strain, then began to heave on the door handle, using the strength of his entire body to separate the door from its frame.

As Sean drove upwards with his legs, the heavy metal door began to move, slowly at first, then gaining momentum. Sweat broke out on Sean's forehead from the exertion, and his face turned red. His knuckles were white from the tightness of his grip on the handle of the door.

With a final heave, Sean pulled the door open to the point of equilibrium. For a moment, the door tottered on its hinges, and Sean worried that it would slam shut again. He didn't want to be in the way of the door if that happened, but he didn't think he would have time to move aside.

Then, to his immense relief, the door started to swing towards the far bulkhead. With another enormous bang, the door slammed into the far wall, sending paint chips flying from the impact.

Sean peered into the compartment from the doorway. He saw the water pouring into the compartment from a giant wound in the side of the ship. Then he saw Ian slumped against a metal support pole, the water already up to his hips and rising fast.

"Ian!" he called, "Are you all right? Come on, man, let's go!"

Ian didn't respond. He didn't even turn his head to look at Sean.

Thinking Ian must be unconscious, Sean jumped through the doorway and landed with a splash in the water on the floor of the compartment. He began to move towards Ian, planning to hoist the younger boy onto his shoulder and carry him up to the deck of the ship.

As he reached Ian, he realised something was very, very wrong. Ian's eyes were open and Sean could see the fear and anger Ian was feeling. How could Ian be unconscious and be able to show emotions?

Right now, the reason why didn't matter. The water level was rising too fast. In the time it took for Sean to move from the hatchway to the support pole, the water had risen from Ian's hips to his waist.

"Time to go, Captain," Sean said, reaching down for Ian's webbing to use as a handhold to lift him up.

"Ankle," Ian whispered hoarsely, barely able to force the word out through his paralysed lips.

Sean stopped at the feeble croak from Ian, and looked at his friend's face. Then, he dropped to his knees, sending up a small splash in the water. Sean ran his hand along Ian's leg until he felt the chain.

Carefully, he lifted up the leg and examined the chain. He was puzzled for a moment when he saw the padlock, then he realised that Ian had been deliberately tied up in this compartment and left to drown. Sean's face contorted in anger.

He could see that there was no way to get the chain off Ian's leg. But maybe, he could free the other end of the chain.

Sean traced the chain back towards the point where it was trapped under the debris. Wrapping the thick chain around his forearm, Sean braced his feet on the deck and began to haul on the chain.

The links went tight, and there was a low, slow creaking sound. It felt like the beam that held the chain fast might be starting to move. Sean gripped the chain even tighter, creating small wounds on his hands from the rough surface. Tiny drops of blood dripped through his fingers and splashed into the water.

Then, with a sickening thud, the wooden beam wedged into a depression in the deck and stuck fast. Sean continued to pull for a moment longer, before realising the chain wouldn't move any further.

He dropped the chain and dove into the water, trying to see if there was a way to manoeuvre the beam out of the depression. When he broke the surface of the water a minute later, Ian could see the frustration on his friend's face.

"It's no good, Ian," he said forlornly, after splashing back to sit next to the stricken boy, "I just can't shift the beam."

"Go." Ian croaked.

Sean shook his head.

"No," he said stubbornly, "there has to be another way."

Chapter 47

Pumicestone Passage, Colony of Queensland, Australia
Monday 24 May 1943

"Can't you get any more speed out of her, Flying Officer?"

Patrick was trying not to let his frustration carry through in his tone, but he was finding it incredibly difficult to keep him emotions under control.

"I'm afraid not, Sir," the pilot replied grimly, "since we've turned south, we've been fighting a massive headwind. I've pushed the engines to full, but she just can't go any faster with this wind."

"Could we get away from the wind at a higher altitude?"

"Possibly, but the time it would take us to climb is longer than the time it will take to get to the tip of the island at this speed."

"How long to get to the point where the vessel was sighted?"

"About 20 minutes, Sir."

Since Leslie had spotted the heat plume of the vessel, it had moved quickly further south. The Lieutenant continued to track it, but the further it got ahead of them the harder it was for her to keep a fix on it.

As frustrated as he was, Patrick couldn't blame the wind. It was just how it was. He needed to look at other options to pursue the fleeing vessel.

"Very well," Patrick said with a sigh, "carry on."

oOo

Bribie Island, Colony of Queensland, Australia
Monday 24 May 1943

Volkov found the *Sea Gypsie* to be very well stocked.

After climbing aboard, he found a storage chest full of soft white towels. He quickly stripped off his wet clothes and used two of the towels to dry himself thoroughly. He threw the wet clothes and the towels into a corner of the saloon.

Rummaging through the lockers, he was able to locate some coveralls, socks and underwear in his size. In a small compartment, he found a rack of soft soled shoes, with canvas uppers and a rippled tread pattern, ideal for standing on a wet, slippery deck.

Once dressed, Volkov moved to the wheelhouse and primed the steam engines. He needed somewhere to hide for a few weeks, before moving on to the next phase of his plan. As much as the *Sea Gypsie* would make an excellent base of operations, the steam yacht was just too big a target for Commander Bowman's forces. No, he had no choice but to abandon the vessel, once he was safely ashore.

A few minutes later, he was able to throttle up the engines and set course for the mainland.

oOo

The water level was rising rapidly. Already, it was half-way up Ian's chest, and Sean thought it would be over his head within the next ten minutes.

Everything Sean had done to open the padlock or break the chain had failed. The padlock was a new, high-quality one, with a tempered steel hasp, and Sean didn't have the foggiest idea about how to pick a lock. Even though the chain was as old as the wreck, this compartment had been completely dry until a few minutes ago. There was no rust on the chain at all, let alone any spots that might have been weakened by exposure to salt and sea.

Sean stopped struggling with the chain, looking around the compartment for something - anything - to help his friend survive. There had to be something he could try!

"Go," Ian managed to gasp, forcing the words out through his still paralysed lips.

Sean ignored him. He wasn't leaving his friend to die while he saved himself. That simply wasn't an option.

Looking around once again, Sean noticed the ventilation shaft. Or at least what was left of the shaft. Almost directly above Ian's head was the broken shaft, wide enough for someone to crawl through.

That wasn't going to work, of course. Ian was attached by the lock and chain to the deck of the compartment. And even if Sean could free him, he was paralysed and couldn't climb out through the shaft on his own.

It was then that inspiration struck. Sean didn't need to get Ian out of the compartment. All he needed to do was to get Ian's head and shoulders into the opening of the ventilation shaft, near the ceiling of the compartment. Ian could then breathe, while Sean worked out their next move.

Reaching down with both hands, Sean grabbed the shoulder straps of Ian's webbing and hauled him upright. Quickly, before the paralysed boy slid back down again, Sean released his grip on the webbing and threw his arms around Ian.

Holding Ian in a bear hug, chest to chest, Sean scrambled to find purchase on the now slippery deck of the compartment.

Over and over again, Sean tried to wedge his feet against some debris on the floor, only to have it roll or slide away. Each time, Sean collapsed back into the water, dragging Ian with him.

Exhausted, Sean gently lowered Ian onto the deck. The water was now lapping at Ian's shoulders. There wasn't much time before Ian would start to drown.

oOo

Pumicestone Passage, Colony of Queensland, Australia
Monday 24 May 1943

"Can you get me radio contact with the *Cooktown*?" Patrick asked.

"I think so, Sir," replied the radio operator, "Navy works on different frequencies to us, so it will have to be via relay through a ground station."

"Is there no way you can get a direct connection with my ship?"

"Not without knowing the classified Navy frequencies, Commander."

Patrick began tapping his knuckles against the map table.

Rat-a-tat-a-tat, rat-a-tat-a tat

It always frustrated him that the different parts of the service didn't share information between themselves. He had Army, Navy and Air Force personnel working in his team, and they talked to each other and shared information constantly.

Then he reminded himself that his team worked across the services because the Chief demanded it. Anyone who brought inter-service rivalries into the Directorate was quickly told to drop their attitude or return to their previous unit.

Suddenly, Patrick stopped his agitated tapping against the table. He worked in a team with Navy personnel. In fact, he had a Navy Officer no more than 15 feet away from him right now.

"Lieutenant Simons!" He shouted down to her, "do you know the current radio frequencies for Navy vessels?"

"They're in my briefing bag, Sir," she shouted back, not taking her eyes off the heat signature, "It's stowed behind the pilot's seat."

Five minutes later, Patrick was in direct radio contact with Captain Calvin aboard *HMS Cooktown*. He quickly brought the Army Captain up to date with their findings.

"What's you're estimated time of arrival, Captain?"

There was silence for a moment, then the reply came back from the catamaran.

"We're still at least 20 minutes away, Sir. We were almost at Caloundra, but have just reversed course and are now heading for the southern tip of Bribie Island."

Still far too long. The *Antelope* would get there first, but how far ahead would the fleeing vessel be by then?

Patrick began rapping his knuckles on the table again.

oOo

Bribie Island, Colony of Queensland, Australia
Monday 24 May 1943

Sean could only see one way left for him to get Ian's paralysed body out of the water and into the ventilation shaft. It was a desperate measure, but it was the only choice he had left.

"Hold tight, Ian," he said, his teeth chattering from the cold of the water, "Just a minute longer and we'll have you up and out of the water."

Sean released the mechanisms on his webbing, loosening both the shoulder straps and the waist belt to their longest length. He then quickly undid the belt and slipped the harness straps off his shoulders.

Gripping the webbing by the belt strap in his right hand, Sean reached back and flung the webbing around the support pole that ran from the floor to the ceiling in the compartment. As the webbing arced around the pole, Sean caught the loose side with his left hand. In a single smooth move, Sean had wrapped the webbing around the pole.

He quickly backed into the webbing, shrugged into the shoulder straps and fastened the buckle on the waist strap. He was now wearing the webbing again, but this time the support pole was trapped between his back and the straps of the webbing harness.

"I'm going to lift you up now, Ian," Sean explained to the younger boy, "I'll duck under the water and then lift you on my shoulders."

Sean took a deep breath, then lowered himself under the water. Being careful not to let the shoulder straps of his webbing slip out of position, Sean manoeuvred Ian into position. His lungs were starting to burn from the exertion, and Sean knew he'd need to surface soon.

With enormous effort, Sean drove upwards with his knees, lifting Ian up on his shoulders. As Sean had connected his webbing to the support pole, Ian's head was perfectly aligned with the ventilation shaft. As Sean rose out of the water, Ian's head went neatly into the opening of the ventilation shaft. When Sean was standing fully upright, Ian's shoulders were inside the shaft, well above the rising level of the water.

Sean began to feel his feet slipping on the decking, and quickly reached his hand around to the adjuster on his webbing. With a twist of the button, the pistons hissed and the cables whirred, pulling the webbing tight against his body.

The adjustment also locked Sean's body onto the support pole. He winced as the hard metal pole slapped into his back, the edges cutting into his flesh. The webbing harness now held him fast to the pole, and Sean could even lift his feet off the deck without sliding down the pole.

"There," he said, panting a little, "that will hold us in place."

The water level in the compartment was at Sean's chest, as he was taller than Ian. Then, Sean realised the water was still rising. For a moment, Sean was silent, catching his breath and feeling the cold from the water working through his body.

"Ian," he called up to the young man on his shoulders, "I know you can't respond, but I hope you can hear me.

"I thought I should tell you how much I appreciate all the time I've been able to spend with you these last few months. It's been an absolute pleasure to get to know you, to be your drill instructor and your Quartermaster."

The water level had reached Sean's shoulders in the short time he'd been speaking. He realised he needed to hurry to get the words out.

"I know we got off to a rocky start," he chuckled, "on the first day of school.

"But I want you to know I'm a different person now, a better person, and a lot of that has to do with the way you and Billy and Jane treated me. You were fair and forgiving, even though you didn't have to be, and it helped more than you can possibly know."

The water was lapping at Sean's chin, and he knew he only had a few moments left before he went under.

"Thank," he spluttered, trying to get the words out as the water tried to find a way into his mouth, "thank you, Mouse."

Sean closed his mouth and drew a deep breath in through his nose, just before the water rose up to cover the rest of his face. For almost two minutes, he was sustained by that breath. Then his body shook violently, before finally going limp in the harness.

Ian wanted to cry out, to scream in anger and grief. But without the ability to move his muscles, all he could do was sit atop Sean's shoulders, letting the tears fall from his eyes.

Chapter 48

Bribie Island, Colony of Queensland, Australia
Monday 24 May 1943

"Do you still have a track on the vessel, Lieutenant?"

"Yes, Sir, although she's close to going out of range."

Patrick turned to the pilot of the airship.

"All possible speed, Flying Officer Davies."

"Yes, Sir. The head wind has eased quite a bit, so we should be able to continue to catch up to the vessel."

Just ahead of the *Antelope* was the southern tip of Bribie Island. Patrick peered through one of the observation windows of the gondola into the late afternoon sunlight. Below them, he could see the untamed forest of the island tapering onto a rocky beach.

He paused. Something looked odd on the beach. He cocked his head to the side and changed his position to look out through a different window.

After a moment, he realised he was looking at a wrecked ship, run aground on the rocky beach. Her bow was above the water, but her stern was submerged, and she was listing to starboard.

"She must be caught on a steep drop-off." Patrick thought distractedly.

He turned away from the window, intending to mark the position of the wreck on the map spread out on the nearby table, when a shout from the loading ramp stopped him in his tracks.

"Commander," Lieutenant Simons called from the ramp, "there's a heat signature inside that wrecked ship!"

Patrick came to kneel next to the Lieutenant on the ramp.

"Do you still have contact with the fleeing vessel?" he asked with an edge in his voice.

"Yes, Sir," Lieutenant Simons replied defensively, "the optical implant is capable of continuing a track on one object, while providing input from another."

Patrick breathed a sigh of relief, then realised he'd spoken to harshly to the Navy Officer.

"I'm sorry, Leslie," he said softly, "I didn't mean to criticise."

"I understand, Sir. You have a lot to deal with at the moment."

Patrick nodded, grateful for the professionalism of this young officer.

"Tell me about the heat signature in the wreck, Lieutenant," Patrick said, returning his voice to his normal calm tone.

"It's too small to be an adult, so it might be one of the missing children."

Patrick considered this for a moment. If they landed to pick up whoever was on the wreck, they'd almost certainly lose their track on the fleeing vessel. The wreck, on the other hand, had been there for years, so they could come back after they apprehended the vessel.

He was about to issue the order to continue the pursuit when Lieutenant Simons spoke up again.

"Sir, I've been watching the heat signature over the last minute," she advised Patrick, "and it's fading quite quickly."

"Fading, like the signal is moving out of range?"

"No, Sir, fading like the person generating the signal is dying."

This changed everything for Patrick. He whirled around and called out to the pilot.

"All stop, Flying Officer! How long will it take you to land the airship?"

"All stop, Commander," the pilot replied instantly, and the *Antelope* shuddered slightly as the propellers reversed to bring her to a hovering position near the wreck.

"It'll take about ten minutes to get her on the ground, Commander. There's no ground crew to assist, so the whole landing process has to be done with thruster controls."

Patrick looked at Leslie, who shook her head.

"He won't last that long, Sir."

oOo

Pumicestone Passage, Colony of Queensland, Australia
Monday 24 May 1943

"I have Commander Bowman on the radio for you, Captain Calvin," the Midshipman called out across the bridge of the *Cooktown*.

Captain Calvin moved lithely across the room, despite the roll of the ship in the swell. For an Army Officer, she was quickly getting her sea legs.

"Go ahead, Commander," she said into the microphone.

"Captain Calvin," Patrick advised, "what is your location?"

"Still approximately ten minutes from the southern tip of Bribie Island, Sir."

Patrick groaned. He'd hoped the *Cooktown* would be close enough to the wreck to undertake the rescue, freeing the airship to continue the pursuit of the fleeing vessel.

"We've located what we believe to be one of the missing children," Patrick reported, "in the wreck of a ship on the southern tip of the island. He appears to be in critical condition and requires urgent intervention."

"We will conduct the rescue attempt, as we're already on-site."

"Understood, Sir."

"The fleeing vessel is steaming on a heading of two-one-three degrees. Your orders are to pursue at all possible speed, and report back to me every 30 minutes on your status."

"Aye, Sir," the Captain replied, before turning away from the radio to pass the new orders to the bridge crew.

oOo

While Patrick was on the radio to the *Cooktown*, he had felt the *Antelope* descending. He had presumed the pilot was bringing her in for a landing and had ignored the sensation while he was briefing Captain Calvin.

Now he was off the radio, he noticed that the descent had stopped. He glanced out one of the observation windows, and saw that the airship was hovering over the ocean, next to the wreck, about twenty-five feet in the air.

"What's going on, Flying Officer?" Patrick barked.

Didn't the pilot realise that time was critical?

"Orders from Lieutenant Simons, Sir," the pilot responded.

Patrick turned towards the loading ramp at the back of the airship, planning to demand an explanation about exactly what Lieutenant Simons thought she was doing.

Instead of shouting at the Lieutenant lying prone on the loading ramp, Patrick found her standing on the ramp, a grim, determined look on her face as she finished undoing the safety harness.

"Sorry Sir, there's no time to lose," she said matter-of-factly, before dropping the harness onto the ramp.

"Thanks Samuel," she called out to the pilot, over Patrick's shoulder.

Patrick whirled to see the Flying Officer giving a 'thumbs-up' sign, then spun back around to see the Lieutenant step backwards off the edge of the loading ramp and drop out of sight towards the ocean below.

Racing to the edge of the ramp, Patrick watched the Lieutenant perform a perfect pin-drop into the ocean, landing just 10 feet from the edge of the wreck. After three or four seconds, she broke the surface of the water, and began a strong overhand stroke towards the side of the wreck.

In that moment, Patrick didn't know whether to be furious or proud of Leslie Simons.

oOo

Leslie hit the water hard, but the pin-drop technique she had learned in basic training meant she sliced into the water like an arrow. She didn't quite expect the water to be so cold, and she needed to stifle a cry of shock as she went under the surface.

As the dive bottomed out, Leslie used her optical implant to scan the wreck. She needed to find the quickest route to get to the boy. Her estimation was that he only had a few more minutes of life left.

"He must be partially submerged," she thought, "for his heat signature to be falling so rapidly."

The instant the Lieutenant broke the surface of the ocean, she started swimming towards the wreck. The distance was only about ten feet, but Leslie knew that if she didn't get out of the water soon, her own body would start to shut down.

"Hope I don't rust," she thought ruefully, with a half-smile on her face.

When Leslie reached the side of the shipwreck, she began to tread water. Lifting up her left arm, she pointed her hand, palm up, at a spot just above the railing on the top deck of the ship. Carefully, Leslie bent her index finger back and touched one of the buttons recessed into her palm.

With a small pop, followed by a hiss, a metal arrow shot out of her left wrist, trailing a thin steel cable behind it. Both the arrow and the cable were stored inside her artificial arm, and scientists had told her the cable was a thin as a piece of twine, but as strong as an anchor cable.

The head of the arrow expanded as it flew, creating tiny barbs that pointed back along the shaft. By the time the arrowhead had travelled ten feet from her wrist, it had taken on the form of a grappling hook.

When the arrow was over the railing, Leslie pulled back on her arm, locking off the cable. The arrowhead arced over the railing and dropped onto the deck. The barbs caught in a gap between two deck plates.

Leslie reached over with her right hand and pressed another button on her left palm. A tiny motor inside her arm spun the drum that held the steel cable, pulling it tight against the wedged arrowhead.

Still holding the button, the cable began to draw Leslie up out of the water. When she was level with the deck, Leslie released the button and flung her hand out to grab the railing.

At first her fingers scrabbled at the rail, struggling to find a grip. Then, she caught hold and hung motionless for a moment. Then, with a graceful swing of her legs, she flipped her entire body up and over the railing to land cat-like on the sloping deck.

Within seconds, Leslie had made her way to the part of the deck just above where she'd detected the heat signature.

"Hang on, kid," she muttered, "I just need a minute more."

Using the powerful mechanisms in her left arm, Leslie drove her metallic fingers into the deck plating. She tightened her grip and, groaning with the effort, began to peel back the metal plating as if it were the lid on a tin of sardines.

Once an opening was made in the deck, Lieutenant Simons scanned inside the compartment with her infra-red vision. She quickly assessed the situation and dropped through the opening in the deck to land in the water flooding the compartment.

The water was only six inches below the ceiling of the compartment, and there was only an inch or two between the bottom of the ventilation shaft and the water. She called out as she swam towards the shaft.

"Can you hear me? Ian? Sean?"

"Ian," came back a feeble reply, "I, I, I'm Ian."

"I'm Lieutenant Leslie Simons, Royal Navy," she called back, "it's good to meet you, Ian. Are you stuck in that shaft?"

"No, but I'm p, p, paralysed. I'm only j, j, just st, starting to be able to t, t, talk again."

Leslie had assumed that Ian's weak voice and stutter were from cold and shock. Now, it seemed he'd been paralysed as well.

"Alright, let's get you out of here."

"An, an, ankle," Ian managed to say.

Leslie ducked under the water and spotted the heavy chain wrapped around Ian's ankle, and the bright new padlock holding it closed. She was about to reach out to break the lock, when she realised that Ian couldn't possibly be standing on the deck of the compartment.

Leslie looked over, and saw the body of Sean Byrne, still holding Ian up above the water's surface on his shoulders. His face was pale in the wavering light that filtered through the water, and Leslie could see that he had strapped himself to the support pole, in an effort to give Ian a fighting chance at living. The realisation of the older boy's sacrifice for his friend broke her heart.

Leslie reached out and snapped the padlock in two. Right now, she needed to save Ian from the crushing cold of the water. Later, she would deal with the anger and bitterness over what had happened to Sean.

As she broke back through the surface, Leslie took a deep breath to calm her voice. She did not need to upset Ian any more by conveying her own emotions to the young man.

"All right, Ian," she said calmly, "I've removed the chain and I'm going to push you up through the shaft to the top deck above. I'll be climbing through behind you."

"S, S, Sean." Ian stammered.

"I know," Leslie said softly, "I'll come back for him once you're safe."

"P, Promise?"

"You have my word."

Chapter 49

Caloundra, Colony of Queensland, Australia
Monday 24 May 1943

"What have I done, Billy?"

Billy came over to the couch where Jane was sitting. She lifted her head out of her hands and was staring at him with red eyes that still glistened with tears. Billy sat beside her, and Jane leaned over slightly, putting the side of her head on his shoulder.

"I have been so foolish," she said softly, "I could see you only wanted to be friends with me, but I pushed for more. I could see how uncomfortable it made you.

"But worse than that," she sobbed, "it drove Ian away from us. From me."

Jane turned her head to look at Billy.

"I love him, Billy, and now I might never see him again."

Billy put his arm around Jane's shoulder, comforting the weeping girl.

oOo

Bribie Island, Colony of Queensland, Australia
Monday 24 May 1943

Ian sat in one of the jump seats in the gondola of the *Antelope*, staring into space.

His wet clothes had been removed and he'd been given a spare set of coveralls from the equipment locker. The coveralls hung off his small frame, and the legs and sleeves had been rolled up several turns. He was wrapped in two blankets, but still shivered in short, uncontrollable spasms every few minutes.

Behind Ian, lying on a portable stretcher, was the body of Sean Byrne. A blanket had been placed over him, like a shroud. The flight crew were doing their best not to stare at Ian or Sean, as they moved about inside the gondola performing their duties.

Lieutenant Simons, dressed in clean dry coveralls, was standing a short distance away from Ian, finishing her report to Commander Bowman.

"You did well, Lieutenant," Patrick said, "you did very well indeed."

"Do you think he'll be all right?" she asked, indicating Ian with a slight tilt of her head.

"Honestly," he said, looking at the stricken boy shivering in the blankets, "I don't know. To watch a friend sacrifice himself to save you and to be powerless to do anything about it, is an incredible burden."

"Sir, could we organise a memorial for Sean Byrne? A simple funeral doesn't seem to be quite enough."

"It's up to his family to decide," Patrick replied, "but I agree that something more formal is appropriate in the circumstances. I'll discuss it with the Chief when we get back."

Patrick turned towards the cockpit of the *Antelope*.

"Take us home, please, Samuel," he said simply, before dropping into a nearby chair, exhausted.

oOo

Caloundra, Colony of Queensland, Australia
Monday 24 May 1943

"Telegram!"

Billy got up from the couch and raced to the door when he heard the messenger call out. The telegram was from his father.

After collecting the telegram from the messenger, Billy went back to sit next to Jane. As his mother came into the living room, Billy unfolded the slip of paper and read the short note aloud.

Enroute back to Caloundra

STOP

Ian safe but has hypothermia

STOP

Meet at hospital

STOP

Jane threw her arms around Billy's neck, bursting into sobs of relief.

"What's hypothermia?" Billy asked his mother.

"It means he's been exposed to the cold and his extremities have probably stopped working. His body will need to be warmed up again, but with medical treatment he should recover."

Jane lifted her head to look at Billy and his mother.

"Can we go to the hospital now, please? I need to see Ian."

"Of course, Dear," Mary replied, "of course."

oOo

Brisbane, Colony of Queensland, Australia
Thursday 27 May 1943

"Volkov seems to have given us the slip again, Chief."

It was rare for the Chief to leave Melbourne, but he had decided to make the journey to Brisbane to hear Commander Bowman's report. He felt that Patrick would be exhausted from the chase and the impact of his family being targeted would be starting to hit home for the Commander.

"I see," the Chief nodded, thoughtfully,

"The *Cooktown* tracked him as far as Coolangatta, on the border with New South Wales.

"It seems he abandoned the *Sea Gypsie* and made his way into the hinterland before the assault team could get ashore. He may have tracked south, but there's no way to be certain at this stage. We've alerted the Sydney office of the Directorate, as a precaution."

Patrick sighed. He wished he could relay better news to the Chief. With Volkov still on the loose, Patrick knew his family and their friends were still at risk.

"Thank you, Commander. There are some other troubling aspects of this situation, but we'll debrief those at another time."

Patrick nodded.

"I'm reassigning Lieutenant Simons to protection duty. As of now, she will shadow your son. I don't have enough agents to assign someone to each of his friends, but I can make sure William has a protector."

"Thank you, Sir, that's very generous."

"Now, I've spoken to the Byrne family and explained the heroic way in which he behaved. I've also spoken to the Commanding Officer of his Cadet Unit. They've agreed to have a military funeral for young Sean."

Patrick felt a sigh of relief, knowing that Sean Byrne would be honoured for his sacrifice.

"I want you to lead the funeral procession, Commander. Ceremonial rig with medals."

Patrick nodded.

oOo

Caloundra, Colony of Queensland, Australia
Tuesday 1 June 1943

The warm winter sunshine didn't match the mood of the people gathered at the Caloundra cemetery this morning. Billy saw a sea of black suits and dresses, and some of the ladies wore black veils over their faces, most notably Sean's mother and his younger sister, Samantha.

Billy saw that Sean's mother was leaning heavily on her husband's arm. Her face was ashen, and Mr Byrne's expression was grim. It was clear to Billy he was fighting to hold his emotions in, so he could support his wife in her grief.

Samantha was crying quietly, standing a little apart from her parents. Billy remembered she was a year younger than he was, and would be starting at Caloundra Colonia College in September as a First Form student. He made a mental note to welcome her to the College and to invite her to spend time with their group, if she wanted.

The only people at the cemetery who were not dressed in black were the members of the military and the Empire Service Scheme Cadets.

Billy stood next to his father, who wore his Navy Officer dress uniform, with gold braid and his service medals, including the bright silver cross and purple diagonal striped ribbon of the Distinguished Flying Cross. His grandfather had come as well, wearing his Navy Captain's uniform and medals.

"I'm proud of you, my boy," Billy had overheard his grandfather say, when he first saw his son in uniform.

Jane was standing on the other side of Billy, and they were both wearing their Cadet dress uniforms. Ian, also in his dress uniform, was standing off to one side of the gathering, keeping his distance from everyone.

The remainder of the cadet unit were standing in formation on the opposite side of the grave to the mourners. The Company Sergeant Major, CSM Golding, stepped forward to address the gathering.

"I had the opportunity," she began her eulogy, "to give Sean some advice earlier this year.

"I wanted him to understand that being a good leader and a good citizen was about taking responsibility not just for yourself, but for others as well.

Sean learned that lesson well, and we've seen him put it into practice every day since.

"The fact that Sean has given his life so that someone else might live is testament to his courage, his character and his leadership. He is an example to us all of what a citizen should be."

CSM Golding took a step towards the coffin, and reverently placed a Sergeant rank insignia on the top of the polished wooden surface. She moved back a step, and saluted.

"We are here to pay our last respects to our colleague," she continued, with a slight quiver in her voice, "and to bid farewell to our friend."

The CSM then turned about, so she was facing the formation of cadets.

"General Salute," she ordered, "Present Arms."

The right arm of every cadet in the formation shot up into a salute. The military members in the gathering did the same. Billy, Jane and Ian saluted as well, while the civilian men removed their hats.

During the minute of silence that followed, the only sound that could be heard was a gentle breeze through the trees and the sobbing of Sean's mother.

oOo

After the funeral service, Billy and Jane made their way to the College grounds and their meeting place under the eucalyptus tree.

The College itself was closed until the new school year started in September, but the grounds remained open. The rowing and rugby teams practiced year-round, and the Empire Service Scheme had a weekly parade, even during the holidays.

Jane and Billy were talking quietly, sitting on the mat under the tree, when they heard a noise from the nearby pathway.

"I say," Ian said, sheepishly, "is there any chance I could talk to you both?"

"Of course, Mouse," Billy said warmly.

Billy noticed a tear well up in Ian's eye when he used his nickname, but Ian brushed it away quickly.

Jane didn't say anything. Instead, she leapt to her feet and ran over to Ian. Throwing her arms around his neck, she hugged him tight.

"I'm so sorry, Mouse," she cried, "I was beastly towards you! Can you ever forgive me?"

Ian returned her hug, just as tightly.

"Of course I can," he replied, with tears streaming down his cheeks, "if you can forgive me for behaving like such a jealous bore."

Jane moved her head back a little, to look into Ian's face. She nodded, as her own tears welled in her eyes.

Suddenly, Billy thought they were going to kiss. He quickly turned his head away, not wanting to witness such an intimate exchange.

A moment later, he heard Ian and Jane laughing, and looked up to see them walking towards him.

"It's all right, old chap," Ian said cheekily, "you can look now."

Jane sat back down on the mat under the tree, but Ian stayed standing. He reached into his backpack and pulled out a slightly weathered wooden board.

"I wonder if I might put this back in its rightful place?" he asked, looking from Jane to Billy and back again.

"Of course, we'd be delighted," Jane enthused.

Ian took a few steps to the eucalyptus tree, and carefully wedged the sign back into the fork in the trunk.

The Caloundra Colonial College 'Explorers Club' had re-convened

End of Book 1
Billy's adventures with his friends continue in Book 2
Land of Hope and Glory

Land of Hope and Glory will be available from 7 September 2020.

Pick up (or pre-order) your limited-edition paperback copy from The Bookshop, Darwin, Amazon or the author's website.

About Stephen Archer

Stephen has been a storyteller for as long as he can remember. A colleague once quipped that he only speaks in anecdotes. Which reminded him of a story! Which he immediately told to everyone within earshot!

Inspired by his love of history, Stephen creates tales of adventure and heroism, set in a fantasy world that's familiar, but at the same time shockingly different to our own.

After growing up in Queensland, Stephen worked as a high school teacher, before joining the Royal Australian Air Force. Since then, he has worked as a university lecturer and a government trainer. He is also a screenwriter and filmmaker in his spare time.

Stephen and his wife, Bec, live in Darwin, in the beautiful and rugged Northern Territory of Australia. They love to travel but are not so keen on being woken at 5am every day by their demanding cats.

Connect with the author

View my website: http://stephenarcherauthor.com/

Friend me on Facebook: https://www.facebook.com/Stephen-Archer-Author-101349358119896

Follow me on Twitter: https://twitter.com/@SArcher_Author

www.ingramcontent.com/pod-product-compliance
Lightning Source LLC
Chambersburg PA
CBHW020328200626
46814CB00006BB/2474